HUNT WITH THE HOUNDS

by *Mignon G. Eberhart*

In *Hunt with the Hounds* Mignon Eberhart again proves herself a master of suspense and romance, creating, against the lovely background of the Virginia fox-hunting country, an atmosphere of terror and intrigue which lasts up to the breath-taking climax.

It had never occurred to Sue Poore that, when Jed Baily was acquitted for the murder of his wife, suspicion would turn on Sue herself. She had come forward and given Jed his alibi, thus placing herself at the scene of the crime. But the prosecution had suggested a motive at Jed's trial: that she and Jed were in love. Indeed, they artfully suggested that she was "the other woman" and Sue's defense of Jed tragically lent color to the accusation. Sue's family had lived in the county for generations, but against this innuendo and against the killer who stalked her from the woods at dusk and among the pink-jacketed hunters, Sue was suddenly terribly defenseless. For the police had decided she was a murderess and not even a bullet scarring the wall beside her could convince them she was in danger.

By the author of *House of Storm, Another Woman's House, The White Dress, Five Passengers from Lisbon, Wings of Fear,* and other outstanding mystery successes.

HUNT WITH THE HOUNDS

Books by Mignon G. Eberhart

HUNT WITH THE HOUNDS

By MIGNON G. EBERHART

RANDOM HOUSE · NEW YORK

FIRST PRINTING

All the persons and events in this book are entirely imaginary.
Nothing in it derives from anything that ever happened.

To Fannie and Dick Bokum

IN FRIENDSHIP AND
GRATITUDE FOR FRIENDSHIP

HUNT WITH THE HOUNDS

1

There had been, as Ruby said later, no other kill that day. That was Wednesday, the ninth of October, an unseasonably cold and rainy day, the day of the Dobberly meet, the day Ernestine was murdered. She was murdered about twilight with the shadows of fog and coming night blurring trees and shrubbery together in an amorphous mass that seemed to advance and watch and then retreat, like unwilling witnesses who would not come forward.

It had not been a good hunting day; a small gray fox had eventually given them a thirty-minute run and gone to earth on the far side of Hollow Hill; so Ruby had been characteristically literal and accurate.

The day Jed Baily's trial ended was much the same kind of day, except it was in the spring, in March. There was red bud and white dogwood along the misty blue hills, and the meadows were vividly green; it was, however, again unseasonably cold and rainy. By chance also it was again the day of the Dobberly meet but probably never in its many years of existence had that particular meet had so sparse a field. The trial took place in the Bedford county courthouse; it was a narrow, cramped white clapboard building with a clock tower.

The aspect of the little town of Bedford was changed very little by the trial; there were more cars along the street; the two garages charged, for the short period, three dollars a day instead of fifty cents for parking, but that was

for strangers, people brought there by the trial, not for natives. The courtroom itself was full but it was a small room. Two extra telephones were rigged up, temporarily, in a coat room. The inn, whose low, red-brick walls had once sheltered General Lee, had a short period of unaccustomed activity. None of the hunts was well attended, but it was near the end of the season; the fields were thinning out as those who came for the winter, merely to hunt, were beginning to leave again. The difference was not remarkable except in the case of the Dobberly meet, with which Ernestine had hunted since she was a child, tagging the field along with her sister Camilla, Sue Poore, Ruby Luddington, on ponies. It was the hunt to which Jed Baily subscribed, the hunt which was the breath of life to Caroline Poore, who, in fact, had been M.F.H. for some years—to all of the little, closely knit circle of intimates whose fathers and grandfathers had also been intimates, who had also followed the Dobberly packs over the green meadows and blue hills and woodlands of the lovely Piedmont country.

Most of these people attended the trial mainly to show their sympathy for Jed Baily; some of them would have attended whether they wished to or not, as they were witnesses, not of the murder—there was only one witness of that—but of a network of small facts that in the end only served, however, to corroborate a very few main and salient facts.

The state rested its case on those facts; the defense had, however, convincingly refuted their significance. At least so everyone felt; whatever else was emerging slowly but with accumulating power, from that trial, there was certainly a growing conviction that Jed Baily had not murdered his wife. Even the judge in summing up did not overlook any just claim but seemed to lean toward the side of the defense. But then the jury retired and did not come back.

The trial had lasted only three days, a short time for a

man on trial for murder, on trial for his life; it had seemed much longer and probably it would have lasted longer had the process of selecting a jury lasted longer. In the whole county probably there was not a person who had not heard of, discussed and formed an opinion of the murder, so the point of previous prejudice was not much stressed. The county was comparatively a small one; it was a land and county where feelings ran rather high, a land of complicated family relationships, of old-time friendships which were as strong as blood bonds. There was also a feeling of loyalty to old residents. Jed Baily was not an old resident; he had come to live in the county only three years before, but married Ernestine Duval. He had bought Duval Hall, with its three hundred (rather impoverished) acres and restored the home of her ancestors to Ernestine; he had farmed after a fashion, he had bred horses, he had hunted and by his marriage to Ernestine he had become automatically one of that small world and thus automatically it rose to his support.

This was an asset, an inadmissible but extremely powerful argument in his favor, the more powerful in that it was Ernestine Duval—his wife then for three years, Ernestine Baily—who had been murdered, and, dying, had accused him of her murder. For her oldest, closest friends to rally to his support was a very potent, if off-the-record, blow in his defense.

In rallying to Jed Baily's defense, that close little, tight little world rallied to the defense of Sue Poore; even if they had accepted the prosecution's stand that Sue Poore and Jed Baily had been acknowledged lovers, they did not believe that Sue Poore could have been the motive, the impetus for murder. As the trial progressed, however, a question, an unspoken implication, began to float in the air. It had no basis exactly; it was like rumor that, really, was not so much as whispered. In fact it was perhaps a kind of private theorem, worked out privately in the minds of those attending the trial; it was based on a simple and incontrovertible fact; Ernestine Baily had been murdered: therefore somebody had murdered her.

The outer world, the world of police and the process of law—and of reporters and photographers and newspapers—was more positive about it; that was the world that was in control and had to be satisfied.

As the jury did not return, it began to look as though there was some kind of hitch; it had all seemed fairly certain. "What has gone wrong?" Sue Poore thought. "Can anything have gone wrong?"

There was a clock, too, on the wall, a round clock fastened on the white plaster just below an arched, old-fashioned window which almost touched the ceiling. During the three days that were so short and yet so long, as if every moment were freighted with a greater weight of living than it could swiftly carry, Sue had learned the face and aspect of the clock; she would be able to see it in her memory all the rest of her life. It had also been a refuge; it gave her a focal point, it enabled her to lift her head with pride and yet reject the avid eyes of all those strangers.

There were phrases, too, which she would never be able to forget. Headlines: The Other Woman. The Woman in the Case. The woman who was herself, Sue Poore.

Words of the prosecuting attorney: "I put it to you, ladies and gentlemen of the jury, did not these lovers conspire to end the life of Ernestine Duval—wife of the accused, intimate and girlhood friend of the woman he so wrongly wished to put in his wife's place. . . ."

There was an objection, quick and hasty; it was sustained. The prosecuting attorney rephrased the same question.

"I ask you then, can you believe the testimony of a woman who admittedly came forward with her story because she knew its importance, because she admittedly believed that it would clear a man who, admittedly again, she met clandestinely, with whom she talked of marriage, the very evening of his wife's murder—within, it has been

6

proved, within a few minutes of his wife's murder? This, remember, at a time when such a marriage would have been impossible, because at that moment, while these two people met in a deserted, lonely cabaña, met secretly, Ernestine Baily still lived. Within the hour, in less than half an hour, Ernestine Baily, this outraged and innocent wife was murdered, in cold blood and in cowardly, despicable fashion. I ask you. . . ." They were scar memories; they would never heal.

She looked at the poignantly familiar face of the clock and the jury had been out for nearly forty-five minutes; the courtroom was restless.

There was an increasing amount of motion, people coming and going, a frank buzz of conversation. Camilla Duval, looking like Ernestine now that Ernestine was dead, rose, her elegant figure slim and erect, and walked out of the courtroom toward the back; probably she intended to try to send a message to Jed whom she, too, along with everyone, supported. Ruby and Wat Luddington, who had sat with Camilla, rose and followed her. Old Dr. Luddington, who had brought Sue into the world—and Ernestine, too, and Camilla, as well as many others of the men and women in the little, crowded room, sat now with his white head in his hands, weary and slumped down in the golden-oak armchair. The trial had been difficult for him; he had showed it in many ways. But his testimony in Jed's defense had been as important as Sue's testimony and there had been no question of prejudice or perjury; if Jed were freed— as he must be freed—it would be due largely, also, to Dr. Luddington.

Caroline Poore sat beside Sue; Woody, five years younger than Sue, had wired frantically on his delayed way, on leave, from San Diego; he was arriving too late for the trial but he did not believe the headlines, and he was coming. Caroline pushed upward her slipping heavy knot of gray hair and a little wave of the scent of violet sachet floated out toward Sue, a delicate fragrance above the

7

courtroom scents of stale air and old floors and, rather curiously, apples. Someone came along the aisle and leaned over to speak to Caroline; it was Fitz Wilson, his brown face kind as always when he spoke to Caroline, but very serious; his crisp, graying hair came near Caroline's as he spoke low in her ear. Had some rumor floated out to him from the locked jury room?

Aunt Caroline's hands, battered and strong and more likely to smell of saddle soap than of the violet that perfumed her white blouse, moved anxiously in her lap as she listened; she nodded and looked at Sue encouragingly. Fitz Wilson bent over Sue. "They've sent out for coffee and sandwiches; the rumor is that they'll be out for a while. Nothing to worry about, but come out with me and get a breath of fresh air. We can slip out the side door. Most of the reporters and photographers went over to Casey's to get something to eat, too."

Sue's lips moved rather stiffly, "I thought—I expected a verdict by now. . . ."

Caroline's blue eyes were comforting and loving. "You'd better go along with Fitz. I'll stay here."

"Do come," Fitz said, and touched Sue's hand; it was a gentle touch, but it had a kind of compulsion; Sue rose. His tall figure offered a kind of protection as she walked along the aisle beside him.

There were strangers, there were friends, in the still crowded courtroom. A woman whose face was familiar and whom Sue associated with hunting, somewhere, lifted a hand to wave at her, although there was something rather reserved in her face. Old Bob Hallock, however, across whose farm land Sue had ridden many times, held out his large red hand to her as she passed and shook her hand silently but with faith and friendship in his blue eyes. Their exit did not seem to attract attention. Bob Hallock's look and his big hand moved her so deeply with gratitude that tears rose suddenly to her eyes. Fitz, guiding her through the entrance hall with its white plastered walls, its

8

knots of people, the printed notices tacked to bulletin boards, saw the tears. He opened a small side door which avoided the front steps, crowded now with clusters of people, and went onto a narrow flight of stairs. But he misunderstood her tears: "I really think he's going to be acquitted."

"It wasn't that."

He didn't question her but led the way again, down the steps to a sidewalk which ran back past the courthouse. "My car's back here."

His car, a long, gray coupe which by now Sue knew very well, stood at the end of the sidewalk, hidden in the alley which they had approached by a fence and the courthouse itself. She saw at once that he had chosen the place purposefully. Neither Jed nor she—nor resolute, lovely Ernestine—were of any importance to anyone except themselves and their friends. But there were certain sensational features of the case; Bedford was not far from Washington and New York and near the fabulous and fashionable hunt country of Warrenton and Middleburg and thus, in a sense, a part of it. So there had been headlines.

"You planned this," she said as he got into the driver's seat beside her.

He started the car and backed out of the niche he had strategically picked and turned into the street toward the outskirts of the little town at a moderate speed so as not to attract attention.

It was foggy and cold with an overcast sky, as it had been on that October day which seemed half a lifetime away. One hand on the wheel, he fumbled in the pocket of his brown tweed coat and pulled out cigarettes, which he held toward her.

"Not now, . . ."

"I'd better tell you. I'm taking you to my house."

"*Is the verdict* . . ."

"No, no! There's no verdict yet, and no rumor, except I think, everybody thinks—it can't be anything but an acquittal. But whatever it is, there's going to be commotion. Photographs. Statements asked from you. . . ."

Excitement, flash bulbs, herself a nucleus. The Other Woman. Are you happy, Miss Poore? What are your plans, Miss Poore? Now if you'll just give us a smile and how about a picture with Baily?

Fitz said, "So we're going home. I've got Jason posted at Casey's. I'll phone to him. He'll know as soon as there's a verdict."

"But—Jed . . ."

The car gathered speed; they had already reached the tree-bordered outskirts of the little village and were climbing the hill that stood protectively above it; she could look down upon the village nestling there and the white, angular clock tower of the courthouse. Fitz said, his brown profile suddenly rather hard, "The courtroom's full of Jed's friends."

They swerved around the hill; the village disappeared. Suddenly it was as if whatever was happening back there, whatever those men and women locked in the bare little jury room were deciding, had really nothing to do with her.

She was obscurely ashamed of that, as if it implied a betrayal. It was always extremely easy to believe anything that Fitz Wilson said. She had known him (as she had known Jed, actually) only since her return to Virginia in the early fall. Fitz (like Jed) was not a native to Bedford county; his mother, however, had been, and when Fitz— who had gone from a professorship in newspaper writing to war correspondent, and then to becoming, in a way, rather an authority on certain phases of international economics—had inherited the old Fitzjames place and come to Virginia to write his articles (near Washington but in peace and quiet) he had fallen naturally into the rhythm and ways of his Virginia neighbors.

She glanced at him now; he was watching the road ahead. He was bareheaded. His black hair was so heavily mixed with gray that it was neither black nor gray but very definitely both and very crisp; she had seen him so often during the winter that even his brown hands, relaxed and easy on the wheel, just hands, had for her identification; she'd have known them anywhere.

He had done things for her and for Caroline that winter that even their kindest, oldest friends had not thought to do. He had ridden with her, coaxing her out on Jeremy, Caroline's old hunter, for long rides that tired Sue so much that, sometimes, she slept; he had dropped in—how many times—at that lonely hour when dusk comes down and two women, living alone, feel the emptiness of even a loved and familiar house, with no man coming home at night. But Fitz had come; he had let Caroline mix for him her famed drink which was mainly good Kentucky Bourbon and pretended to like it better than any drink he had ever tasted; he had sat with his riding boots stretched out before the fire; often as not he had stayed to dinner.

Always he had been there, too—somehow, mysteriously getting wind of it—when the police came to question; when the defense lawyer, Judge Shepson, came to plot the course which he'd hoped would save Jed.

The car swerved again, leaving the wet and glistening highway. They were taking a winding and familiar road which led across country, a short cut back to the tiny, sleepy village of Dobberly, whose cluster of old red-brick and white clapboard houses, sheltered by trees, made a tranquil, familiar center for wider-flung country places— her own home, two miles from Dobberly, Duval Hall, a little to the east and not far from Fitz's place and nearer, almost touching the edges of the village, the impressive show place which Ruby and Wat Luddington had recently bought from a rich New Yorker and renamed Luddington Farms.

What were they doing back in the courtroom they had left?

A monstrous shape stirred in a dark pool into which as a

rule Sue would not permit herself to look. "Fitz, if the verdict . . ."

"It'll be acquittal."

"Jed would need . . ."

Fitz said abruptly, "You've done enough for Jed. I told Caroline what I was going to do. You can't walk back and I won't take you." He turned off the highway into the narrow road that led directly to his own place. Hedges crowded close to the car; thin young greens of foliage were hazy in the fog.

But when they reached the house and the white stables and white-railed paddocks with rolling green meadows beyond, when they evaded the dogs who leaped upon them joyfully as if it were any day, a happy day, and entered the long, gracious white house with its wide chimneys and thick wistaria, Fitz went directly to the phone.

Sue waited in his study. She stood by the table, looking down at some thick reference books and not seeing them; she was indeed not aware of any physical sensation at all. She did hear Fitz's voice in the distance and then his footsteps along the hall. It was dusky in the room; she could not read his face when he came into sight in the doorway. But then he cried, "It's an acquittal."

He took her hands, drew her to a chair near the fireplace. He lighted a fire and flames crawled slowly along the paper and kindling. He stood then and looked down at her.

The dusky room, with the tall figure of the man before her outlined against the growing, rosy light of the fire became slowly clear and real. The dogs outside were clamoring to be let in. The mist had turned to a light rain that whispered against the windows. The trial was over. Jed was free; so in another, different way she was free.

Fitz was watching her. He said, in a voice that was very quiet in that quiet room, with the whisper of rain on the windows and the soft crackle of the fire, "Now that Jed is free, there's something I want to say to you. I love you, Sue.

I'll always love you. I think you love me. I want you to marry me."

A bit of kindling snapped and flared; the rain was louder. Jed took her hand.

She'd been wrong to think that she was free.

"You can't mean that, Fitz. You've forgotten. I'm the woman in the case. I'll always be that. Marked and . . . You can't want to marry me. Besides . . ." How very wrong she'd been! ". . . besides there's Jed."

2

AFTER A PAUSE he put her hand down upon the chair arm. "Yes, well, there's Jed."

He crossed the room and touched a bell; he stood there, not looking at Sue, his face and attitude unrevealing until a colored maid, neat and attractive in her uniform and crisp white apron, came to the door. "Jason isn't here. Can I get you something, Mr. Fitz?"

"Jason's at Bedford. He'll be home as soon as he takes Miss Poore home." The girl's eyes went to Sue and she smiled as Sue spoke to her; Fitz said, "Miss Caroline Poore, I mean. I brought Miss Sue here and she needs some tea, we both need tea. Mamie, you'll be glad to know that the verdict is in and Mr. Baily is acquitted."

"Oh, I am glad. Oh, that's good." Her dark eyes beamed with sympathy and with recognition of Sue's widely published place in Jed's life. "Miss Sue, I'm so glad for you. Now you just rest. I'll have tea here soon as I can. Why that's good news, Mr. Fitz, that's good news. Everybody's going to be happy about that."

She whisked away. Fitz came slowly back to the rosy circle of light around the fireplace. He sat down in the deep chair with its hollowed red-leather cushions, its reading table and light, its ash trays and papers, its stacks of books and magazines where obviously, habitually, he sat and read or worked.

Sue said huskily: "You think of everything . . . Aunt

Caroline. I'm glad Jason will take her home. She's been wonderful, like a rock. But you know that, you've seen her. You—how can I ever thank you for everything you've done for me!"

"I'll tell you how. You can listen to me. There are some things you've got to get straight. Both for your own sake and for mine."

He paused, staring at the fire, thinking. A telephone rang distantly and was answered; Fitz turned toward the door as Mamie appeared again. "It was Mrs. Luddington. She wanted to know if you'd heard; I told her yes. Do you want to speak to her, Mr. Fitz?"

"No; not now. Thank her; tell her I've heard. And Mamie, if the telephone rings again, say I've heard about the acquittal; say I'm not here. Understand?"

"Oh, yes, sir." Again she whisked away. Fitz said, without looking at Sue, "Take off your hat."

She hesitated, vaguely surprised, then took off her small hat, gray like her suit, and put it on the table beside her; she ran her hands through her short, light hair, fluffing it out. She had worn the gray suit with fresh white blouses and the same gray hat every day of the trial; it did not seem possible that it was over, and the removal of her hat was like a proof of it. She leaned her head back against the chair and let the peace of the book-lined room enfold her. Seeming very far away, the telephone rang again and was silenced.

Fitz was watching her. He said quietly, "I want you there always, Sue. There are things I want to say and I will when you're ready to talk. But all of them sum up to that."

She wouldn't look at him. But when she closed her eyes she could still see the red armchair and the books, symbols of the center of Fitz's life. She could feel the warmth, she could hear the rain, shut out; the scuffle of the dogs who wanted in.

"You are crying, Sue. . . ." Fitz's voice came nearer. He was kneeling beside her; his arms took her against him

15

and his hard cheek pressed down upon her own. "Don't. I'm never going to let anyone hurt you again. Don't . . ."

He stopped then and held her without speaking.

She could no longer hear the whisper of the fire or the soft murmur of the rain. Fitz turned her face and kissed her and kissed her again as if for all his life and all that life held for either of them.

"You do love me, Sue. Don't you?"

She moved her face against his shoulder, pushing it down into the warmth and roughness of his coat.

He said, "I love you so much."

A silvery tinkle came along the hall. He put his hand under her chin, lifted her face, looked into her eyes, with a very serious, direct question in his own gaze and then as if she'd replied to him, kissed her again lightly and got to his feet. He was standing before the fire when Mamie entered with a tea tray.

"Put it here, Mamie. Miss Sue will pour."

Mamie put down the tray; the shining silver and china caught highlights from the fire. Something smelled of hot bread and cinnamon. Mamie said, touching the teapot with an inquiring brown hand, "That was Miss Duval on the phone. Miss Camilla Duval."

Everyone, to the day of her death—to the day of her murder—had called Ernestine by her maiden name, Ernestine Duval, almost never Ernestine Baily; even now Mamie felt it necessary to distinguish between the Duval girls, Ernestine and Camilla, yet Ernestine had been dead now for months.

"What did she want?"

"She said she missed you, couldn't see you anywhere. She said did you know about the verdict. She said there was a lot going on." Mamie arranged a spoon carefully, her pretty face bent. "She said there was pictures and reporters and everybody congratulating Mr. Jed. She said she never saw such excitement; she said they are going down to Hollow Hill club."

"Hollow Hill!"

"Yes, sir. She said only a few of them, but she said they just have to do something to show Mr. Jed how glad they are."

"Well . . . I suppose that's right."

"Yes, sir. She said please to tell you to come."

"Thank you, Mamie."

The maid's face, which had held a certain tentativeness, cleared. "Yes, sir. I knew you'd feel that way. I told her you were out and wouldn't be back in time, but I'd tell you when you did come. There's the hot water, Miss Sue, and cinnamon toast and cake." At ease now, Mamie went away again.

Fitz pulled a chair up to the shining little table.

Sue said: "But they mustn't . . . it's like a celebration, it's . . ."

"Oh, that's all right. Natural. Blow off steam."

"Ernestine," Sue said and stopped. Fitz gave her a quick, perceiving glance.

"Come on, Sue dear. Pour the tea. And may it be the first of many—oh, my darling, many times."

Again she wouldn't look at him; she went to the straight chair at the tea table; he moved the cups, held them as she tipped the silver teapot with the satiny, soft sheen of age upon it. He said in a conversational way, "Yes, Ernestine. She was a part of everything here and now she isn't; it was tragic and dreadful, yes. But that is in the past, Sue. Everybody's got to look upon it as something in the past, and as soon as possible to be put away, finally; nobody can go on all his life thinking, this person, this friend is not here, therefore life may not close over the abyss. This tragedy, this horror has made a wound, a terrible scar. That is wrong. Scars heal, dear Sue. Milk?"

At her nod he poured milk into her cup, uncovered the muffin dish. "Drink your tea."

Someone at last let the dogs in; they came like cavalry, thudding along the hall and hurling themselves into the room, upon Fitz, upon Sue, threatening the tea table, the chairs, the room. There were, when they quieted, only two hounds and a strong, stocky Kerry Blue terrier, who perceived the muffin dish and came to put his whiskered head upon Sue's knee and look at her with eyes that were purple with longing.

"It's all right. Give him a piece if you like. . . . Now then you—settle down!" They quieted, all three of them, tolerantly, after Sue had divided a slice of cake in three parts, the Kerry Blue swallowing his share in a gulp and then eyeing the others in a still and menacing manner until he decided that they, too, had finished, when he lay down himself at last with a thump.

It was wrong; it stored up pain; but she let herself savor what she might not keep, the firelight and the dogs—the consciousness of the man who sat opposite her at ease, his legs stretched out toward the fire.

They sat for a while in silence except for the murmur of the rain, the thud of old Sally's leg as she scratched her ear, sighed and flopped over on her side. The Kerry Blue put his head upon his black paws and eyed Sue and the muffin dish resolutely. When Fitz at last lighted a fresh cigarette, rose and went to stand before the fire again, he began to talk quietly, as if merely continuing a conversation. "Now then, Sue, dear, let's put things as they actually are. Not as you, just now, see them."

"It's the way everybody . . ."

"Wait. In the first place, you see, you did a very brave and courageous thing, in coming forward as you did, at some cost to yourself in order to help save a man's life."

"I had to."

"Yes. But some women would not have seen it like that."

"He didn't kill her."

"Because of your courage and honesty, you have been put through a very bad time. . . . And very unjustly."

Her eyes jerked up to meet his. He smiled. "My dear, my

dear, can you possibly think for one moment that I believe that you and Jed were lovers?"

She said after a moment, slowly, "But—the testimony . . ."

"My dear Sue," Fitz said briskly, "if you told me yourself that you had fallen in love with the husband of one of your closest friends, that you led, connived, inspired him to murder his wife, I'd never believe a syllable of it. Now don't be a fool, Sue. I've learned to know you this winter very well. You've got some nonsense in your head about this trial and about yourself; you think you're a marked woman, that you'll always be—there never was such a pack of nonsense!" He turned abruptly to the fire; after a moment he said over his shoulder shortly: "It's you that's important. Marry me, Sue."

"I am a marked woman. It's true. I can't do that to you." But how easy, how fatally easy it would be to say something else!

She stiffened her hands on the arms of her chair. "I must go home. Aunt Caroline will be there and . . ."

"I've got to make you listen to me, Sue. I love you. I want you to be my wife. I should be very proud for you to take my name. Please believe me."

She didn't answer because she couldn't. He moved to look at her. She was sitting very still, very small in the high-backed chair, her chin which he had seen lifted so straightly that it betrayed her terror in the witness chair, was lowered now, her whole face was lowered so it was soft and young with the light rosy on her slender cheekbones and shading her eyes softly. The Kerry Blue, single-minded dog, had returned to put his head on her knee and she was patting him absently. The light made her short hair shine softly too; she wore a string of small pearls, fastened with an old-fashioned clasp which had slipped around so he could see it; probably it had belonged to her mother or her aunt. The little string of pearls gave him a kind of wrench, for it gave him an insight, a small measure of the special horror that the trial, the whole ugly concoction of accusation, publicity, police, cross-examination, photographs had meant to her; she felt that she had betrayed not only herself but everyone close to her. "Was Jed B ily worth it?" he thought, with a stab of bitterness.

His face tightened; for a moment he lost himself in thinking over paths that were already well worn. He saw Sue's motion, however, when she lifted her hand and touched her eyes and his heart smote him.

"Jed . . ." She began and stopped.

"Have you promised to marry Jed?"

"No. We never talked of marriage until that night, but he expects—he believes . . ."

Fitz made an impatient move and controlled it. "Do you feel in any way bound to him?"

"He depends on me. He said so. All winter . . ."

"But what about you? Are you in love with him?"

"I thought I loved him. I thought . . ." she stopped, thinking of those far away weeks before Ernestine's death; she had been bewildered, torn and perplexed, resolving at last to put an end to that perplexity.

Fitz watched her for a moment. "There's no disloyalty in you, my dear, if that's what's bothering you."

She said, troubled, staring at the fire: "I didn't think then that I would change."

"Perhaps you haven't changed. Perhaps it wasn't the real thing. Do you want to marry me, Sue?"

"Yes, oh, yes," she said and caught herself. "But I can't, Fitz. I can't . . ."

Fitz started toward her, and stopped; he had to go very lightly, very cautiously; if only there had been more time!

But there wasn't time, he remembered; he had to build his bridges, gather ammunition, map out a defense which might well be costly.

He would not have told her, however, just then; he

would have given her a few more moments of peace. But away off in the kitchen he heard a bell which he knew was not the telephone. The dogs, recognizing it, jumped up; his heart moved again, but this time in fright. Surely they had not come so soon.

Sue didn't hear the doorbell; she had no idea of what it might mean; she did not move. He watched her but his whole being was rigidly alert; he was aware of the flutter of Mamie's white apron along the hall, of her tentative pause for an order, as if Mamie herself, sensitive and gentle, understood that now, just now, was an important segment of time which must not be disturbed.

He turned to speak to her. But then the front door of the house burst open, the dogs hurled themselves out of the room, there were people, voices, "Fitz, Mamie, is Mr. Fitz at home? Hi, Fitz, where are you?"

Sue looked up. Fitz took a quick breath. "Sue, my darling, I must tell you something at once. The jury freed Jed; it was an acquittal. But there was something else."

Her eyes from blue had leaped to a frightened black. "The jury added a recommendation. They strongly recommended that the police immediately resume and prosecute to the fullest of their powers an investigation into Ernestine's murder. They particularly recommended to them investigation of any persons known to have been in the immediate vicinity at the time of her murder."

"Oh, there you are, Fitz!" Camilla stood in the doorway. She looked, in the firelight, so like Ernestine that it was rather shocking. Jed came behind her and pulled her out of the way and came into the room—Jed, handsome, smiling, his slender face, his shining dark eyes, his gleaming black head, the arrogance of his young and handsome body all lighted with triumph. "Sue! I've been looking everywhere for you. Sue—what's the matter?"

Fitz moved so he stood near Sue, almost between them. "I've been telling Sue about the jury's recommendation."

There was a short pause. The dogs surged around the room. Camilla came forward then and slid out of her raincoat. "Oh, that! That doesn't mean anything."

Jed, with the firelight now picking up ruby reflections in his dark eyes, laughed. "Why, that's nothing, Fitz! They had to say something like that."

Fitz said nothing; Sue looked up into his face and caught there the fear and shadow of the thing he foresaw.

He smiled, trying to reassure her; his heart ached to see the soft and gentle peace leave her face; if personal hatred could have availed, if it were ever anything but destructive and futile, he would have hated Jed Baily.

"I understand," Sue said all at once, clearly. "They meant me. I'm the only other . . ." she swallowed and said, ". . . suspect."

3

THERE WAS another short silence; even the flames seemed to pause and wait, briefly arrested. The dogs, ever sensitive to human voices and human emotions, turned wondering and slightly troubled eyes to Sue, to their master; Jed took a step forward and cried, "Sue, why what an idea! Who made you think . . ." he whirled around to Fitz, accusing and angry. "You did this! You've frightened her."

Sue heard him and didn't hear him. Fitz's eyes were dark gray and troubled. "You tried to tell me. You tried to prepare me," she said, stumbling over the words, and then she saw that Fitz had also tried to give her the most complete protection a man can give a woman.

He had offered it knowingly, in advance of her need; in advance of the catstrophe which he had foreseen and feared. Why hadn't she seen the danger! Another trial, herself as the accused. Accused of the murder of a woman who, they would say, was her rival.

But then there was brightness everywhere; someone had turned on lights.

Camilla had moved to the tea table; it was Camilla who had turned on the lights. Her stubby, white hands with their scarlet nails moved among the tea things; her ash-blonde hair was thick and shining (now that Ernestine's lovely, great coronet was not there to outshine her sister's); her lips were scarlet, too. She said, coldly, "As Jed says, the jury had to do something like that; they couldn't just let it

23

drop, Fitz, darling—I'm going to ask Mamie to bring fresh tea." There was ever so slightly in Camilla's manner a kind of proprietorship; Fitz nodded shortly.

Camilla crossed the room again with a swish of silk; except when hunting (for she'd felt, she said, that an occasional hunt would cheer her and that everyone would understand) she'd worn black since Ernestine's death, very chic black, very smart black, which Jed, her brother-in-law, must have paid for; Ernestine had had nothing when she married Jed; Camilla had had nothing and still had only what Jed gave her. She was now slender and silken and undeniably attractive; the dress was demure, decorous and smart. She knew exactly where the bell was; she went to it directly and put her finger on it with, again, the faintest hint of authority.

Jed had been standing perfectly still, hands thrust in his pockets, black head unmoving, dark eyes on Fitz. He was wearing the same suit he had worn during the trial, a brown, sleekly tailored sack suit, a city suit which seemed out of the way and wrong on Jed who rarely wore anything but riding clothes. He was unchanged, however, as far as anyone could see, as far as Sue herself had been able to see, looking from her own chair in the courtroom to Jed, unwontedly quiet, alert and listening all the time, but handsome and as composed as anyone could expect. His face, as a rule, was brown and weathered; usually his fully curved lips had a slight and pleasant smile. Now his face was pale; that came from those months, waiting, confined, instead of as usual riding and hunting and in a rather desultory way, farming the land he had bought with Duval Hall.

He moved suddenly as if he'd made up his mind, and came to Sue; he dragged up a footstool and sat down beside her. "Nobody's going to accuse you. Look at me, Sue. Why, darling, I won't let them accuse you. Fitz has thought this up himself. He's trying to frighten you! Why in the hell are you taking that line, Fitz? I don't like it, I'll tell you that."

Fitz said to Mamie, who had appeared in the doorway, "More tea please, Mamie."

Camilla, who had started to speak to the maid, closed her lips, hesitated and then moved back to the tea table.

Jed said, "I've been looking everywhere for you, Sue. I looked for you when they announced the verdict; I thought you'd be there. I thought you'd want to be there."

"I took her away," Fitz said dryly, standing before the fire again.

Jed's shining, sleek, black head jerked around; he stared up at Fitz. "What did you do that for?"

"I thought she'd had enough."

"Enough—what?"

Pillory, shot through Fitz's mind. He bit back the word. "I thought she'd had enough of everything," he said easily. "I knew there'd be all sorts of excitement whatever the verdict."

Camilla touched the high coronet her braided hair made; it struck Sue suddenly, and in a tangential, unimportant filament of thought, that Camilla had started to wear her hair like that only since Ernestine's death; it had been Ernestine's own, unique hairdress, it had been on Ernestine like a crown. It was so, now, on Camilla; she touched it, withdrew a gold pin and replaced it again.

"Oh, there was excitement! You never saw such a hubbub. Everybody crowding around, shaking Jed's hand, hugging him, patting his back. Kissing him. Everybody in the county was there, I think. And pictures. I thought they'd never stop the flash bulbs. Asking him to pose this way, that way, with me . . ." She shook her head and smiled. Her voice was high and rather thin and although its lazy, elliptical accent was perfectly natural, it seemed then to Sue, whose ears after those years in New York had grown accustomed to northern tongues, exaggeratedly and almost affectedly southern.

Camilla added rather regretfully: "Of course, I couldn't, being Ernestine's sister."

For a moment or two, the familiarity of Camilla's voice, the way the scene had, with a click, dropped back to a natural and accustomed one, people she knew around her, firelight and dogs and tea tray, pushed back the black and confusing waters. How could anybody accuse her of murdering Ernestine!

But they had so accused Jed.

She glanced at Fitz, unconsciously seeking reassurance, but he was watching Camilla, his face without expression. Jed leaned toward her: "Sue, you haven't said you're glad! Everybody else has said so. And I looked first for you! It was you I wanted to be there."

Fitz said, "Here's the tea."

"Oh, I expect Jed'll want a highball," Camilla said, all charm and grace. "Poor boy hasn't had a drink since . . ." She caught herself and said smoothly, "Mamie, Mr. Jed would like a highball."

Mamie's soft, intelligent eyes went to Fitz; she'd take orders from her employer, that glance said. Fitz nodded and she put down the fresh tea and went away. Camilla began to pour. "Have you had tea, Fitz? Oh, I see you have. Where were you when I phoned? We thought we'd stop and get you, Jed and I; the rest of them went on to the club. Of course, I do suppose it doesn't sound quite right to celebrate like that, but it won't be a real celebration, I mean not really gay, you know; just very quiet and among ourselves. Poor Jed! It's as I've said all along, two wrongs don't make a right. We can't bring Ernestine back; and she wouldn't want Jed to suffer for something so dreadful and terrible that he didn't do."

The obvious fact that that was apparently exactly what Ernestine had wanted seemed to strike her; she stopped abruptly, but the impact was a slight one; it glanced off; she went on with scarcely more than a breath: "Poor dear Ernestine—but I always say what's done is done. We have our lives to live; Jed, here is your highball."

Mamie came in with another glittering, tinkling tray

and put it down on a table beside Fitz; he poured Jed a generous drink and one for himself. Jed took the glass, swirled it, and smiled and lifted his triumphant glance to Sue. "Here's to my brave darling!"

Fitz put his glass down with a click as unexpected and sharp as the click of a revolver. "Jed, stop thinking of yourself, think about Sue for a change."

Camilla's blonde head went back in a startled way. Jed's face darkened: "What's the matter with you, Fitz? What are you trying to do! Spoil everything? I've been in prison for months; I've just been freed. I'm acquitted. . . . I— want to talk to Sue. I want to talk to her alone. I haven't had a chance for a word alone with her for months. Not since the—for months! Come on home, Sue. I don't want Fitz's liquor and I don't want any more of his company. . . ."

"You are in my house, you know," interposed Fitz suddenly with a half-amused, yet dry note. Jed paid no attention to it or the words. He didn't get up; he took a hasty but hearty drink and said, "And I've got a right to be with Sue and I'm going to take her home so we can be alone."

"Exactly what right?" Fitz said.

"Right!" Jed stared at him. "If you think that after all this publicity about her I'm not going to marry Sue, then you don't know the rules of a gentleman. . . ."

"Fitz, don't!" cried Sue. The dogs scrambled up with interest. Camilla gave a faint scream. Fitz looked at Sue and suddenly, and with genuine although rather wry amusement, smiled. He lowered his arm. Jed looked astonished. "Why, Fitz, you were going to hit me!"

"M'hm," Fitz said. "I may yet."

"But Sue—what did I say you didn't like? All I said was I'm going to marry Sue—right away if she wants to . . ."

Fitz interrupted crisply. "You've overlooked something rather important. In fact two things. First, Sue may not want to marry you . . ."

Camilla and Jed spoke at once.

Camilla cried, "My goodness' sake, Sue Poore, you better be glad he wants to marry you!"

Jed said easily: "Oh, but she'll almost have to. And you do want to, don't you, Sue? You wouldn't have done all that for me and besides . . ."

"And second, you've got her into this terrible thing, Jed, and you've got to help get her out. The police mean business."

"Oh, now, Fitz, you're exaggerating," Camilla glanced at Sue. Her pale but extremely pretty blue eyes showed no alarm. "Tell him, so, Sue, or we won't have any peace. Nobody's going to bother you. It can't bring Ernestine back. Investigation, pooh! You mark my words, they'll drop the whole thing right off. Now you two men stop your quarrelling. Goodness me, we ought to be so thankful and . . ."

Jed got up and came to Sue. "You're not scared, are you, honey? Don't let Fitz scare you. I'll not let him."

"Who do you think killed your wife?" Fitz asked.

His voice was extremely quiet; it was remarkable how it seemed to whip across the room. Jed's dark eyebrows drew down angrily. Camilla gave a kind of smothered cry and broke off some more cinnamon toast.

And another thing happened that was remarkable, at least to Sue, for Fitz's question evoked a sudden presence of Ernestine, her blonde braid brighter than Camilla's, her eyes lovelier and deeper, her lips redder—her will more decisive and sure. Then the image vanished; Camilla was there instead. Jed said with a heavy, thick voice of anger, "Ernestine killed herself. I've always said so. Nothing else could have happened."

There were cogent arguments against that; Sue, wearily and well, knew every one of them. Fitz appeared to consider and reject the litany of their enumeration and arrived at the most potent of all. "The police say it's murder."

"Oh, for Heaven's sake, Fitz, do you have to keep talking like this? I've had a hellish winter, today's the first release, the first . . ."

"It hasn't been an easy winter for any of us."

"If you mean Sue—but I tell you I love her. She—I'll make it up to her. I'll marry her and . . ."

Jason stopped in the doorway; he was an old, kind, black-faced, white-haired butler; he wore a raincoat and carried his hat. At one time, long ago, when Sue and Woody's father had been alive and sent a regular apportionment of his Navy pay to Caroline for the care of his children, Jason had worked for the Poores; lately Caroline could not afford a butler, but he still regarded Sue and Caroline and Woody with a proprietory affection. He said now as Fitz's look questioned him: "Miss Ca'line she want Miss Sue to come home. I brought the cyar."

"I'll go with you." Jed took Sue's arm and started for the door.

Camilla half rose, dismay in her face. "But, Jed, those people. They're waiting at the club."

Jed's handsomely curved lips set themselves stubbornly. "I want to go with Sue. We've not had one minute alone. Let 'em wait."

Fitz, Sue knew, was watching the little scene. The Kerry Blue got up courteously, although with roving black eyes toward the cake. But the door of escape had opened; Sue flung it wide. "No, no, Jed. They're waiting for you and I —honestly, Jed, I want to be alone."

He looked hurt and surprised. "Don't you want me to go with you?"

Jason, however, fumbling with his hat, his old eyes troubled, ended it. "They two men there, Miss Sue. They want to see you. Miss Ca'line, she's upset."

A spell of arrested motion laid itself abruptly upon the room; even the dogs stopped, struck by something paralyzing in the air. Fitz said then: "Two men?"

And Jason, troubled, twisting his hat, replied: "Yes, Mr. Fitz. Police."

Camilla rose, dropping a spoon with a clatter. Fitz picked up Sue's hat and put his hand under her elbow.

Jed said: "But see here—I'm going with her—see here . . ." He took another hasty but generous drink and Fitz, already with Sue at the door, said easily, "Not at all, Jed. You must see that. Worst thing in the world both of you could do. I'll take her—I'll report later at the club or— Jason, see to Miss Camilla and Mr. Jed. This way, Sue, it's stopped raining. No need to put your hat on."

The dogs galloped after them to the door; Jed followed, his glass in his hand, saying something. Camilla came too; then they were outside and down the steps. She was in Caroline's car, Fitz was at the wheel. The house seemed to slide behind them; the wet, blue stone driveway glistened; it was not raining, Fitz was right, but a heavy mist lay over everything. He said: "Lean back, Sue," and chuckled a little. "Jed didn't quite see my argument but didn't quite not see it. Don't worry about him, honey. He'll be all right. Pull down your window, will you, maybe we can clear off the windshield."

"The wiper doesn't work," Sue said, and rolled down the window. Later it struck her that Fitz's swift, yet matter-of-fact action was far more restorative than heroics, drama or spirits of ammonia. "I didn't think they'd come so soon . . ."

"Well, I didn't either. Old Benny must have got his dander up."

Old Benny was Robert Lee Benjamin, the county sheriff; he was a tall, spare man of about sixty, with white hair and faded blue eyes which nevertheless were piercing and honest; Sue liked him and respected him and he had known her since she wore two fat pigtails; she now feared him. He had held office peaceably for many years. He rarely had a murder case, never one such as this; he had called in state police, with all the scientific equipment at their disposal.

The car was speeding and puffing. No one could take better care of a horse or a dog than Caroline, but she felt strongly that a machine once assembled and in working order should stay that way; by the time Sue had returned and got the laboring little car to the garage, it was too late to do much about it; it wheezed to a crossroad, a dirt road which again was a short cut. The country was interwoven and brought together by many criss-cross, wandering dirt roads, useful for people who spent a large portion of their lives in the saddle and who hated the concrete highways. There Fitz slowed the car. The concrete road went on down into Dobberly. "I'm debating," he said. "Shall we go direct, or shall I go down into town and phone to Judge Shepson?"

Judge Shepson was the lawyer who had defended Jed; twenty years ago he had been for a short time in politics; he had been Judge, in fact, of the circuit court. Times had changed and he had resumed private practice, yet he was still and always would be called Judge. Sue thought, "A lawyer—in my defense. *My* defense!"

"Is it that bad? Already. Do I need a lawyer?"

"Certainly not." Fitz turned into the red dirt road. "You've told everything you know, anyway. You can't add anything to it, so whatever you say can't be incriminating."

She was confused and frightened. She did not see the warning until they had gone another mile or so, and indeed had turned between the gateposts, so heavily overgrown with ivy that their weathered stones were visible only in patches, that led to the winding, gradually ascending and rather badly repaired driveway of the Poore place —once called proudly "The Laurels," once a plantation, now dwindled to two or three hundred acres of meadow and pine woods and rather sparse orchards. Then she said: "Why, yes, Fitz, yes! I can't think of anything I haven't told."

"That's all right then. Just repeat it. In case of any—oh, questions they haven't thought up till now, think twice. If they take a new tack, a new slant, you've got a right to refuse to answer, if you want to."

The house came into view as they rounded the great

curving hedge of laurels whose trunks had already been matured and thick the year the guns had fired at Fort Sumter, whose blood-red flowers had blossomed long before the retreat and advance and retreat of Bull Run, not many miles away. The laurels were green now, the great red blossoms would come later. The white house was low and rambling; there were long windows and a wide, covered veranda, shaded with glossy ivy and Virginia creeper and wistaria which was as yet a delicate brown tracery.

She had been born in that house and, five years later, Woody, Sue's brother, had been born there, in the same gabled room with the sprigged rose wallpaper and small white mantel and so had Caroline and all the Poores for a long time. Three chimneys, built in the days when chimneys were of practical use, wide and high, stood above the house.

Behind it were the stables, where now only Caroline's two hunters dwelt; the paddock fences and stables rather needed a new coat of paint. It was a scene so familiar to Sue that she did not actually see it then, yet its presence and nearness was comforting like the nearness of a person whose tried faithfulness is like a fortress. Two cars stood in the graveled circle before the steps.

One was a police car; its radio aerial glistened with moisture. The other was easily distinguishable for reasons of its long and shining opulence; it was a foreign car, a Renault, with which Ruby had stunned the countryside. So Ruby and Wat Luddington were there, too.

Fitz muttered something and brought Caroline's shabby little car to a halt. Then Sue saw that Ruby and Wat were not in the house; they were sitting in the car in silence, apparently waiting, Wat at the wheel, Ruby huddled in a creamy, long cashmere coat, with a red scarf over her lovely head. Both got out and started toward them.

Fitz turned off the engine. He said quickly, watching Wat and Ruby's advance, "Jed and Camilla came before I'd said my say. Nothing has changed you; you are Sue

Poore; you are fine and brave and—very dear to me," Fitz said, "and you are going to be my wife."

He opened the car door. Sue could hear the gravel crunch under Ruby's high-heeled red pumps. She could smell a faint whiff of wood smoke from one of the fireplaces. Wat Luddington was brushing his mustache rather nervously; his thin politician's face was anxious.

Fitz's wife! The other woman? A marked woman in a murder trial, and now questioned as a suspect?

Wat Luddington said: "We've been waiting for you. Pa's in there, and the police."

As she got out of the car truth unveiled itself; the jury for Jed's trial had in all but fact judged her guilty. In another trial that judgment would not take the form of a recommendation; it would be a verdict. A strange and terrible thought assailed Sue. Suppose another trial did not end as Jed's had done; suppose they found her guilty.

4

SHE STOOD on the damp gravel, holding her hat with suddenly cold hands, looking up at the house.

Ruby was talking, Wat was talking. Ruby came up and linked her arm through Sue's.

Ruby had slipped off the red scarf; her beauty was as stunning as her newly and rather curiously acquired wealth and almost as surprising. She had been a lumpish, unattractive child, slow and phlegmatic but always in love with Wat, who in those days was more embarrassed than anything by her obstinate devotion. She was now a beauty; she must always have had beauty's integrants, but Ruby herself, an independent Galatea, had extricated them. Her black hair was brushed and shining, smoothly parted and done in an enormous bun, her brown eyes were like two calm midnight pools, long lashes brushed the soft pink glow in her cheeks. She gave Sue a slow although rather troubled smile and said nothing.

Wat, behind her, was talking quickly and nervously; Wat's talent was articulateness. It was one of the reasons, everyone thought, that his ambitions had turned toward politics. That and, of course, his marriage to Ruby, who with her beauty, her county birth and her first husband's money, was not exactly a handicap to a political career. Certainly he had given up the profession of medicine for which his father, old Dr. Luddington, had destined him; he had come home after his marriage to Ruby, for he had to start his career, naturally, from his native state. He was then trying to get himself elected to Congress.

". . . waited at the club—then Miss Caroline phoned to Pa; so we brought him over. He's inside—I don't know, Fitz, do you think we need to stay? It's not that I mind, or Ruby. Except—well, you know how the newspapers are. But if there's anything in the world we can do—although I do hope this is nothing. It can't be anything serious, can it?" There was real anxiety in his sharp eyes, peering a Fitz but he raced on, "The police have to do something since the jury recommended it. Can't just let it go by. Maybe the whole thing will die down, blow over. Tough on Sue, of course, but . . ." Wat's thin, rather nasal voice, slicing through the misty air stopped; there was the effect of a deletion, a slight embarrassment with a quick recovery. "Not that Sue brought it on herself, I didn't mean that. Everybody knows Jed's been crazy about her ever since she came home; Sue didn't encourage it . . ." again there was a slight gap and Wat said, ". . . intentionally. But mark my words . . ."

Fitz said crisply, "Why don't you and Ruby go home!"

"Well, but—that's what I'm saying but—why, Fitz Wilson, you sound as if you want to get rid of us! There's no call to get mad. I didn't say anything against Sue."

Ruby pressed Sue's arm. Suddenly Sue realized that there was real anxiety hidden under Ruby's placid exterior, too; the hand on her arm was trembling. But Ruby said, calmly enough, "I think Wat's right. You'll see that the doctor gets home. We'll go now."

She turned in slow and stately fashion toward the car. Wat sprang to open the door. "But now you two come along to the club as soon as you can. We'll expect you, do you hear?"

Fitz walked up the steps with Sue. The car door banged. At the top of the steps he turned around and said mildly, "You can go to the club, Wat, or you can go right to hell for all I care."

"Why, Fitz Wilson!" cried Wat, startled, from the driver's seat. He'd had his hand on the starter; the engine whirled over smoothly and they could see Wat's protesting face, his mouth moving, but could not hear his voice above the sound of the engine. Fitz smiled in a pleased way. "We've got to keep Wat down. He's going to be the county's stuffedest stuffed shirt, if we don't."

She looked up at him rather sadly. "You're going to have plenty of fights on your hands, Fitz, if you try to fight everybody that says or thinks what Wat . . ."

"There's nothing the matter with a fight! And you've got a fine long line of fighters back of you. Come on. Keep your head . . ." He opened the door with the eagle on the knocker—a one-eyed eagle whose head was turned and who had watched out of that one eye blue and gray lines, trudging, limping, straggling along the road below. The hall was lighted; the stairway down which Woody had once fallen and nearly cracked his skull, whose steps were faintly hollowed by the years, glimmered—white banisters and mahogany railing. There was the familiar blended scent of pot-pourri and floor wax, old rugs and camphor from the head of a deer over the mirror; there was also a faint ghost of pipe tobacco and always, permeating everything, wood smoke. Light came from a door down the hall, beyond the old-fashioned, delicately formal and sentimentally cluttered drawing room; it was the door to the so-called library which indeed had once been a library but was now Caroline's special refuge—Caroline's and her dogs. Two dogs tumbled out now—Sister Britches, the old, indulged beagle bitch in the lead, Reveller, stiff and rather bored, following. Sister Britches started a shrill tongue and was silenced by Caroline's voice from the library. She then came to the door.

Caroline Poore, fifty-odd, with a goodness and kindness that shone around her like a halo, was now distraught and trying not to show it. She stood there, pushing up the untidy mass of her gray hair, her blue eyes distressed, obviously at a loss for exactly what to say.

In the saddle that hair was neatly netted, her hat severely and smartly adjusted, her sometimes shabby skirt always brushed. She rode so well that her thick little body took on grace and flexibility. Out of the saddle she never looked quite assembled. She wore now the suit she had worn to the trial, but she had removed the jacket. Her white blouse was rumpled mysteriously, her black skirt was rumpled mysteriously, her hair looked as if it had not been brushed for a week and she had in the meantime lost her hairpins.

The dogs pattered around them. A waiting, listening silence seemed to emanate from the library. As they came nearer Caroline finally achieved utterance. She said: "I got out your Uncle Willie's port."

In the Poore family code this was, of course, perfectly clear; it meant an occasion of the first magnitude—funerals, weddings, births, Woody's passing his examinations. It must have rather puzzled those invisible listening ears in the library.

And now Uncle Willie's port was got out for an investigation into murder. There was a catch at Sue's throat, like the quaver of a half-hysterical laugh. Fitz looked at her sharply and said, "Steady," and Caroline made a kind of helpless gesture with her hands and preceded them into the library.

The dogs crowded in with them and then bounded onto the old, hollowed couch. Three men were standing in the library.

They had risen as Caroline had risen; they were standing in tentative attitudes, expecting to resume their chairs. They were Dr. Luddington and two men in the uniform of the state police. One of them was a Captain Henley whom Sue knew from the repeated series of questionings during the months preceding Jed's trial; the other had appeared briefly the first day of the trial to testify. Dr. Luddington, of course, had stood almost in the place of a father to her more than once in times of need, when Sue's and Woody's own parents had been at the far side of the world and Caroline, alone and perplexed, had sought his help.

He had aged that winter; his once ruddy cheeks had sagged, his eyes were shadowed. But he came to Sue and took her hand.

"My child, these gentlemen wish to question you. You have told everything you know of Ernestine's death so many times that I cannot possibly imagine what more you can tell, but here they are. Hello, Fitz."

Captain Henley said briskly: "Miss Poore, this is Captain Wilkins of Richmond. You heard him testify at the trial."

Sue had expected Sheriff Benny; her heart sank. She did not like Captain Wilkins. He was thin, dark and saturnine in his expression, with thick black eyebrows that met over his nose and an expression that was at once probing and cynical, as if he intended to dissect with zeal and yet already knew in advance what he should discover. His nod was offhand, subtly disparaging; yet he clearly believed himself to be polite, reserving his conclusions.

Actually his saturnine expression was due to a bad digestion. It was true, however, that he did not feel that anybody should be let off the penalty for murder because she was young, pretty and a native of the county and likely to be judged by a jury of her countrymen who might confuse chivalry with justice.

Captain Henley explained, "As you'll remember, Captain Wilkins testified about the gun. He's the head of the laboratory. I asked him to come with me. We wish to question you. Alone, if you please." He looked pointedly at Caroline and Fitz and Dr. Luddington.

Dr. Luddington relinquished Sue's hand. She rather expected him to fire up in what Woody called his Kentucky-colonel manner, polite but coldly and furiously outraged. Instead he lifted his glass of port with a rather shaky hand, put it down and said: "I—we'd like to be present."

"Alone," Captain Henley said and sat down, filling his chair tightly in spite of the spruce way he carried himself; he had a fat face, and thin, hawk-like nose.

Fitz said: "Look here, I want to suggest that your position be made clear, Captain Henley. If there is any reason why Miss Poore might require the presence of her lawyer, then you'll have to give her time and permission to get him here."

Captain Henley looked at Fitz. "I haven't got a warrant in my pocket, if that's what you mean."

"Warrant!" whispered Caroline. The dogs lifted their heads and looked at her anxiously. Captain Henley said: "You know what the situation is: Jed Baily was acquitted. We can't let it drop at that. The woman's dead. She was murdered . . ." At this point Captain Wilkins defined his position more positively than Captain Henley had defined it; he gave a brief and very certain nod.

Captain Henley went on: ". . . there was the recommendation of the jury. We've got to resume the investigation and we are—there is a certain pressure of—er . . ." he floundered and Captain Wilkins said: "public opinion."

"Exactly. Public opinion. A question of our sworn duty. It's true that I have talked to Miss Poore many times before, but from another angle, another viewpoint; that was when Baily was charged and waiting trial. I want to go over the ground again."

Captain Wilkins' eyes, almost hidden under the bushy cover of his eyebrows, sparkled deeply and rather scornfully as he glanced at his colleague. Dr. Luddington said: "But—surely you have no new evidence. And if not what can you ask her that you've not already . . ."

Captain Henley had exhausted his patience. "I'll leave if you insist, but I'll have to ask Miss Poore to come with me to the sheriff's office."

Caroline was on her feet. "Come, Tom," she begged. "Come, Fitz."

Fitz said, "Sue, if there is any question which you do not wish to answer, remember that you can refuse. Don't let them try to trip or trap you."

"I'm not trying to trip or trap anybody," Captain Henley said.

Caroline drew Dr. Luddington toward the door; she put

her hand beseechingly upon Fitz's arm, too. Henley's threat of arrest had thoroughly routed her. Sue sat down suddenly in Caroline's chair; her knees were shaking.

Captain Henley rose and in a sort of martial step that showed off his spruce and tightly fitting uniform, crossed the room and closed the door to the hall.

Captain Wilkins said, "It's rather late."

"I know. I'll see that you get your train." Captain Henley sat down again. "Now, Miss Poore, you've told your story of the murder many times, I realize. I want you to tell it again."

"Not—all of it surely."

"All of it."

"But I—you heard it, all of it, in court, here, you have records."

"We have not much time, Miss Poore."

Sue was still carrying her small gray hat; she put it down on the table. "Where shall I begin?"

"With the evening Ernestine Baily was murdered, when she telephoned to you, you said, asking you to come to her house."

"Yes. . . . Yes, she did. You know . . ."

"Please go on as if I didn't know. Captain Wilkins has not heard it in full. If there is any detail that you now remember that you may have forgotten or omitted from your previous statements, please do not omit it now." Captain Henley looked at her rather worriedly and got up and took a turn up and down the worn old Turkey rug. "I'm going to be frank with you. You heard the jury's recommendation?"

"Yes . . ."

"You know what it means?"

"I—yes, that is, I was there, at Duval Hall, but I . . ."

Captain Wilkins said, "It was as close as they could come to recommending your arrest. Surely you know that."

"But I—I didn't, there wasn't . . ."

"Just a minute, Captain Wilkins. I'd like to explain the

situation." Captain Wilkins leaned back again with a rather scornful look; Captain Henley took another turn across the room and went on, "When we questioned you before we were frankly trying to find corroborative evidence to support the arrest of Jed Baily. The situation is now completely changed. If he did not murder her then obviously someone did. You were at the house; you were present. Anything that you may be able to remember may now be very important to you. I don't wish to frighten you . . ." Captain Wilkins stirred; Captain Henley went stubbornly on. "You may have, without knowing it, some clue or indication to the identity of the murderer. Put everything else out of your mind."

It was a fair speech even with its reservations; Sue felt that Captain Wilkins disapproved of it. She said, "Thank you, Captain Henley. I do understand."

"Very well then," he sat down, crossing his knees in their handsomely, if tightly, tailored breeches, and waited.

Sue took a long breath. "Well, then . . . Ernestine phoned to me early in the evening."

"It was foggy," Captain Henley addressed Wilkins, yet certainly he knew her story so well that he could prompt.

"It was very foggy." She had told it so often that it had fallen into set phrases, like the remarks of a habitual after-dinner speaker. "It was Wednesday, the day of the Dobberly meet."

"You'd been hunting."

"Yes. Ernestine . . ." She knew exactly what the next question would be so she answered it before it was asked. "Ernestine was there; I don't remember speaking to her, anything special. I mean, I don't remember that she seemed any different. We'd had one or two runs, but no kill." (Except Ernestine; Ruby had said that, hadn't she? Sue would not let herself remember that. She went on.) "Late in the afternoon hounds found in the hollow below the Dobberly schoolhouse; we had about a thirty-minute run and then the fox started for the ridge above Hollow Hill. I was tailing the field, really; I was never a very good horsewoman and I've been away . . ."

Captain Henley interrupted: "She's been living in New York. Early this fall she came back to live with her aunt here."

Captain Wilkins' look indicated that she might better have stayed in New York. He said nothing. Sue took up the familiar lines, as familiar as lines in a repeated drama, except there were no footlights and police for audience. "I was tired and it began to drizzle; I thought the fox was going to earth there behind Hollow Hill but if he didn't, I didn't want to be in at the death anyway. I came home. I'd been here some time, over an hour; I was dressing when Ernestine phoned and she said she wanted me to stop at Duval Hall on my way to the hunt dinner."

"Hunt ball?" asked Captain Wilkins in a sepulchral voice.

"Not exactly, but there was going to be dancing."

She thought fleetingly of herself, in emerald green taffeta and a short fur cape (which looked rather like, but wasn't, mink) going to be introduced to murder.

Captain Wilkins knew more of the outlines of the story than he or Captain Henley pretended; he said, watching Sue, "Did Mrs. Baily say why she wanted to see you?"

They had asked that many times. "No."

"Did you guess?"

"No."

"How did she seem over the phone?"

Judge Shepson had warned her about that, yet the reply he had rehearsed her in was the truth. "She sounded hurried and brusque; it was a very short conversation, only a few words."

Wilkins' face was frankly skeptical. Captain Henley said, "Well—and then . . ."

"I went to Duval Hall as soon as I had finished dressing; I drove Aunt Caroline's car, intending to come back and pick her up after I'd seen Ernestine. I parked the car at the gate. . . ."

"Now why did you do that?" asked Captain Wilkins.

Both men knew that. It was still a difficult story to tell. "Because Jed came along the driveway from the house. His car was there at the gate, too. He saw me. He said he wanted to talk to me."

Her lips were dry. Captain Henley said, "You went then with Baily to the cabaña."

She nodded.

"Why did you do that?"

"He said he wanted to talk to me. I wanted to talk to him."

Wilkins said, "Cabaña? Where is this cabaña? With relation to the house, I mean."

It had been pointed out at the trial; a map, a diagram had been drawn and shown the jury. Sue knew the measurements now as she had never known them before. "It's about a hundred yards from the house; there's a small pool there; the people from whom Jed bought the place had it built; the cabaña is about twenty feet from the side of the pool, toward the house."

Henley said, "There are shrubs all around it and a mass of evergreens; there are heavy shrubs all around the house, too, and the house is not visible from the cabaña or vice versa. The driveway, though, goes straight from the house to the gate; the gate is perfectly visible even on a foggy evening."

Captain Wilkins said, "So you went with Baily to the cabaña; naturally you didn't want to be seen. It was lonely there, I take it, deserted. What happened in this convenient cabaña?"

5

It was the cabaña that had been so significantly empha-
sized during the trial, vividly and brightly spotlighted,
photographed, written about in the newspapers. It was
small and ordinary, with summer terrace furniture stacked
in ghostly angular shapes; Jed had taken her in his arms
there, briefly, for the first, and as it happened, the last
time. When the prosecution finished with the cabaña it
was a sinister and ugly rendezvous; nobody would have
believed that Sue and Jed had met there only once and
that mainly because of the cold fog and the nearness of
the cabaña. Yet it was true, too, that she wanted to say the
thing she had decided she must say to Jed, apart from any
other listening ears. She had not hesitated; she had not
given his suggestion a second thought. The wet shrubs had
brushed her green taffeta skirt and she drew it aside; the
door of the cabaña stuck and Jed thrust against it with his
shoulder to open it. How was she to know that every moment of that short meeting was to be probed and pictured,
exposed relentlessly, but in distorted lines and colors that
did not exist?

"Well," said Wilkins in sharp impatience, "well?"

Her statement was on record, not once but many times;
stick to it then, word for word. It could not be unsaid. Anything added might turn itself into a snare. "Jed told me
that he had—had fallen in love with me."

Captain Henley said, hurrying her to the point, "He
said he wished to divorce Ernestine and marry you."

"Yes. But—we—it wasn't going to happen that way. I've told all this . . ."

Captain Wilkins glanced curiously at Henley. "How did you extract—I mean—how did you know this, Henley? Did she admit it at once or Baily or . . ."

"We had an idea from this and that, a few allusions, that Baily had been paying her attentions. We inquired; Baily had to admit it. When we had Miss Poore on oath and asked why she'd gone to the cabaña with him, she admitted, at least she claimed, that it was because she wanted to tell him they were seeing each other too often, that there was nothing doing and that she was going away; she claimed that she wouldn't hear to a divorce."

Claims is an invidious word. Sue looked up. "That is true. I told Jed that I was going away."

Henley said, "The fact is Ernestine—that is, Mrs. Baily, knew that her husband had been attentive to Miss Poore. Her accusation may have been a matter of revenge, but she did know that."

"Everybody seems to have known that," Wilkins said dryly. "Does Baily admit a quarrel with his wife?"

"No. But he had the advice of counsel. It would have been a dangerous admission. Yet a quarrel with his wife, whether he admitted it or not, wouldn't prove he shot her. You'd better hear it as it happened. Please go on, Miss Poore."

Her cheeks were hot with anger at Wilkins' tone. There was nothing she could do. She said, "We talked for perhaps twenty minutes. He was going to the club; Camilla —that's Ernestine's sister—was going to Fitz Wilson's for cocktails. Jed was taking his car; he had to go early for a committee meeting, so Fitz and Camilla were going to pick up Ernestine later. Oh, yes, and the servants were out; they'd been given a night out, except the stable-man."

"So the house was empty except for Ernestine," Wilkins said, "and you knew it."

"Why, I—yes, I suppose I did. I didn't think of it until I tried to get help and nobody was there and I . . ."

Henley interrupted; "Let's keep to the events as they happened."

"Well—well, then, I had said—what I'd planned to say to Jed. I didn't want to talk any longer. I . . ."

"Did he yield to this high-minded entreaty of yours?" Wilkins asked. "Did he agree to let you go?"

Again her face grew hot with anger and humiliation; she said, "Everything that I can remember of our conversation is on record, Captain Wilkins. You can read it if you like. . . . He did not agree but there was no point in prolonging our talk. Besides, there was no time. We left the cabaña; he went on to the driveway. I stopped; there's a little porch, so it was dry, and smoked a cigarette."

They had stressed the element of time. She told them now painstakingly, "I stayed there perhaps ten minutes; I'm not sure. I wasn't thinking of time. Then I put out my cigarette and started for the house. As I walked to the house, I mean as I reached the house and could see the driveway from the front steps, I could see Jed, sitting in his car. He had a cigarette, too."

"You said it was very foggy."

"Yes, it was, but I could see the whole length of the drive; Jed's pink coat—"

"Pink!" said Wilkins. "Oh—I'm from the west myself." He paused and added thoughtfully: "We've got a lot of coyotes but the only kind of foxes we have are the two-legged kind."

He looked as if, in his opinion, the west and the east were not so different in that respect and Henley said, "Well, scarlet, really. Easily visible. I may as well tell you, Wilkins, I thought Baily was guilty at first; I thought Miss Poore . . ." he looked at Sue with a kind of bright objectivity as if she were a specimen to be analyzed. "I thought the young lady here was—mistakenly but from loyalty to Baily—well, frankly, cooking up her story. But I

46

have to say that, during the trial, I became convinced as the jury that we were barking up the wrong tree. In any case we'd have to accept their decision. And their recommendations. Usually . . ." He stopped, his lips closed tightly. A glint of cynical knowledge flashed from under Wilkins' bushy eyebrows. Usually, obviously, when the police brought in a suspect whom the jury acquitted, the police were of the same opinion still and the case lapsed; this time it was different.

Henley resumed: "I know Baily would have been visible from the doorway. I experimented . . . but—go on, Miss Poore."

"I—then I heard the shot."

Wilkins sat up. "You heard it!"

Henley looked faintly smug; he had at last surprised the visiting expert. "Please continue, Miss Poore."

These words were, like a well learned lesson, quick and automatic. "It came from inside the house. I was standing at the door, about to ring. Jed was in the car. I could see him. He dropped his cigarette and I could see it. I was looking at him when I heard the shot."

Wilkins thought for a moment and said, "It must have been an emotional meeting there in the cabaña . . . both of you taking time out to smoke. However—so you heard the shot and then what did you do?"

"I didn't do anything for a minute. I thought—I never thought of anything like . . ." anything like Ernestine, her hand at her back, anything like Ernestine, her fair head rigid, staring at the red on her withdrawn fingers. Sue's mouth was dry. "I thought that someone was cleaning or looking at a gun, accidentally shooting it. I—but then I heard a scream and I—I opened the door and ran inside. She was in the garden room at the back of the house and she . . ."

Even now, even after so many repetitions, even after the courtroom and the listening silence and the scribbling fingers of the reporters, she had to force out the words. "Ernestine was standing there, with her hands at her back and she pulled one of them away and looked at it and it—I saw then—it was red and she said, 'I've been shot.' I ran to her."

Wilkins was sitting up. The coldness and cynicism about him was gone. He looked still and shocked, touched with murder; it was as if he, too, with Sue, had been transported to that room, that charming room with all the great baskets of hanging ferns and the gay yellow chairs and sofas and the French door open upon the misty, walled garden—and Ernestine, in her yellow dress and the Duval garnets and her hand redder than the garnets, brighter. "I've been shot," she had said in astounded, accusing fury. There was no fear, then, only anger; she did not intend to die; she had not thought of death.

"What," said Wilkins after a moment, "did you do?"

"I tried to help her; I didn't know what—I tried to get her to a chair—she wouldn't lie down or move; she put her hand to her back again and said to get help, to get somebody. I ran to the bell. She said the servants were out; I thought of Jed and ran to call him and the stableman—"

"Sam Bronson," interjected Henley.

"He had heard the shot, too; he was coming to the house but from the stables. I called to him and told him and then Jed had seen me and the stableman. He guessed something was wrong. He was coming, running back along the driveway to the house. I told him and he ran to the garden room. The stableman was already there and Ernestine, of course, and she said to get the doctor."

"Dr. Luddington," interjected Henley again.

"So I phoned for him. He was at home. He came right away."

There was a pause. All of them seemed to see, superimposed upon Caroline's library, another picture—the garden room and its green ferns; Ernestine in her long, silken dinner dress, her eyes sunken and deep with anger and astonishment—and the blood on her hand.

48

Wilkins said suddenly, "The gun."

"Oh, yes." Sue swallowed. Her fingers were working, pleating a fold of her gray tweed skirt. "It was by the door —it was on the floor. I picked it up."

"*Why?*"

Why? Everybody had asked that; she didn't know why. The gun was there, glimmering wickedly, on the red tiled floor. She saw it; Jed and the stableman were trying to get Ernestine to lie down and Ernestine was in frozen, stony silence. She would not speak or move her hand. Sue went around to the door and there was the gun. She picked it up and put it on the table with its glittering ornaments and the great red mass of carnations. "I don't know why."

Wilkins looked at her and looked at Henley; they exchanged a long glance.

"Well, look here," began Wilkins and Henley said, "We asked her that, of course; go on, Miss Poore. Did you recognize the gun?"

"No. I supposed it belonged in the house; I thought still that it was an accident. At least—I didn't *think*, I suppose; Ernestine had said that she was shot but I couldn't . . ." She sought for a word and said ". . . couldn't comprehend it. It was all very quick and shocking and . . ."

"Did you know it was Baily's gun?"

"No. I didn't know anything about it. I don't know much about guns"

Wilkins said shortly, "Somebody knew enough."

He was, of course, the expert; he had testified about the gun and why Ernestine could not have shot herself. He had also testified as to the fingerprints on the gun. "But you didn't try to rub out any fingerprints?"

"No. I didn't even think of fingerprints."

Wilkins sat forward again. "Oh, come now, Miss Poore, you can't have been as innocent as all that. Any child knows about fingerprints. Any . . ."

"It's a point in her favor," Henley said as if Sue were not there.

"Remember she'd have rubbed off other fingerprints at the same time."

Henley scratched his nose. "You mean she'd have thought of that?"

Wilkins said shortly: "Henley, I checked the fingerprints myself. There were Baily's, Mrs. Baily's, her sister's, the Duval woman's. One or two other smudges which so far you don't seem able to identify . . ."

"We can't check every fingerprint in the county," Henley said in a wave of rebellion.

Wilkins shrugged, ". . . and this girl's. Normally we'd expect to find somebody's prints—anybody's who lived in the house. I say that the girl would have thought quickly enough to realize that the presence of fingerprints on that gun would strengthen her story. However—it's a debatable point both ways, I'll grant you. Let's get on with this. I've got to make my train."

Captain Henley's thin lips tightened; he said to Sue, "When did the doctor get there?"

"It was only a few minutes. Jed had got towels and I was getting ice from the pantry when he came. I ran to tell him she was in the garden room. We went in and then—and then . . ."

"And then Ernestine said . . ."

"She said that—Jed had shot her."

"Wait a minute." Wilkins crossed one hand over the other, regarded it minutely and said, "I take it that no one else was seen in the—what you call the garden room or—you said the French doors were open—on the steps or garden or whatever is immediately outside the room?"

"There's a terrace and then two or three steps down to the garden," offered Henley. "The garden is small with a high stone wall on three sides. Anybody could get over it of course but—there's a gate from it into a paddock that's beyond it; the paddock's got a high fence, too—rails—it runs around two sides of the garden. The house is along the third side and the lawn is beyond the fourth. The only point is that the garden is not easily accessible."

50

"Except from the house or paddocks."

Henley nodded. Wilkins said, "Well, then, Miss Poore, was there anything to suggest that anybody else had been there?"

She knew the only answer. "I didn't look; Ernestine—I never thought to look. But of course it would have been too late. And then when the doctor had got there and Ernestine was—was saying . . ." Her voice caught.

Henley said suddenly, "Would you like some of the—er—port your aunt brought?"

Uncle Willie's port in the best decanter was at Henley's elbow. "No, thank you. She—well, the doctor was dressing the wound, you see; or rather, I realized later, examining it. The bullet he said—but that was afterward, too—was still in the wound. And Ernestine . . ."

Wilkins was learning forward. "Was it then that she made her accusation?"

If it had not been for Ernestine's accusation, Jed would not have been arrested and charged with murder. She said, "Mrs. Baily said that Jed had shot her. She said they had quarreled about . . ." She could feel a flush mount like a flame to her face. ". . . about me."

Captain Henley said, turning his foot this way and that, appearing to admire his beautiful boots, "The stableman heard it; Baily and the doctor heard her. The words of their sworn testimony almost exactly coincide. She—the murdered woman said, 'Oh, Doctor Luddington, he shot me, Jed shot me. He's in love with Sue—he wants to get rid of me. We quarreled. He shot me . . .' That's almost exactly what she said, isn't it, Miss Poore?"

"Yes," Sue said.

"Well, well. But you saw him with your own eyes at the time the shot was fired."

"Yes."

"Did he," said Captain Wilkins in a purring way, "see you?"

6

THIS WAS a divergence; this was new and treacherous ground. If they had ever asked that before, Sue did not remember it. Perhaps they had, it was a reasonable and a likely question; but now it was important. She had given Jed a full, complete and certain alibi. But could Jed give her such an alibi? Had he turned in that moment when she entered the house? And even if Jed could give her an alibi, would they now believe it?

Captain Henley said, "Can you answer that, Miss Poore? Did Baily see you at the same time when you say that you saw him?"

"I don't know."

Wilkins said, "There's another question I'd like to ask. Do you intend to marry Baily now that he is acquitted?"

Sue knotted her fingers together. "I—no, we have no such plan."

"What!" exclaimed Wilkins. "But that was the whole purpose of the famous talk in the cabaña, wasn't it?"

"I told you the purpose of that. I explained to him then that I was going to go away . . ."

"Ah, yes. You were running away. You didn't expect him to pursue you, of course. You didn't expect that he would, under such a threat on your part take some kind of action. You didn't . . ."

Sue got up. "I did not. I have told you the truth only because you are an officer of the law. But it is the truth."

Her hands were shaking—her voice, to her horror, shook, too—her cheeks were flaming and hot. Captain Henley got up, too. "Now, now, Miss Poore. This is our duty—we have to inquire."

Wilkins remained seated, not quite smiling. "And you didn't, since your lover took no action at all, take matters into your own hands? I should say, literally a gun . . ."

She turned and started for the door.

Captain Henley sprang forward, his face red and flustered. "Where are you going? See here . . ."

"I am going to telephone to a lawyer." She was shaking inwardly. She managed to control her voice; anger helped her. Later, of course, cold fear would creep in and nibble at her defenses.

Captain Henley passed a hand across his balding forehead, took a deep breath and got control of the situation and of himself adroitly; he stood up as if at salute, his rather pigeon-like chest thrust out. "Miss Poore, if you refuse to continue the story I shall be obliged to take you to Bedford and question you further."

It was as efficacious a threat as when he first made it; Sue could see Caroline's face. Her niece, Sue Poore, detained by the police. Besides she thought again, it was, all of it, already a matter of record.

She said, "There is not much more to tell. They took Ernestine upstairs—Jed and the stableman carried her—Dr. Luddington went with them. I turned down the bed and brought what he wanted, towels, ice, a big bulb for the bed lamp. That was because he—when she was quiet—he said he'd have to probe for the bullet. But then—we waited outside, Jed and the stableman and I. In the hall. Dr. Luddington said one of us would have to help him give her ether, but then she—died. While we waited."

She remembered the wide hall upstairs, the closed door into Ernestine's room and the way its ivory painted panels had caught the light. The cigarettes Jed had smoked. The stableman in whipcord breeches and gray, turtle-neck sweater, thin, scraggy, his small dark eyes alert, smoking, too. And then Dr. Luddington came out and closed the door behind him and his face and the way he closed the door told them.

"Wasn't there any question of taking her to a hospital?" asked Wilkins suddenly.

"No. That is, I think Dr. Luddington knew how serious it was. I think he was afraid to move her. The rest of us didn't know. Ernestine didn't know. He said so; he said that was why she accused Jed. I mean—she didn't realize that she was dying; Dr. Luddington didn't tell her and he hoped to save her."

Captain Wilkins began, "But why would she accuse Baily if . . ."

"The motive offered was spite. Sheer spite," Captain Henley looked at his boots.

"Spite? But then she must have hated him."

Captain Henley still examined his handsome boots. "Ernestine was older than her husband; may have been jealous, may have been . . ." he stopped, brooded, and said, "May have been anything. But that was the doctor's testimony. He said she didn't know she was going to die. He said she wasn't in a condition to speak or think rationally. He said she had a quick temper. Obviously she knew nothing of Baily's infatuation for Miss Poore. He said it was in his opinion entirely a matter of personal vengeance and spite and an accusation which, if she lived, she'd have retracted."

Wilkins said, scornfully again, but after a thoughtful moment, "Opinion! Opinions don't carry much weight."

"Dr. Luddington's does," Henley said briefly and conclusively.

The outcome of the trial had proved that. Wilkins had to accept it; he turned in a disgruntled way to Sue. "Well —what then?"

"We—Dr. Luddington that is, called the police. Sheriff

Benjamin came. Some state troopers got there first." She remembered all of it, as clearly as if she were seeing it, like a colored scene on a small television screen, played before her eyes. Jed, sunk in a deep chair, staring at the floor; Sam, the stableman, hovering on the outskirts, his small eyes bright; Dr. Luddington looking gray and drawn, going about his duty. Herself—and then the police.

"What about the woman's sister? The Duval woman? Didn't you send for her? Didn't you tell her her sister was shot? Dying?"

Sue's mouth and throat were dry again. "No, not at once. I mean—we didn't realize that she was dying, you see. Dr. Luddington had told us to be quiet."

"But the woman's own sister! Surely . . ."

It annoyed Sue for him to refer to Ernestine as "the woman"—the dead woman, the murdered woman. "We did not realize Mrs. Baily was dying. We simply didn't send for her sister. She came later."

She could remember Camilla's voice and Fitz's but that was later, after Ernestine had, inconceivably, died, when the police were there. After the alarm had gone out and all at once, immediately, the whole county had known it. She had had only a glimpse of Fitz that night; it seemed strange now.

Captain Wilkins said suddenly, "What I don't see is why you arrested the husband in the first place."

"Now see here, Wilkins, the woman accused him. The stableman heard it; everybody heard it . . ."

"If it hadn't been for the stableman you'd never have heard it," observed Wilkins sardonically. He rose. "The woman was murdered. No question of it; that's my opinion —you'll grant it's expert—that gun killed her. No human being could fire a gun into his own back at that angle. The girl was there; she had been summoned by Ernestine who in all likelihood was jealous, admittedly quarrelsome and determined to put an end to the thing, warn the girl off.

The girl goes to the house after an admittedly emotional scene, in the cabaña, where no one could see them, a surreptitious meeting . . ."

"No," whispered Sue.

". . . during which the girl, as a last resort perhaps, threatened to leave, to go away. A dodge as old as the world, a lure as ancient as the stars. But Baily doesn't fall for it; he goes away himself, ends the scene, perhaps angrily —how do we know?"

"No," cried Sue again. "It wasn't that way."

". . . He intends to go on, unperturbed, to the hunt dinner, the hunt ball. The girl goes to the house; she's going to fight it out. The wife tackles her; they quarrel, the girl is desperate; she is in love with Baily—obviously frantically in love with him; she would never have testified in his behalf as she did if she had not been in love with him, had not still been hoping to save him and marry him. And maybe his money, who knows . . ."

Henley interrupted, "Baily's not a rich man."

"He bought that house for his wife. He doesn't do anything."

Henley had informed himself. "The house is an old one, architecturally a prize, it's famous for that. But in fact it didn't cost him much and the land is poor. He's got enough to live as he wants to live apparently, but he's by no means rich."

"All right, all right. He's got that much—And in the end, in the midst of a violent quarrel with Ernestine, the girl snatches up the gun . . ."

"How'd she know where it was?" interjected Henley.

Wilkins shrugged. "These people, the way they know each other, I'll bet they could find their way around each other's houses in the dark. Besides . . ." his low forehead wrinkled; his heavy eyebrows drew together. "Wasn't there some mention of a gun cabinet?"

There was, of course; it had been made much of, the gun cabinet in the hall, barely outside the door to the garden room. Nobody, though had remembered or at least admitted any helpful knowledge about the revolver.

She heard Captain Henley explaining it. She heard Wilkins say, "Ernestine accused him all right. You arrested him because of that and the gun. But if now you dismiss that accusation as spite, I can't see what you're waiting for, why you dragged me over here, why . . ." he gave his coat a shrug, looked at his watch, and started for the door. "I'll miss my train."

Sue was standing, holding the back of her chair; the door from the hall opened and Dr. Luddington came into the room. Again, however, where she would have expected fire and thunder, he seemed only beaten and tired. He said, "Gentlemen, you are making a grave mistake."

Caroline expected a storm too. "Now, Tom," she pled from the doorway. Fitz came in, glanced at Sue and made the sketch of a wink, as if to belittle the monstrous things Wilkins had said, but he was sober, too.

Wilkins said, "Will you answer a question or two, Dr. Luddington? You've been listening at the door so you know the course of the inquiry."

"I—it depends . . ."

"Let's not argue, doctor. For one thing I haven't time. For another thing we hold the winning hand. You must realize that."

"He is perfectly willing to reply to any questions," Fitz said.

Henley said to Caroline, "Miss Poore, we have to do this. It's our sworn duty. And there's—" he touched his forehead where there was a glisten of sweat and said— "pressure."

Dr. Luddington said wearily, "Pressure! You arrested and tried an innocent man. Now you are threatening to put another victim through the same ordeal. Pressure!"

"Somebody shot her," Wilkins said. "You're a doctor; you've seen a lot of wounds of one kind and another. You knew that she couldn't have shot herself."

Dr. Luddington sighed, "I was afraid of it."

"You said then it was murder, didn't you?"

The record, typed out, sworn to; he must feel as Sue herself had felt, helpless and hemmed in by that record. "I said so, yes. I called the police. It was a violent death; a death by gunshot. But I had not time to consider whether or not it could possibly have been by her own hand."

"It couldn't," Wilkins said.

"You don't know . . ."

"As it happens I do know. That's my job. . . . You heard Mrs. Baily accuse her husband of killing her."

"Of shooting her. There's a vast difference there, sir. As I testified. She accused Jed, yes, but she didn't know she was dying. She didn't know she was accusing him of murder. Ernestine, I'm sorry to say this, sir, but justice—I'm sorry to say that in my opinion Ernestine spoke out of spite. In actual fact she was in no condition to make any lucid statement."

"That seems lucid enough."

"It was not. I've stated that. I took my oath upon it." The doctor's face had a gray shadow; he said simply and rather drearily, "and that is no small matter to anybody."

Captain Henley looked up from his boots. "Dr. Luddington, please tell Captain Wilkins just why you thought it was spite on the part of the murdered woman."

"Because it was. Sue, here, saw Jed at the instant the shot was fired."

"She says she saw him," interpolated Wilkins softly. Dr. Luddington looked up quickly, with a flash of old-time fire in his eyes. Henley said: "Do you think if Ernestine had had time she could have taken back her statement? Admitted that she had lied?"

The flash of fire subsided. Again there was a gray shadow in the doctor's face. He said, "I'm sure of it. If she remembered she'd made it. Her pulse was very weak by the time I got there. But the point is she didn't know she was dying. She . . ."

"Now look here, doctor, it seems to me an extraordinary kind of thing for a woman so shocked and wounded, dying indeed, to give way to revenge."

"Her mind was already wandering; she was dying even if she didn't know it. No statement made like that can be depended upon for an instant. I am a man of experience; I think my neighbors will tell you that, also." He passed a rather unsteady hand wearily over his eyes. "Also I have always been a man of—honesty and some standing." He took a long breath, lifted his head and said, "Her accusation was not only false but it was made by a woman who at that moment was in no condition to speak with any degree of truth. Her testimony is entirely without value. Consider her wound . . ."

"I saw the pictures; I—well, go on."

"Then you certainly will realize that a woman in such a condition is not an accurate witness."

He had so testified; his manner, his earnest, nearly fervid conviction and more than anything the way the county people knew and believed him had gone far to free Jed.

Henley glanced at Wilkins. "Of course the fact is she may not have known who shot her—that was brought out —since she was shot in the back. . . ."

Wilkins said shortly, "I can reason that, too. What did you do, Dr. Luddington, before you called the police? Didn't you warn Miss Poore? I seem to have heard . . ."

Sam, the stableman, again; he'd told it, of course, merely because it was a fact and the police had asked him about it. Dr. Luddington said, "I would have failed in my duty if I had not told Sue to go home before the police came."

"In fact you wanted to get her out of it. You wanted to keep her presence in the house at the time the woman, her rival, was murdered, a secret. You didn't want people to know that she and her lover . . ."

Once he would have blazed into wrath. Now his words were a tired gesture of wrath. "I object to that word. I may be old, sir, but a horsewhipping . . ."

59

Fitz said, "Stick to facts that are proved, Wilkins."

Perhaps the word horsewhipping still hovered in the air; perhaps there was a harsher echo of it in Fitz's voice, a younger man with a poised and able-looking body. Wilkins said rather rapidly, "It's a criminal offense to assault an officer of the law. I'll say what I please."

"But you might find that southern tempers are supposed to run high," Fitz said with composure. "We're an impulsive race. I'll thank you to use language suitable to a lady's ears."

Wilkins stood very straight, seeming to gather to himself the force and authority of his uniform. "She'll hear worse language than mine, if she goes where, for my money, she ought to go," he said flatly. "Henley, I've got to get to my train. You asked for my advice and I'll give it. I'd arrest that girl, like that." He snapped his fingers, walked toward the door and turned. "She's guilty as hell and everybody in the county knows it."

He disappeared into the hall; Captain Henley wiped his face and hurried after him. Apparently he had an abrupt encounter with Chrisy in the hall. There was an explosive murmur; Chrisy, Caroline's cook, came to the door, wiping her hands on her apron as if inadvertently she had touched poison in the shape of Captain Henley. She said, staring after them: "Would you like dinner now, Miss Caroline? I've got waffles, if the doctor and Mr. Wilson want to stay."

The telephone at Caroline's elbow began to ring.

7

It was Jed. Caroline handed the telephone to Sue and went into the hall, following the doctor and Fitz.

"I waited and waited," Jed said. "Why didn't you phone me?"

"They're just leaving."

"Do you mean to say they've been there all this time? What on earth were they doing?"

"Questioning."

"Sue, you sound—what's the matter? What'd they want to know? I've got to talk to you. I'm coming."

"No . . ."

"But I've got to hear. I'll be there in fifteen minutes."

Fitz came in. He took the telephone away from her. "Jed? She can't talk to you now; she's exhausted. . . . No, don't come. . . . Well, I don't think it's advisable. . . . No, there was no new evidence. Dr. Luddington's going to give her a sedative and put her to bed. Of course he's here. . . ." He listened as Jed's voice went on in insistent tones. He said to Sue, "Do you want him to come?"

She shook her head. Fitz said into the telephone, "I'll tell you why, when I see you!" He listened for a second or two and then, quietly, in the middle of something Jed was saying, hung up.

"He'll ring again," Sue said unexpectedly.

"Let him. Sue, there's got to be a way out of this. You didn't kill Ernestine; hold to that. And—hold to me if you can." He leaned over and put his hands around her face, gently, like an embrace. "Caroline's going to put you to bed. I'll go now."

He went into the hall. There were voices; then Dr. Luddington and Caroline came in, the doctor with the shabby black leather bag, the same one probably, out of which he'd taken cough drops and thermometers and bottles of pink and white pills ever since Sue could remember.

Night had come and the windows were black. Dr. Luddington's tired face was ashy gray. He tried, however, to smile. "Now, my dear, remember that you didn't murder Ernestine. Think of that and—trust me. Will you?"

What could he do? And then his smile was so troubled, his eyes so anxious, pleading for her to believe in his omnipotence as she had as a child, that she smiled, too.

"Now, that's better. Here—take this now—and these later, one at a time if you can't sleep. The first thing you've got to do is sleep; Caroline . . ."

Caroline was there with a glass of water. Sue was far more docile than she had been as a child, grateful for their pretense that they could protect her. In her own gabled room, with the rosebuds on the wall, Caroline helped her out of the gray suit she had put on, it seemed to Sue, a million years ago. Chrisy came, puffing up the stairs with a tray in her kind hands, her dark face heavy with anger. Chrisy led Caroline away, downstairs. She made her eat and she came back to Sue, took the tray, gave her an admonishing look and reached for another pill. "Take this, Miss Sue. Mr. Fitz, he came with his car and took the doctor home. I just put your aunt to bed. She's mighty done up. Now, take this."

It was comforting only to obey; Chrisy turned out the light but left the door into the hall open. Shortly after that it began to rain. She would think, now; there had to be a way out. Fitz had said, "Hold to the thought that you didn't kill Ernestine." Kill Ernestine! How could anybody think she could kill anybody?

All at once, with the rain drumming softly on the roof of the porch below the windows, Sue went to sleep.

She slept while it rained, a long, cold spring rain on the meadows, the blue hills, the red clay roads and the roof of the house where she was born. She slept while Fitz and Judge Shepson sat around a table in the lawyer's study, far into the night. She slept while in another room, in the other direction, in the sheriff's office in the Bedford courthouse with the clock in the tower sounding the hours, men sat far into the night, too. There was debate; there was a repetition of facts, while Captain Henley, his spruceness gone, his tunic over a chair, the hollows around his shrewd eyes growing deeper and grayer, went over and over the evidence. Captain Wilkins, who had got his train, might as well have been there in person; Henley quoted Wilkins who was the expert. The sheriff, looking old and troubled, listened.

At two o'clock Woody, his flight delayed at Memphis by foggy, bad weather, sent a telegram to Sue, standing at the Western Union counter, a thin young figure in his blue uniform, the one gold stripe on his cuff shining as he scribbled and chewed the pencil and scribbled again.

If there were other lights amid the rain and night, if there were other wakeful, debating minds, then there was no one to know; the party at Hollow Hill Club, however, had fizzled out, had ended early, was, in fact, no party at all.

It rained all night. Sister Britches, outside Caroline's door, was restless. She heard actually nothing but the rain; it sounded like footsteps but in truth that night, was not. But she listened to the patter of rain and the ticking of the clock in the hall. And out in the stable old Jeremy was uneasy too; he knew as well as Caroline that there had been a hunt that day and they had missed it. He was old and authoritative; the dull sound of his restless feet was like very soft thunder.

It was still raining in the morning, but lightly, much as it had rained the night of Ernestine's murder.

Since almost the first month of Sue's return home, there had been a kind of hurdle for her to take when she first awoke, a fact that had to be looked at and taken as she would take a jump. At first it had been Jed—all during the early fall with its lazy Indian summer days, with its crisp frosty mornings, with cubbing over and the hunt season opening and herself riding old Jeremy, avoiding—yet not quite avoiding—Jed; meeting him so much, so often, seeing him when, at the end of a hunt, they gathered, all of them, for those endless post mortems, those gay suppers.

And then Ernestine was killed. And that was the hurdle of the winter, the long and dreadful winter, Ernestine's death, Ernestine's murder—and a coming trial which might mean Jed's life.

There was, of course, now, the most dangerous hurdle of all. But when she awoke that morning she thought first of Fitz.

In the space of a few seconds the whole tapestry of a life may seem to present itself, its threads interwoven and their pictures clear and all but simultaneous. It was so with Sue that morning, for she thought of Fitz and wondered that she had not known before the thing that now was so clear in her heart. She wondered how she could have believed herself in love with Jed. Was it because she had only feared it, and had fought a shadow, without pausing to examine its substance? At the same time she thought, "But they can't arrest me; they can't charge me with Ernestine's murder." It was, in the morning, incomprehensible. They had been frightened; they had let the mere required formality of the police stampede them.

So she argued, reasonably. She got into a white shirt and jodhpurs and went downstairs. There was coffee in the dining room; Chrisy heard her and came in from the kitchen with a plate of popovers. "You better, Miss Sue?"

"Yes, I am, Chrisy. I was frightened last night—and tired —and . . ." She saw then that there was no morning paper in its usual place beside Caroline's plate. "Oh," she said and looked at Chrisy.

"No sense reading truck like that. Now you eat breakfast. Miss Caroline, she's out in the tack room working off her spleen. Oh, yes," she paused at the door to the kitchen. "And there was a telegram from Woody early this morning. Came from Memphis. He'll be here, he said, tonight. If you want to read it it's in Miss Caroline's study; I wrote it down. Now you mind you eat something. You just don't look like nothing this morning, Miss Sue."

The door swung to. What had the newspapers said? She drank coffee; she crumbled, deceptively, what she couldn't eat. The rain had stopped by the time she rose from the table; the dogs were probably with Caroline; the house seemed quiet and empty. What did one do when one was about to be arrested for murder?

But that, too, was panic.

She went to Caroline's study and looked at Woody's telegram, written in Chrisy's sprawling handwriting, as generous as her heart. Woody had been delayed by bad weather. He had heard the news; he would arrive sometime that day, weather permitting. There was no telephone message from Fitz.

For Woody the message was laconic. What would he say when he knew how matters really stood? She was beginning to lose her early morning's sense of reassurance; she'd find Caroline.

She went out the side door; there was a path from the side door, between laurels that were glistening with silvery beads of moisture, to the stables, long and rambling, which one time had sheltered riding horses and hunters and carriage horses, and now held only the Geneva mare (Caroline's favorite hunter, light on her feet as a cat) and old Jeremy. Jeremy put his head out of the open half door in his loose box and looked at her thoughtfully as if wondering whether she meant to saddle him and take him for one of the long rides of the past winter. Sister Britches lay in the doorway of the tack room; she was never far from Caroline. Sue had almost reached the door when she heard voices and then it was too late to withdraw, for Jed heard her coming and came to the door.

"Sue," he cried, his slender, handsome face lighting.

"Sue . . ." He ran to meet her; he took her hands eagerly. "I came right away, as soon as I could. Caroline wouldn't let me wake you."

His black hair shone from the fog; he looked like himself again, natural and young and still invincibly triumphant. He was wearing riding breeches and a yellow pullover beneath his brown coat; he had not ridden over, however. She saw the end of his car standing in the driveway, projecting from behind the laurels. He drew her inside the tack room. Caroline was working with saddle stuffing, her square, sturdy hands going about their business expertly and energetically; it was like Caroline to seek solace of the things she loved best. Her blue eyes were still grave and worried; she said, "Good morning, Sue. Did you manage to sleep?"

Jed said, "Miss Caroline, I've got to talk to Sue. They wouldn't let me yesterday; Fitz and Camilla and—darling Miss Caroline, I've waited so long."

Whatever happened, she must make Jed understand the truth; Sue said quickly, "I want to talk to you."

Caroline pushed back the heavy, slipping wad of her gray hair and gave Jed a long considering look. "Well," she said then, "if Sue wants it. But I don't want you to upset her."

"I won't upset her."

Caroline was still troubled. "I'm not sure you ought to be here, Jed, to tell you the truth. The way they talked last night."

"But don't you see that's why I've got to be here?" Saddles, cared and tended and satiny in their gloss, hung neatly on pegs behind him; he put his hand on one, leaning easily against it. "I want to tell you, Miss Caroline, exactly how things were between me and Sue."

"You don't need to tell me anything." Caroline picked up a cleaning cloth and put it down.

"Yes, but see here, you're Sue's aunt. I couldn't talk to you before now, not the—not the ghastly way things were."

"I don't see that they're much better now."

They were arguing about a shadow; something that no longer existed. Perhaps it had never existed. Sue had to stop them. She said: "Aunt Caroline—Jed—there's no need to talk of this. We aren't going to be married . . ."

Perhaps Caroline heard; all Jed's attention, however, was focussed on Caroline and impetuously, almost angrily, trying to win his point, he said: "Well, but now I'm free! Now things are different! I love Sue just the same and besides everybody expects it! I've been acquitted and Ernestine . . ."

He stopped rather abruptly; Caroline said, "If you mean that now Ernestine's dead you're free to come courting Sue, then I don't think this is the time to say it. No, I don't."

A swinging light bulb, caged in wire, threw the tack room with its cupboards, its shelves, its rows of bridles and saddles, into bold relief; the dangling leathers of reins and martingales and stirrups made a pattern of sharp black lines against the wooden walls. Jed lounged against the saddle near him, his dark face alight and eager. "But Miss Caroline, that's the very reason I've got to explain. I mean, all the things the papers said, and the way they questioned Sue and implied—and I couldn't do anything then, I couldn't . . ."

"Listen to me, Jed Baily," Caroline said. "If you think I wondered whether or not any of those things were true, then I didn't. Not for a minute. Sue never did anything to be ashamed of. I didn't even ask her. I didn't have to. We never talked of it once." She pushed back her hair again. "So I'm not going to now."

Sue felt a tightness in her throat; she went to Caroline but then could only stand there, silent, beside her. Jed said: "Well, that's all very well, Miss Caroline. And it's true, of course. Sue and I—weren't—there was never . . ."

"You shut up, Jed Baily," said Caroline with sudden fierceness.

She gathered up the saddle before her; Jed sprang forward but before he could take the saddle she had replaced it heavily on its accustomed peg. She bent to scrutinize a stirrup carefully. Jed said, "Please don't treat me like this, Miss Caroline. I can't help the way things are. And I can't help being in love with Sue. I fell in love with her the first minute I saw her; I tried not to, and Sue tried not to. . . ."

"You had a wife," snapped Caroline. "You ought not to have made love to Sue. But you did, you know you did. You wouldn't let her alone. You were after her day in and day out. Everybody knew it—how could they help it? I knew it; of course I knew it. But I knew it wouldn't be long before Sue sent you packing. Except she—Sue—I was afraid she was going to be hurt." Her voice faltered.

"Sue was in love with me," Jed said. "There was nothing wrong about it, Miss Caroline. Sue told me that night, in the cabaña, that she was going to go away. It's just the way she told it at the trial. I asked her to stay; I asked her to be patient. I told her I was going to ask Ernestine for a divorce."

"I don't want to hear," Caroline said.

With a sense of rushing toward a climax which was unnecessary, like a dangerous curve on the wrong road, Sue tried again to steer them onto the right road. "Jed, things are different! We were wrong then, we didn't realize . . ." It was unsuccessful.

Jed, swiftly, went on, "Sue wouldn't hear of it, Miss Caroline." Caroline turned piteous yet steely blue eyes to Sue. Jed said, "And that was the situation. But now it's different. I'm free and I've been acquitted. Sue needs me. This whole terrible thing—Sue wouldn't have been in it at all if it hadn't been for me and I realize that. And if she hadn't loved me she wouldn't have insisted on testifying as she did; that night, the very night Ernestine—died—both of us, Dr. Luddington and I both did our best to make Sue go away, leave; we could have fixed Sam Bronson so he wouldn't talk; but Sue wouldn't. That shows she loves me, doesn't it? That shows . . ."

Caroline's blue eyes went to Jed. "Who murdered Ernestine? Who murdered your wife? That's what you've got to find out. If they arrest Sue . . ."

Jed stood up; again triumph was alight around him. "If they arrest Sue, I'll tell them I did it myself. I'll do anything for her. They can't hold Sue for Ernestine's murder if I say I did it."

They had not heard approaching footsteps, but Sister Britches scrambled up then and waved her stern. Fitz stood in the doorway. "That's an excellent idea, Jed," he said cheerily. "Why don't you try it? Good morning, Miss Caroline. How are you, Sue? Is there any chance of some food? I'm famished."

8

He had been up most of the night consulting with the lawyer, going over and over every detail. Since they had already covered that ground, the lawyer directly for Jed, Fitz almost as directly during the many times when he had heard the police question Sue, there were not many details that they had failed to collect—except, however, the most important one of all, which was not, Fitz said rather wryly, exactly a detail.

Fitz told them quietly over breakfast. They went into the house with him, all of them. "I was looking for you, Jed," he said. "Camilla said you were here."

Caroline absently and troubled polished the gleaming silver coffee pot. Jed stared across at Fitz, his bright dark eyes incredulous.

"But they simply can't be going to arrest Sue. It's fantastic."

"It's fantastic." Fitz gave a sort of shrug; his hair was wet still, from the shower, his face had a refreshed look from shaving, but fatigue showed in the sharper lines around his mouth and in his casual yet rather resolutely restrained manner. "It's fantastic, but she was there, Jed, and while they may not have a case against her that would stand up in court"—he glanced at Sue reassuringly as if to soften the effect of his words—"still it's a case. There's undoubtedly political pressure behind them, too; there's the recommendation of the jury, which had only one possible interpretation. There's—the point is we've got to work fast."

"Work fast!" Jed repeated. "But what can anybody do? It's so absurdly wrong, Fitz. I can't believe that any reasonable person . . ."

"Well, try to believe it," Fitz said shortly.

Chrisy brought in a plate of eggs and bacon. "But what . . ." Jed began and Fitz said, "Find out who killed Ernestine."

"But Ernestine . . ."

"Listen, Jed. Get this into your head. Ernestine was murdered. She didn't kill herself."

"Nobody would . . ."

Fitz put down his coffee cup and looked across at Jed with level, considering gray eyes. "Nobody will ever accept a theory that she killed herself; it would be convenient and fine if they would, but it simply is not true. The police are going to have Sue charged with murder if we don't get out some evidence, dig up some detail, some motive, anything in God's world to prove, even to suggest that she didn't do it. Do you realize how things stand?"

"Certainly I do. I can't believe it, because Sue—well, she didn't, but . . ." Jed's handsome, dark face cleared. "You heard me; I meant it. I'll stick by Sue the way she stuck by me. If Sue's arrested I'll go to them and say that I did it."

Fitz's gray eyes were rather fixed and cold; actually he was thinking again how easy it would be to hate this handsome boy, with his dark, sparkling and triumphant eyes, this man who had, really, never stopped being a boy. He said, however, tranquilly again, "All right. It might confuse; it certainly would confuse. I don't see what else it would do. Try it if you like."

"But you sound as if you think they're going to arrest her, this very minute, this very day. . . ."

"I'm sorry," Fitz put his hand, firm and hard, upon Sue's hand. "I'm sorry, but I do think that. Unless we stop it."

"Stop it! All right; I'll do it now then, right away. Where's the telephone?"

Sue cried, "But he can't do that. He didn't murder her. This time he'd get the death penalty."

"Oh, no," Fitz said, putting sugar in his coffee, his brown face rather fixed but tranquil too. "It's safe. He can't be tried again for the same crime."

Jed, half rising, stopped short.

"But—but . . ." Jed thought and said, "Why, that's silly. Suppose some new evidence came up, suppose . . ."

"I don't think you could convince them; I think they'd put it down to what it is."

"If I confess they've got to believe it," Jed said stubbornly.

Fitz drank some coffee thoughtfully. "What would you say? How would you convince them exactly?"

"Well." Some of the triumph went out of Jed's eager face. "Well—I don't know. I'd make it fit. I can think up a way!"

Fitz gave a kind of sigh, small and weary, which probably nobody but Sue heard. "Jed, this can't be settled or solved by dramatics. We've got to have facts. Go ahead, do anything you like. They can't hang you for it . . ."

"I won't let him do it," Sue said.

". . . they may get you for perjury or something, but . . ."

Sue turned to Fitz, "You said to hold to the fact that I didn't do it. They can't prove I did."

"That's right, too. Hang on to it. Now, Jed—as I told you we talked most of the night . . ."

"I don't see why you didn't include me," murmured Jed rather sulkily.

Fitz went on: "You've been all over the thing with Judge Shepson, many times; he knows the case thoroughly, naturally, but—as the police said, from the angle of defending you; from your angle. We found simply no loopholes; the point is that you or Camilla might know of a motive, of some small clue, of—well, anything, that might point the way to the murderer."

72

"I'd have told them; I'd have tried to save myself!"

"Yes, naturally. But we can't leave anything untried; we've got to follow any, every trail that might, just might, provide a clue."

"Well, all right. I see that. But I can't think of anything . . ."

"Well, first, I asked Shepson about your giving Sue the kind of alibi that she gave you. . . ."

Jed started up. "Why, of course, I'll say that I saw her when the shot was fired. I'll say . . ."

Wilkins had asked that. Sue said, "That's what the police said. Wilkins said, had Jed seen me . . ."

"Did you see her, Jed? At that very minute?"

"That doesn't matter! I can say so, can't I . . ."

"No, you can't. The record is already sworn to. You said you were not watching the house, that somebody could have entered it without your knowledge. You can't change it."

"I can change it and I will, I'll . . ."

Fitz was shaking his head. "And, he says, nobody would believe it anyway. He thinks it would seem so flagrantly cooked up that it would work against Sue instead of for her. I'm afraid he's right."

"But—but it's an alibi . . ."

"What about the stableman?"

"Sam Bronson! Oh, he's all right. He didn't kill Ernestine."

"Well, I don't think he did. For one thing, there's the time element; I don't see how he could have got from the garden door, through the gate, across the paddock, and then back around the house to exactly where he was when Sue saw him; there might be some way nobody's discovered, but he told what he knew with an effect of truth. He was a good witness; there was no motive that anybody knows of." He looked at Jed. "You're perfectly sure he had no quarrel of any kind with Ernestine?"

Jed frowned; he said slowly, "I was sure; Shepson asked

me that. But I suppose I might not have known it. Maybe after all he . . ." He stopped though, blankly.

Fitz said: "Robbery is ruled out . . ." Again there was a kind of hope in the look he gave Jed.

Jed shook his black head. "Not a single thing gone. Camilla knew every bit of jewelry and every trinket Ernestine had; I gave them all to her—except, oh, one or two pieces. There wasn't much of value; I haven't got that kind of money."

"Well, then—are you absolutely sure that there was nobody strange around the place? I mean, of course, you can't be perfectly sure of that—but if we could prove even a tramp or hobo prowling around it would help."

Eagerness flared into Jed's face again. "What's wrong with inventing one? In a case like this . . ."

"I told you, Jed, we've got to have the truth. Something solid, probable, facts. Don't act like a child!"

Jed's face flushed. He got up. "I'll do this my way and I'll do it; I'll fix it. I'll . . ."

"You'll sit down," said Fitz, suddenly weary. "And try to use your head. What about Ernestine, then? What about a motive? Was there anybody—anybody at all, Jed, who might have wanted to get rid of her for any possible reason?"

Jed sat down slowly and rather sullenly; he leaned his head on his hand and stared at the white cloth. "You're asking me to do a difficult thing; we didn't get along, we— but she was my wife."

"On the face of it I don't like it, either—none of us does —but the need outweighs everything else. . . . Shepson questioned you about motives."

"Yes. Oh, yes, over and over."

Fitz's gray eyes were again rather fixed. "And you couldn't think of anything. Any—quarrel she'd had with anybody. Any hold she had perhaps . . ."

"My wife was not a blackmailer," cried Jed, jerking up his head.

74

"For our present purpose we've got to think she might have been. The fact is, if this wasn't a purposeless, wanton murder—by some stranger, some stray who merely happened on the scene, merely happened to snatch up your gun . . ."

"Maybe Ernestine snatched it, to defend herself."

"That's right. That's a good point and it adds to the intruder theory. It's still a thin theory, though, if we can't produce the intruder. And if it wasn't an intruder then it had to be somebody Ernestine knew and who knew her well enough to want to murder her."

They knew that; they'd known it from the beginning, but it yet had the impact of a very peculiar horror. It limited murder to someone within a small circle.

Caroline's hand on the table was trembling; Sue saw it and wanted to take it and tell her it wasn't so, that nobody they knew, none of that close circle, had crossed a terrible barrier which man has set up for his own protection. But they'd thought of it, that winter—how could they have not thought of it? At cold and desolate moments, the question would strike. Do these eyes meeting mine so frankly actually conceal the knowledge of murder? Does this hand clasping mine in friendship have dreadful recollection of death?

Sue said quickly, "But Ernestine knew so many people. Not just us, but all those outsiders, all the people who come to hunt, so many newcomers, so many . . ."

"That's true," Fitz said, "but someone close to her might have a clue. You, Sue, and Camilla and Ruby knew her so long and so well. Jed, Wat Luddington—I, myself; we were closest to her. Among us we might discover some hint, some faint clue."

Jed, staring at the table, said suddenly, "We might. Yes —there might be something—I'm not sure . . ."

Fitz's control slipped; there was sharp impatience in his voice. "Jed, can't you see how important it is? What are you talking about?"

But the impatience aroused Jed's instinctive sense of combat; he lifted obstinate and angry eyes to Fitz. "I'm only trying to think—trying to remember. Ernestine—you all knew her; as you say it's not a time for—well, she was difficult; she was—high-handed. She made people furious when she wanted to, and she was ambitious. She knew of course that I liked Sue, she wasn't very pleasant about it— Shepson wouldn't let me admit that. She might have had a quarrel with almost anybody, really, but if she had I didn't know it."

Caroline said suddenly, "How was she ambitious, Jed? What did she want?"

It was an important question. Fitz flashed Caroline a look of approval. It was like Caroline's honesty to put her finger on what could be the crux, the motivating force which had led—but by what dark ways?—to Ernestine's murder. Suddenly it occurred to Sue that they had never inquired like that before about Ernestine herself; yet if her murder was an affair of motive (maddened and twisted though it might be) and not a wanton, chance and brutal thing, then that motive had to lie in something Ernestine wanted, or didn't want—desired or opposed or threatened. Perhaps they had been, up to then, mainly taken up with clearing Jed. It had preoccupied them; its urgency had both obscured and denied paths of inquiry which did not appear to lead directly to that end, or which might be dangerous to Jed.

Fitz said to Caroline, "That's right! Now Jed's acquitted there's no reason not to proceed on that line. Before now Ernestine—well, there was no point in emphasizing anything which might seem, then, to add to the case against him, I mean to provide fuel for quarrels between them, that sort of thing. So Shepson said. But now . . ." He got up. "Thanks for breakfast, Miss Caroline. Do you want to come with me, Jed?"

"Where are you going?"

"I thought I'd go and see the sheriff. Find out if there's any news."

"He wouldn't tell you."

"Maybe not. But he's friendly, he might."

Jed looked at Sue, looked at Fitz. "Well, all right, I'll come back, Sue, just as soon as I can."

There was nothing so overt as proprietorship in his tone; there was an easy acceptance, a kind of recognition of mutual claims upon each other. Fitz flashed a quick look at her, and then went with Caroline into the hall. Jed was about to follow; Sue braced her hands on the table. "Jed—wait . . ."

He turned. "Why, Sue . . ."

"I want you to know. Jed, what we felt for each other wasn't—wasn't real. We—I don't know how it happened or what but it wasn't real, I know that now, and I . . ."

"What are you talking about?"

"I'm trying to say, that I—I can't—we don't really love each other, so . . ."

Incredulous surprise flashed into his eyes. "Why, Sue Poore! Are you trying to say you don't want to marry me?"

"We were wrong, Jed. We were mistaken. We . . ."

"Well, I never heard of such a thing! Of course we're going to be married. We're engaged, aren't we?"

"No, we're not. No . . ."

He interrupted, "Well, we are. You've just got yourself worked up, Sue honey—it's been rough. I realize it, but we're in the clear now. I'll . . ." The hall door closed; he cried, "There goes Fitz. Listen, Sue, I'll come back. I'll soon talk you out of this."

"Jed, I mean it. It's true. I mean it."

"Why—why, Sue! You can't let me down like that. Why I . . ." He came back a step or two, his face flushed, his voice shaken and vehement. "You can't. I need you, Sue. I love you. I've depended on you all this time. You . . ." His face cleared. "You're tired and worried and don't

77

mean it! Sue, darling, we'll get you out of this. . . . I'll be back as soon as I can."

He waved and smiled and dashed out the door, down the hall. There was a word with Caroline; the front door closed again.

She was still standing there when Caroline came back. She sighed and pushed up her hair. "I wonder," she said, "what Ernestine was up to."

"Ernestine! But what could she . . ."

"I don't know what. But we all knew Ernestine." Caroline added thoughtfully, "I told Fitz to question Camilla; Camilla's not as smart as Ernestine but she's—and then besides," said Caroline not really on a tangent, "Camilla certainly does like Fitz. Ernestine snapped up Jed soon as he came down here and didn't have anything to do but spend his money; maybe Ernestine thought he had more than he had. Anyway it was the best match that offered itself. Young men around here, young men with money, aren't too plentiful; it's always rich but married men. If Camilla's not set her cap for Fitz I can't see straight!"

Sue said, astonished, "I never heard you say anything mean about anybody."

"Well, then," Caroline said, "it's high time," and unexpectedly a little ghost of a giggle caught them both. In the very midst of it, however, Sue thought, "But that's right, Camilla does like Fitz."

In the afternoon Camilla came.

It was a curiously divided day. On the one hand there was the familiar and comforting presence of the house, of all its tangible reminders that life was sweet and secure and gracious, that it had always been safe, that it would go on like that. It surrounded them with a layer of kindness and of reassurance; it fought off a very dark and dreadful shadow with its reminders of sunshine and warmth.

But on the other hand the telephone might ring at any moment. A police car might drive up. Their ears were attuned to that possibility.

As the day wore on the silence began to seem rather ominous. Fitz did not telephone; Jed did not telephone. So probably the sheriff either had or gave them no news. It was Thursday; ordinarily Caroline would have joined the Beaufort meet. Caroline subscribed to the Dobberly hunt; it was by now almost her child. She had been M.F.H., she loved the Dobberly hunt, the Dobberly packs, the acres of hills and meadows over which they hunted, she knew the hounds, their names and dispositions as well as she knew the dispositions and names of friends: old Reveller, his toenails worn down and too old and stiff to hunt, had been a leader of the pack, brought home by Caroline to be given a peaceful old age. (Sister Britches was a pet; she had never hunted except for private excursions of her own into the woods behind the stables.) But Caroline was well known also and popular among the neighboring hunts; her dressing-table mirror was always studded with invitations. There was scarcely a day during the whole season when she did not join some hunt; she was restless that day, missing the hunt, missing the usual vigorous and happy routine of her life.

She gave Geneva and Jeremy in turn some rather desultory exercise around and around a track that had been worn down, in the long meadow behind the house, by other horses long ago. She found a thorn in one of Reveller's old feet and worked at it energetically.

Even the horses were restless. Once the Beaufort hunt in full cry swept fairly near, over the ridge toward Dobberly; old Jeremy thumped about crossly in his loose box. Caroline looked wistful. "They're heading toward the Luddington woods," she said and listened. "The fox will cross Osbaldeston Run the other side of Dobberly, strike for the Luddington woods and get to Hollow Hill again. I wonder if we ought to have more of those earths stopped."

She knew the country better than any topographer; she knew what the fox was likely to do at any given point. She listened to the faraway cry with an intent yet dreamy smile of longing; to Sue the music was merely a remote and rather eerie wail, pitched on a high note. "I've been away for too long," Sue thought, "it's the land of my birth and I feel like a stranger." She offered, apologetically, to exercise Jeremy.

"N-no," Caroline said. "He's had enough. . . . Someone might come," and went back to the stables to berate, insofar as Caroline was able to berate, her only stableman, who was not a stableman at all but a boy of fourteen or so, Chrisy's grandson, Lij.

Camilla drove up about four in Jed's car; she got out and hurried up the steps. For the first time since Ernestine's death she was wearing a color, a beige tweed suit that, as a matter of fact, had belonged to Ernestine. Again Sue had the illusion of a stronger, more forceful Camilla, clothed literally in Ernestine's suit and in Ernestine's authority. Camilla said, stripping off her gloves, "Who's that man parked down by the road? Sue, I want to talk to you about Jed."

9

THE MAN parked down by the road, out of sight of the house, was a policeman. Chrisy went down to see, creeping along in her blue starchy uniform, behind the laurels, to peer at him. Camilla had whirled past too rapidly to see the uniform; he had made, however, no attempt to stop her.

And Camilla had come, not as Jed's emissary, but to plead his case. "Jed doesn't know I've come. Sue Poore, you can't be serious." She appealed to Caroline. "Jed says that Sue said she'd changed her mind; she said she doesn't want to marry him. Oh, of course, Jed doesn't think she means it but I think it's outrageous for Sue to talk like that. What has got into you, Sue! You can't let him down like this. He's depending on you; you mean everything to him. He said so. He said, all this horrible winter, the poor boy, he's got through it only by thinking of you. You'll just have to marry him, Sue. And if you ask me, I think you ought to be thankful he wants to marry you!"

Caroline bristled. Sue cried, "Wait, Aunt Caroline. Camilla, this is between me and Jed and . . ."

"It's my business, too," snapped Camilla. "I was Ernestine's sister. Jed is more than a brother to me. He loves you and you gave him every reason to think you loved him just as much and that you'd marry him. Even before Ernestine died, that very night when he talked of divorce, you . . ."

Caroline uttered a threatening sound.

Sue said, "No, that's wrong, Camilla. I meant what I said to him then; I was going away. I . . ."

"Going away, nothing! You were just leading him on. Besides Jed's a good match. Where would you hope to make a better one? There's not another unattached man in the county!"

Caroline got a word in there before Sue could stop her. "There's Fitz," she said mildly, but with a cold sparkle in her blue eyes.

It checked Camilla; she came to a full, blank stop as if all her instincts sent out little questions like groping tentacles; she said then, "Fitz! Do you mean to imply, Miss Caroline, that Fitz Wilson and Sue . . ."

Caroline adroitly and with a pleased glint in her eyes, side-stepped. "Not at all! What on earth made you think of that, Camilla? You said Jed was the only unattached man in the county and I said no, there was Fitz."

"Well," said Camilla, "but—and besides, Fitz—well, at any rate, Miss Caroline, I think you ought to make Sue see her duty to Jed. As well as her duty to herself. Good gracious, after all that publicity and their meeting in the cabaña and—everybody perfectly sure that . . ."

Caroline suddenly was dangerous; she stood, looking like a rather tousled but militant duchess and advanced upon Camilla. "Camilla Duval, if I hadn't known your mother and grandmother before you, I'd smack your face . . ."

Sue caught her square little hand. "Darling, let me talk . . ."

"I've got plenty to say myself," snapped Caroline, "and I've got a right to say it. You listen to me now, Camilla Duval."

Camilla was looking uneasy. "I didn't mean to hurt your feelings, Miss Caroline. But I do think Sue ought to marry him, and I think as much for her own sake as Jed's. Everybody thinks so; they expect it. It's the only thing for Sue to do. I'm one of Sue's oldest friends, and—and Jed needs her so much, he told me so; it's her duty . . ."

The telephone at last rang.

Caroline turned ashy white. She forgot Camilla; she swept to the telephone and picked it up. But it must be Fitz, thought Sue; or Jed, or . . .

Caroline said, "Oh. Sheriff Benjamin . . ." in a stifled voice. She listened for a second or two and sat down as if her sturdy knees wouldn't hold her. She turned stricken eyes to Sue. "He wants to talk to you, he—here," she held the telephone to Sue.

Sue moved. She crossed the room; her hand touched Caroline's, she saw Caroline's imploring, tragic gaze; she spoke into the telephone and Sheriff Benjamin said, "Miss Sue?"

"Yes?"

"I've told your aunt. I'm afraid I've got bad news." He cleared his throat; he was reluctant, hating his duty. The words were forced out, "I wanted to warn you ahead of time in case—I've known your people, Miss Sue, all my life and I—but the fact is I was overridden in this, I—the fact is"—he cleared his throat again—"I've just sworn out a warrant for your arrest."

The room was so still that the beating of her pulse in Sue's ears was like a drum; somewhere Sister Britches was scratching at a screen wanting to be let in; in the distance, away off, the Sheriff's voice said finally: "Did you hear me?"

"Yes."

"I wanted to warn you. I've fixed it so they won't be along for another two or three hours; I'd suggest you get in touch immediately with a lawyer, maybe Judge Shepson." He hesitated. "I am doing this as a matter of personal friendship; ex officio. They, the state police, Captain Henley, in fact, and a Captain Wilkins, feel that I am prejudiced in your favor. I—well, at any rate—I'll see that you have some time to do what you can to prepare."

Sue whispered, after a moment, "Thank you."

Later it occurred to her that he was doing a bold and courageous thing. There had been strong pressure; his present action might endanger his own job. He said, "I'm sorry. I wish I could do more."

She said, "Thank you," again as she put down the telephone.

Camilla was beside her, listening; Caroline stood up, stiffly, her face frozen and white with only her eyes alive and, again, imploring. Sue thought, if I could only tell her that it was wrong, that she was mistaken, that he didn't say that. Camilla said shrilly, "What did he say? What's wrong? What did he say—Sue, have they found out . . ."

Sue turned. "He's sworn out a warrant . . ." Her voice stopped. Camilla searched her face with those bright, sharp eyes and cried, "A warrant—he's going to make an arrest—you!"

There was a long moment of silence; Camilla said, "Oh, my God!"

Caroline said: "I'm going to phone Fitz," and took up the telephone.

Afterward it seemed to Sue that she listened and watched as if none of it had anything to do with her. Even the room was strange, the colors had changed, the dimensions were different; she felt lightheaded, so some things were obscured and some things painfully clear. Caroline was asking for Fitz's number, repeating it, Camilla was pacing up and down, pausing to watch and listen, too, twisting her gloves, smoothing Ernestine's skirt nervously; her eyes seemed to have retreated in her head, under that fair coronet of braids, above that thick, wide jaw. Sue thought blankly, "Arrested, that means charged with murder, Ernestine's murder. Me!"

Caroline said sharply to Camilla, "Tell Chrisy to bring some whiskey, quick."

Camilla hurried to the door but then paused to listen as someone answered the telephone at Fitz's house. It was Jason but Fitz was not there.

"Ask him to call me when he gets back." Caroline put down the telephone. "He doesn't know where he is."

Camilla vanished toward the dining room. Caroline

lifted the telephone again, "Dobberly one three five."

It was a familiar number, the number Caroline always had called in times of crisis, Dr. Luddington. Camilla, followed by Chrisy, came back as he answered. Chrisy's face was like a thundercloud; her lower lip was shaking. She carried a decanter of whiskey and a glass and she poured out a drink—which she placed on the table. Caroline said, "The sheriff phoned. It's come. They made him swear out a warrant. Oh, Tom—what are we going to do?"

Sue said, "Tell him we've got several hours. Tell him Sheriff Benny's holding off the police as long as he can. Tell him . . ." Caroline nodded and repeated it word for word in short quick bursts. She listened, then; all of them listened. Camilla's perfume—rose, like the perfume Ernestine had always used, Sue thought queerly—floated out and around them like a ghost of Ernestine, like an avenging presence. Ernestine would want to be revenged.

Caroline put down the telephone again. "He said he'd do something. He said to wait."

Camilla said rapidly, "I'm going home. I'm going home now, Sue. I—I think I'd better go home."

Chrisy looked at her with dark fury and reproach. "Well, then, Miss Camilla, you go on home. Nobody's stopping you."

Camilla gave her a cold glance. "Oh, there's nothing I can do. I—I was thinking of Jed. I . . ."

Caroline did not answer; Camilla in Ernestine's beige suit, trailing rose perfume, went away. They heard her high heels tap on the hall floor; they heard the front door bang; they heard Jed's car start up and sweep down the drive with a roar. Chrisy said, biting her angry underlip: "Ain't that like her now! Off like a scared cat. Them Duval girls never was any account, if you ask me." But, valiant though she was, she turned to Caroline like a frightened child, "What we going to do now, Miss Caroline?"

Caroline said firmly, as if it answered everything, as she had done so many times in the past, "I've called Dr. Luddington."

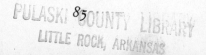

So they waited, the three women, while a man in a police car at the gate, down by the roadside, waited, too.

An hour later they were still waiting; nothing had happened except the Beaufort hunt, foiled, as Caroline had predicted they would be, of their original fox, had found again and had swept back across the ridge toward Dobberly. The eerie music of the hounds wailed closer; Caroline did not appear to hear it. Drearily it began to rain.

The heavy sky, the rain, the walls of the house, closed in upon them. Caroline again tried to telephone Fitz and he had not returned. A few minutes later the telephone rang at last, but it was not Fitz. It was not as a matter of fact, Dr. Luddington, but it was a message from him. "It's a patient," Caroline said past the telephone to Sue, and listened and presently put it down. "He's a patient; he says Dr. Luddington asked him to tell you that he was held up by an emergency and that you're to come to his office right away; he'll meet you there." Caroline frowned. "He said you're to come alone."

It was, for an instant, perplexing; Chrisy, who had remained with them in spite of its being Thursday, her day off, suggested an answer. "That man down there in the car, that policeman. Maybe the doctor knows he's there; maybe he don't want him to stop you, Miss Sue."

Was the waiting policeman, then, empowered to arrest her if she left the place? Caroline said, "I'll take you in the car. I'll drive and you can get down in the back seat and hide . . ."

Chrisy was shaking her head. "Ain't no good, Miss Caroline. He'll see her."

It was a queer, small problem; their pent-up anxiety sharpened its urgency. It made imperative the need to obey Dr. Luddington to the letter. Caroline said, "Take old Jeremy! It's easy; by the lane behind Wat's place; nobody will even see you and if they do . . ." she frowned and said: "Of course, get into riding coat and hat; they'll think you're part of the hunt. The policeman will never think of stopping you if he sees you at a distance; he'll never—hurry, Sue."

Chrisy was already puffing heavily up the stairs; Caroline went to get Jeremy saddled. It could have been little more than five minutes, ten at the most, before Sue, in coat and hurriedly tied stock, her hair and hat properly netted, ran across the gap in the driveway made in the laurels, to where Lij held Jeremy. She was sure that the policeman had not seen her.

"Hurry," said Caroline and thrust a crop into her hands, "You'll need this for the gates."

Sue was in the saddle. The rain was a drizzle, cold on her face. Caroline said, "There's only one fence, Sue, and two —no, three—gates. Give Jeremy his head at the Luddington lower pasture, it's swampy. Take it easy. . . ."

Jeremy shook his head and Sue gave him a looser rein. He set off contentedly, with long, easy strides, around the stables, out on the dirt lane and then into a zestful gallop. To Caroline, of course, this was the most practical form of transportation, but it added to Sue's feeling of unreality. Sue Poore, galloping off across meadows she'd known all her life, to try to save herself from being charged with murder. They ought to have waited.

It was a vague feeling, due probably to her slight sense of the theatrical. Jeremy pricked his ears forward. The Beaufort hunt could not be far away; the shrill music was clear and sounded near. She swerved Jeremy who showed (and had) every intention of joining the hunt, across a small stream which he jumped with pleasure and so eagerly that Sue did not manage quite to avoid the willows; her hat was knocked on one side, her thin but wiry veil torn, her cheek lashed by the sting. She righted her hat and took Jeremy more deliberately across grazing land of the adjoining farm, keeping to the lower ground in case of observation from the now distant main highway; she came out at the bridge over Dobberly Run, took Jeremy onto the country road, up the hill, and, then, beyond the great Wat Luddington place, she could see Dobberly village.

It was a village of two or three main streets. Dr. Luddington's red brick house was at its outskirts with perhaps forty acres or so of meadow and woodland behind it, a woodland which merged into the Wat Luddington woods.

She went slowly along the road. The whole Luddington place was fenced—a post and rail, newly painted a gleaming white, built for a hunting country and easy for a rider as expert as Caroline. Sue never liked to jump. She had to cross the fence however, in order to reach the lane which wandered erratically behind the great show place—which Ruby had bought with her first husband's money and Wat managed with the lavishness for which the place was well equipped—and on, following the lower ground, into the Luddington woods. At length she turned Jeremy, who was a born jumper, took one pleased look at the fence, gave himself a run, and sailed over it; Sue's knees relaxed and her heart settled back down; for her always there was a moment of suspense just before she jumped. She took a long breath and looked around her; the grazing land there was firm but she turned Jeremy toward the lower, swampier meadow where it was slower going but less easily visible from the house and stables.

They reached higher ground again behind the white stables, a gate which opened and closed readily, a short lane between paddock rails, another gate and at last the long lane which eventually wound through the woods where Dr. Luddington's place and Wat's and Ruby's adjoined— one of the reasons for Ruby's purchase of the place. Another, of course, was its magnificence. The lane here was not much used; it was wet and choppy, but it was a lane and she made better time. Better, at least, until she entered the woods.

The drizzle had slackened to a rather bewildering mist. She was not too familiar with the woods; the gray-brown shapes of trees, the masses of laurels and pines were alike confusing. The lane eventually petered out; if she bore to the right she would go at least in the direction of Dr.

Luddington's house. She did so and came to the bank of a tiny stream heavily bordered with willows and green, glossy laurels, the Dobberly Run, which wound leisurely all through the woods. The Beaufort hunt had passed that way and not long before; the marks of horses' hooves were sharp and deep in the red clay and the sound of the hounds seemed to linger in the air. The stream curved out of sight behind willows and laurels and it, too, had to be jumped.

Fast at water; slow at woodland. This was not, even for Sue, a difficult jump; it had, however, apparently been difficult for a straggler from the Beaufort hunt, for in the very second that Jeremy jumped the narrow stream she caught a flashing glimpse of the red coat, the black and white staccato notes of collar and stock, of another rider. He was beyond the curve, barely visible through the screen of laurels and willows, getting onto his horse. Obviously he had taken a spill; she did not think he saw her. He disappeared instantly behind the laurels. She turned old Jeremy again and followed the course of the stream.

She came out quite suddenly in view of the village and in view of the paddocks where Dr. Luddington's old riding horse grazed peacefully in fair weather. The stables obscured her view of the house; she followed the paddock rail, reached a gate and, this time, dismounted to lead Jeremy through it. She led him the rest of the way; no one was in the stable, but Dr. Luddington's car, a new and glistening car which Wat had insisted on presenting him, stood in the graveled drive behind the house. There was a light in his consulting room.

She tied old Jeremy securely as Caroline had taught her to do and walked around the house, following the gravel drive. She came out for an instant on the street. The house was flush with the sidewalk, its brass knocker worn by the pressure through the years of many seeking hands; she rang, but then remembered it was Thursday, no one would answer, it was maid's day out. Anyway, the door to the office wing of the house was always unlocked. She opened

89

the door and slid quickly inside, feeling hunted as any fox, casting a glance over her shoulder to make sure no stray trooper had seen her. The street was deserted; the sky was heavy and dark. She closed the door.

She was in a small square hall with an old-fashioned hat rack and below it an umbrella stand made of majolica ware; she knew them both as one knows old and familiar faces. A small waiting room was at the right and she went in quickly. The door across the room, the door which led to his consulting room, was closed.

It meant that he was engaged with a patient. Probably, she thought, the same patient who had telephoned his message.

That room, too, was familiar; it was extremely ugly, with its dark, mission-oak chairs and settee, its shiny brown linoleum, the great fern in its green pot. She knew every detail of it and loved it. There was no sound of voices from beyond the consulting-room door. She debated knocking, in order to let Dr. Luddington know that she had arrived but he knew that; the bell at the door rang also in the consulting room. He was still occupied with the emergency.

Had she tied Jeremy securely? She was sure she had. She wondered if anyone had seen her. Suppose they had; it didn't matter. Again she had a vague feeling that they had been too hurried, she and Caroline and Chrisy, too frightened. Probably she could have simply driven out in the car, straight to Dr. Luddington's office. There was still no sound from behind the closed door. She walked nervously around the room.

Magazines all but covered the table (of the mission-oak period, again) magazines which were, in this office, heavily interlarded with hunt and horse magazines; a picture of Ruby, lovely and calm, mounted on the fabulous hunter Rocking Horse which she had bought at a fabulous price looked out from the front page of one of them.

She put it down beside a stack of *Chronicles* with their familiar banner—Breeding, Farming, Hunting: Showing

Chacing, Racing. Dr. Luddington's first diploma still hung on the wall where he'd placed it—how long ago, now? Near it was a faded picture of his young wife, who had been Sadie Carew, who had died shortly after Wat, their only son, was born. Wat had been destined to follow his father's footsteps and then—because he met Ruby again (after her unexpected widowhood had lasted a year or so) in New York and married her, had come back to Virginia, to build the career Wat himself had chosen, with the money that actually had come to Ruby through the death of her first husband. Perhaps Ruby had engineered that meeting. Wat had come first with her, since the day when, a remote and orphaned connection of the Duvals, a child who showed little promise of the beauty she was to become, she had been sent to Dobberly and the care of Mrs. Duval (a faded and discontented edition of Ernestine and Camilla, who after Ernestine's marriage had taken herself, a small annuity, and an obscure but convenient ailment to a sanitarium in Italy from which, comfortably, she refused to emerge).

Wat, of course, in those days had had eyes for no one but Ernestine—glittering, charming Ernestine, who outshone everybody (especially fat little Ruby with her slow, dull ways) but who frankly intended to make a good match. There was, beside the picture of Wat's mother, another picture, a snapshot of the four girls.

It, too, was indescribably familiar to Sue, but she looked at it now with a feeling of poignant strangeness; four laughing, squinting girls with blown hair and tennis rackets, Ruby standing behind Ernestine so her fat little legs would not show. How inextricably their lives had been entangled even then!

But it was Ruby who, unexpectedly, had made the astounding marriage, Ruby who resolutely had become the beauty, Ruby who had taken her small inheritance and a world cruise and there met Jacob DeJong, the extremely rich Hollander, much older than Ruby, who had fallen in love with her and with her beauty and eighteen months after their marriage had died. It still seemed surprising, too, that it was Ruby who had married twice in that short —yet very long—time, first Jacob DeJong and then Wat Luddington whom Sue—all of them—had known all their lives and whom Ruby had always frankly wanted to marry.

Ernestine, smiling so complacently in the picture, was dead, and she, Sue Poore, was about to be charged with her murder.

She moved away from the picture. Suddenly she felt that much time had passed since she entered the waiting room. The patient in the consulting room ought to be bandaged or splinted by now—splinted probably; most of Dr. Luddington's emergency calls were on hunting days and, while he had brought many babies into the world, he had also set and wired an inordinate number of broken bones.

She stood for a long time again staring at the door before she went to it and knocked. No one replied.

He must be there; his car was outside. How long, really, could Sheriff Benjamin hold off her arrest? She knocked again and then suddenly, overcome by something that came out of that silence, flung open the door.

There was no patient there. Dr. Luddington sat at his desk. He did not look up. There was a dark, wet looking patch on the back of his gray coat.

The silence was like a cloth laid down upon her, upon the figure at the desk, upon the world. That cloth, however, was suddenly torn by the sound of a horse galloping off somewhere in the dusk outside, galloping wildly in furious haste as if he had a rider. Jeremy?

She saw, at the same time, the revolver on the desk. It gave her a blinding sense of repetition; she had experienced this before. The only difference was the sound of those wildly galloping hooves which died away as she listened.

This time she did not touch the revolver.

10

THERE WAS actually, however, another very important difference in the circumstances surrounding the murder of Ernestine Baily and the circumstances surrounding the murder of Dr. Thomas Luddington. Ernestine with her fingers pressed to her back, had moved; she had talked before she died.

Dr. Luddington had died at once, before he could talk or move or summon help. The bullet had gone, this time, straight to the heart.

Yet he could not be dead. Sue's instinct was to deny it. A small mirrored surface, a box of some kind, stood on the desk amid shuffled papers; she held it near his lips. There was not the faintest misting on its bright surface.

She straightened up; the black window panes winked at her, reflecting the bright overhead light, reflecting the doctor's bowed, slumped-down figure—reflecting a girl in riding habit, dark coat and light breeches, with a stock that was no whiter than her face. And terror emerged from the silence and the dusk.

She moved back, toward the waiting room, glancing from side to side. No one was there. No patient, no—her eyes glanced over the telephone, returned. Telephone, of course. She reached across his old typewriter; she lifted the telephone.

Suddenly terror washed over her; she must get out of the house, out into the street, scream, shout for help. Her lips were shaking against the telephone.

She did not hear the car stop outside the house, but she heard the sound of the front door as it opened and someone came into the waiting room. The footsteps were loud and candid; there was nothing furtive or stealthy about them; a man's voice said, "Dr. Luddington? I came as soon as I could," and Jed came to the door, saw her, stopped abruptly and then ran across; the whole room jarred; the instruments on the table tinkled. He bent over Dr. Luddington; he knelt on the floor.

He had knelt like that beside Ernestine, when she sat on the couch and refused to die and then said that he had shot her.

The dusky, foggy twilight, the revolver, the wound in the back—Jed and herself. The grim repetition struck her with a savage new terror, inexorable, as if once launched the insistent train of likeness could not be stopped. She cried wildly, "You must go! They'll arrest you! This time they'll never let you go. They'll—Oh, Jed, why did you come like that. . . ."

He was getting to his feet; he knocked against a chair that scraped backward with a screech so loud that it covered her words, too loud in that silent house which murder had entered. He caught her shaking hands. "Sue—what were you doing?—What . . ."

"I was going to telephone. The operator—she'll know what to do. The—the police. *The police, Jed!* You must get away first or they'll . . ."

"What about you?"

The whirling dark waters had closed over her indeed; she stared at Jed.

"I'm all right," he said. "It's you that—come on, Sue." He turned with a jerk toward the door. "I'm going to get you out of here. You don't realize. The whole county'll be in arms. . . ."

The telephone rang. It was sharp and shrill across the sodden figure of the man in the chair who would never

94

lean forward to be summoned forth again upon an errand of mercy and of skill.

Jed dropped her hands and went to pick up the telephone. "Hello. . . ."

It was a woman; it was the operator. Jed said, "Why, yes —yes, someone did try to call from here. There's been a serious accident—No, the doctor is—call the police. We want the police. This is Jed Baily, tell them—listen, don't call the state troopers. Get Sheriff Benjamin over in Bedford first. It's important—that's right."

He put down the telephone; Sue moved blindly into the waiting room; she could not stay in the brightly lighted consulting room near that bowed figure, which was now so strangely different. Out of chaos emerged an age-old question—where has he gone? This is the face I knew, the hand I've touched, but where is he? She sat down in one of the mission-oak chairs; they must tell Caroline, they must tell Wat. Jed came to the door.

"Sue, you must get out of here. . . ."

"He was like a father to me, Jed. He—always—he was so dear to me."

"Yes, Sue, I know, but . . ."

"We've got to let Wat know."

He came across to her, putting his hand on her shoulder. "Don't you understand, Sue, how necessary . . ."

Someone again came quickly into the hall, closing the outer door; there was no time to move or speak; heels tapped across the hall and Ruby Luddington came in, saw them and stopped abruptly. "Why, Sue! Jed—I—didn't expect—I . . ." Ruby was never very quick on the uptake, but she caught an uneasy breath; her lovely dark eyes went from Sue to Jed. "Is anything wrong?" She started toward the consulting room as if she guessed; Jed tried to stop her. "No, Ruby, don't—it's too late. . . ."

"Too late? Too—what's happened? It's the doctor—what . . ."

Jed took her arm but she brushed past both of them. She was in riding clothes. They saw her stop in the doorway, her shoulders stiffening, her hands clenching at her sides. Then she went into the room, and out of sight. There was not a sound, not a breath of motion; Jed said, "Do you suppose she's fainted? I'd better go . . ." he went into the room and said: "Ruby, I tried to tell you. . . ."

"He's dead," said Ruby in a stunned way.

"I'm so sorry, Ruby. It's a shock . . ."

"What happened?"

"We don't know."

"It's like Ernestine," Ruby said in a kind of whisper.

"Come out, Ruby. You can't help him now. Don't touch anything. . . ."

"He can't be dead. He can't—he sent for me, he told me to come, I don't understand. . . ."

"He sent for me, too, he—then he was like that. Ruby, we've got to let Wat know. . . ."

"What have you done?"

"There wasn't anything to do. He was dead. We phoned for the police. . . ."

There was a sharp silence; then Ruby said, "Police?"

"Well, it does look like Ernestine. I mean—it's in the back. . . ."

Ruby came back to the doorway; she looked stonily at Sue, her dark eyes very large in her white face.

"His gun is there." Jed came back into the room. "It's on the desk. I didn't touch it." He looked at Sue and at Ruby. "See here, Ruby, I'll talk fast but—it's like this. They're about to arrest Sue for Ernestine's murder. . . ."

"Sue!"

"At least that's what Camilla said. Is it true, Sue?"

She nodded; Jed went on hurriedly. "The point is, Ruby, if the police find her here—I mean—there's not time to plan—the only thing is for her to get out quick. I'm going to make her leave and, Ruby, will you swear that she was not here?"

"No, Jed, we can't. . . ." Sue began.

Jed said hurriedly, "Ruby, I'll explain later. I'll tell you exactly why it is so important. But just this minute, before the police come, we've got to get Sue out of the way."

"Why, of course," Ruby said. "If you think it's right. But I don't understand. . . ."

"I can't go," Sue said.

Jed stared at her. "Why, but Sue . . ."

She said inadequately, "It's Dr. Luddington . . ."

"It's too late anyway," Ruby said, listening. "There's somebody now."

Jed said, "It's the police. It's the state police—I can see their lights. . . ."

Ruby, thick and stolid, in her perfectly tailored black coat, did a queer thing; she looked all around the room and said in a slow, calm voice, "That fern needs water," and went over to touch the fern in a dazed, sleepwalking way.

So Ruby, Sue thought fleetingly, felt more than she showed. Then heavy, authoritative feet thumped up the steps and men, uniforms, shining leather belts seemed to crowd the little hall. She and Ruby and Jed stood, as if at bay, to meet them.

They were state troopers. Jed had reckoned without the radio in their patrol car. Sheriff Benjamin had sent them immediately; there were, in fact, only two of them and they quickly questioned Jed, who went into the consulting room with them. Ruby said vaguely, "I've got to phone to Wat," and then did not move to do so.

Later Sue realized that what seemed at the time confusion was actually an extremely orderly procedure; the men were excited but knew what they were to do and did it promptly; she heard them telephoning; she heard them questioning Jed. They did not question her or Ruby; they were still in the consulting room when another car and still another came roaring up the little street which suddenly was full of shifting lights and uniforms and people as the neighbors along the street, seeing the lights, hearing what

97

had happened, began to gather in excited groups outside the house.

Captain Henley and Sheriff Benjamin came in the second car. Sheriff Benjamin gave her a quick nod; Captain Henley's excited eyes were like two bright daggers pinioning her with guilt. He went through hurriedly into the consulting room. Sue thought, "I can't stay, I can't listen, I can't sit here and look at his diploma—at that picture of me and Ernestine and Camilla and Ruby." And there was nothing else to do; she had to stay.

Somehow she must tell Caroline; she stopped a trooper. He would not let her phone Caroline; he promised, though, hurriedly, to see that Miss Poore was told. And immediately Sue regretted it; it would have been better to wait. She said, "Let Chrisy—that's the maid, let her tell my aunt. . . ." The trooper was young, excited, but seemed to accept it; he nodded and hurried on, into the consulting room.

And then they took the three of them away, out the back door on account of all the people in the street. "We don't want any trouble," Captain Henley said to Sheriff Benjamin. "There's the making of a mob out there. Everybody loved him."

A mob, thought Sue; and it could not be and was. Ruby rose, seeming perfectly collected. She linked her arm in Sue's; they went out through the consulting room, through a tiny hall and into a kitchen and then quickly, into a police car. It took a route around the stables and then to a highway. Sue felt as if she were in a nightmare, speeding frantically through unfamiliar and frightening space which had no end. Yet Ruby beside her was familiar, her white face clear in the dusk; Jed, on the other side of Sue, took her hand tightly. They arrived at Bedford; they went to the same side entrance where, during the last moments of Jed's trial, before the acquittal, she and Fitz had hurried to Fitz's car, to escape.

They went into the courthouse—it was dimly lighted and musty and smelled of cleaning compounds—they were in Sheriff Benjamin's office.

They remained there until nearly morning.

They did not begin to question them (beyond Jed's first statement) either singly or separately, at once; they put them under guard. About eight Jed induced one of the troopers sitting with them to send out for sandwiches and coffee. Hot, thick hamburgers came and coffee in paper containers. Ruby ate hers firmly, all the way through and a faint color came into her lovely face. They looked strange and out of place, the two women in black coats and beige breeches; Jed in slacks and a sweater and sport coat, sitting there in the bare, brightly lighted room. There was an inner office, too; men came and went; there must have been a telephone there, for it rang often; once when the door was opened, Sue caught a glimpse of a great, black safe with a picture painted on its door, standing in a corner and laden with magazines and hats and a dangling fly swatter.

Eventually, after the telephone had rung again, a trooper came to the door. "Miss Poore?"

All Sue's body seemed to jerk to attention; were they going to question her now, were they going to take her away somewhere, put into effect that warrant which had been sworn out for her arrest in that very office? The trooper had seen her involuntary move; she did not need to reply. He said, "That was a lady, says she's your aunt. No, sit still. I told her you were not hurt. She was afraid you'd been run away with. Seems a horse you were riding came home without you, had a big cut on his leg."

Jeremy. She had forgotten those galloping hooves. She started out of her chair; she must tell them immediately. Jed was watching her; Ruby was watching her. The trooper said, "And they want you in here, Miss Poore. The Captain's got back."

Jed wanted to go with her; he got out of his chair; Ruby

made some confused move, too; the trooper would have none of it. "You come in here, Miss Poore, and you"—he looked at Jed and at Ruby, firmly—"you stay here."

Captain Henley must have come in by a back entrance. She had not seen him pass through the outer office, but there he was, alert, suspicious, spruce and very excited, in an armchair beside Sheriff Benjamin's roll-top desk. Sheriff Benjamin was there, too, looking old and pale, his white hair disheveled, the wrinkles in his face standing out sharply.

"Sit here," he said, and the trooper pushed a chair up closer. Sue sat down.

The overhead light there was even brighter than where she had waited. It beat down into her face; it dazzled her eyes.

Captain Henley said: "Why did you kill him?"

11

It seemed then to Sue that every question they asked came back to that one, "Why did you kill him?"

Not *did* you kill him, *how* did you kill him, *when* did you kill him, but *why?*

Sometimes it varied. What did Dr. Luddington know of the Baily woman's murder? Why did you have to keep him quiet?

Most of the questions came from Captain Henley. pounding away, breaking the case, attacking with the foretaste of triumph. Sheriff Benjamin, his old face troubled and worn, for the most part listened. She told her story not once but, it began to seem to Sue, a hundred times—as if she had never done anything, never lived any other life than that one, under the bright, dazzling light, replying, repeating, replying. Once she turned to Sheriff Benjamin half-sobbing: "Sheriff Benny, you know I couldn't have killed him. Dr. Luddington . . ."

"What did he know?" pounced Captain Henley. "What did he know?"

There were other questions; hundreds of reshapings of the same questions.

"Why did you go to his office?"

"I wanted to see him. I was going to be arrested."

Sheriff Benjamin had already claimed his responsibility there. "I told her she was about to be arrested," he had said flatly to Captain Henley. "I thought it my duty."

It had angered Captain Henley; she could see that; a flush rose in his fat, shiny face; he had said nothing, however; the sheriff was the sheriff; he had continued remorselessly, "Why did you want to see him?"

"I thought he might help me."

"How?"

"I don't know, I don't know. I had to see somebody. . . ."

"What did you want to ask him? What did he know? What were you afraid of?"

"I wasn't, I tell you. I wanted his advice. I didn't know what to do."

"But he didn't come to your house; you went there."

"Yes, yes, I told you, somebody phoned, a patient . . ."

"Who was this patient?"

"I don't know. Aunt Caroline talked to him!" They had gone into that; they had sent somebody to telephone Caroline; Sue was thankful they had not yet brought Caroline, too, to the Sheriff's office.

"We can round up the patient," said Sheriff Benjamin.

Captain Henley ignored it; there was no such patient, his manner said brusquely. "So you rode over from your house; why?"

"I've told you . . ."

"Why?"

"So I wouldn't be stopped; so the police you had at our gate wouldn't see me and stop me. . . ."

"It wasn't so nobody else would see you, was it?"

"No—no, I tell you . . ."

"You went by back ways, didn't you? You never went out on the highway. Why did you sneak through the woods like that? Nobody was following you. Why didn't you come out in the open?"

"I've told you, I've told you. . . ."

"Did anybody see you?"

"No, I don't think so. Unless the man who was in the woods . . ."

"Oh, yes, our convenient rider." Captain Henley went to the door, his chest puffed up smartly, his black boots shining; Sheriff Benjamin would not look at her. Captain Henley opened the door, said crisply to somebody outside: "Have you checked on the Beaufort hunt yet? I don't care how many people you wake up. Find out who—if anybody—took a spill in the Luddington woods this afternoon, late."

He slammed the door; he came back. "How long do you claim you were in the waiting room?"

"I don't know, . . ."

"Ten minutes or an hour?"

"Nearer—I don't know. Half an hour."

"You said twenty minutes before."

"I tell you I don't know."

"What were you doing there?"

"I told you. Nothing—looking at pictures. . . ."

"You were looking at pictures! Looking at pictures!" He leaned forward. "Why did you kill him?"

"I didn't—I didn't . . ." She put her hands over her eyes, shutting out Henley's accusing, red face, shutting out the glare of the lights. Heavy footsteps crossed the outer office; Sheriff Benjamin stared down at the floor. A car raced along the street below, at top speed. The whole village, the county seat, was alive and shocked, the streets were lined with cars; clusters of men stood, waiting for news, around the courthouse steps and on street corners. Murder in the dusky twilight; murder in the night.

Captain Henley said, "You knew he kept his gun in his car. You came up on your horse; the doctor's car was parked there in the driveway; you took the gun out of the glove compartment."

They had already established that. It was Dr. Luddington's custom. A loaded revolver always went with him on night calls, or any calls, loaded and kept in the glove compartment of his car. It wasn't that he feared attack, Sheriff Benjamin had said, coldly; doctors often did that, particularly in lonely country districts when they had night calls.

"He was afraid for his life," snapped Captain Henley, "that proves it. A loaded gun in his car at all times."

The sheriff shook his head and looked at the floor.

Eventually they questioned Ruby; they brought her into the room where she sat, her thick figure composed, not a hair out of place, her lovely face quiet. She answered all their questions quietly. She knew nothing that, as far as Sue could see, could be called a clue except that her father-in-law had telephoned her and said he wished to see her.

He had not talked to her—she had been out—he had left the message with a maid. By telephoning, then and there, to the maid, Henley established the approximate time when Dr. Luddington had telephoned Ruby; it was shortly after, perhaps twenty minutes after, Caroline herself had talked to Dr. Luddington. He established also the exact words of the message, but they were not revealing; Dr. Luddington had asked for Ruby and on being told that she was out had told the maid to tell Ruby he wanted to see her.

"I didn't telephone when I came in," Ruby said. "I'd been riding, the horse was still saddled; I simply rode over." She paused and said, "I hope someone has seen to my horse."

The sheriff said, "Wat saw to him, Mrs. Luddington."

"He knows, then?" asked Ruby.

"I told him," said the sheriff.

Ruby waited a moment, her soft, dark eyes thoughtful. "It must have been a great shock," she said then. "I realize you have to question us, but I—I'd like to go home as soon as possible."

Captain Henley said, "The maid is sure it was Dr. Luddington." He looked at the sheriff. "Baily says that whoever phoned him said he was a patient. Didn't give his name. Just said he was a patient and that Dr. Luddington couldn't talk himself because he had an emergency case, but that he wanted Baily to come to the office as soon as he could."

"That," Sue said, her voice unsteady, "is exactly what the patient said to Aunt Caroline, the very words. If you could find him . . ."

The sheriff sat up, rubbed his hands together and leaned forward again, his elbows on his knees. So far, of course, there had been no proof that such a patient existed. Yet Caroline would have known Tom Luddington's voice anywhere.

The sheriff said, "Why should he have wanted to talk to you, Mrs. Luddington, to Miss Poore and to Jed Baily, all at the same time?"

Henley flashed him an impatient look. "The only thing we know to be fact is that he phoned Mrs. Luddington; her testimony is corroborated by the maid."

The sheriff looked at him, his faded eyes angry. "We have Miss Caroline Poore's word for it that someone calling himself a patient phoned. . . ."

"Her unprejudiced word?" interrupted Henley.

"You forget that she had no opportunity to talk to her niece; no opportunity for them to invent such a story."

It was true, of course. But Captain Henley was not satisfied. "Where's the patient?" he said. "Where's the patient?"

The sheriff said to Ruby, "Do you have any idea at all as to what he wanted to see you about?"

Ruby shook her head. "No, I'm sorry."

"Had you ever, you and Dr. Luddington, talked of the Baily murder?"

"Oh, yes. I suppose we talked of it many times."

"Please think carefully, Mrs. Luddington. Did he ever, at any time, give you an impression that he knew something of the murder that he was withholding? . . . Please take your time; perhaps it was only a word or a look."

Ruby never thought quickly or easily; Sue knew the look of unhurried, plodding concentration in her face; her conclusions were, however, literal and accurate. She shook her head. "No. We knew that he had been with Ernestine at the last. Once or twice Wat questioned him. But there was never anything."

Henley said suddenly, his eyes bright and agate hard in his hot, red face, "Mrs. Luddington, what exactly were your relations with the murdered woman?"

Ruby looked at him slowly. "Ernestine? Why, she was one of my oldest friends. She and Sue, and Camilla Duval and I—we were always friends. We went to school together. . . ."

"I know that!" Henley's voice sounded irritable. "I've been told it a thousand times. But did you get along? Had you ever any quarrels?"

Ruby looked blank. After the instant or two which Ruby always seemed to require for complete comprehension, her shining black eyebrows lifted a little. "I didn't quarrel with Ernestine," she said flatly.

Sue could have told him that Ruby was not likely to stir sufficiently from her monumental calm to quarrel with anybody. The sheriff said, "Do you know whether or not any of his patients fancied he had a grudge at the doctor? That has happened, you know."

Henley said quickly and scornfully, "It's exactly like the Baily murder. Same thing exactly: door open, dusk, revolver near him, his own revolver, shot in the back."

"That doesn't mean the same person did it," said the sheriff mildly.

Henley gave a kind of derisive snort. "It's got to be linked with the Baily murder, no matter how you look at it. He was the important witness; he gave testimony that helped free Jed Baily; he was with Ernestine Baily alone for an hour or so before she died."

"Somebody could have taken advantage of that very fact. Everybody knows the circumstances, down to the last detail. It would be easy to duplicate them with the very conclusion in view that you are taking. Someone else—someone who had nothing to do with Ernestine Baily's murder —could have duplicated the same set of circumstances in the hope of making us believe it was the same murderer."

"He could have," Henley said shortly, "but I don't believe anybody did, and you'd never get a jury to believe it. No—it's too close to the Baily case and you didn't let me finish—did or did not Dr. Luddington throw his weight at the trial to get Jed Baily off? Certainly. Well, then, he knows Sue Poore is to be arrested. . . ."

Ruby stirred to give a kind of indignant murmur at that point. Henley went on ". . . he will be put on the witness stand again; he is a man who could not under any circumstances give false testimony; he knows Sue Poore killed the Baily woman, we know that the motive and the opportunity were there. He protected her so far as he could. But she phones that she is to be arrested, she wants to see him. He knows that she intends to plead with him to contrive to protect her even to the point of perjury. She goes to see him; he refuses to lie point-blank for her; she kills him the way she killed the Baily woman. . . ."

Ruby, shocked, was standing. "Sue never killed him! Sue couldn't kill anybody. This is perfectly outrageous!"

She came over to Sue and stood, her heavy figure itself like a protective wall, between Sue and Henley. The sheriff sighed. Someone had opened a window near-by. It was still misty and wet outside; in the silence that followed what was practically an outbreak of hysteria on Ruby's part, a murmur of voices drifted up from the street below. It was a curious murmur; there was an angry, rather threatening, undertone. Henley said, "Hear that. We're going to have trouble, Sheriff, if we don't act quickly. The Baily murder was bad enough; but this one—everybody in the county knew Dr. Luddington."

"Everybody in the county loved him," the sheriff said heavily. "But I'm not going to act too quickly, Henley, and you can't make me."

"You're going to arrest this woman."

Ruby said, "If you arrest Sue Poore you'll be making a terrible—a terrible mistake."

"Your loyalty does you credit, Mrs. Luddington." Henley got up and opened the door to the waiting room. "That's all now; you can go home. . . . Unless Sheriff Benjamin wishes to question you further," he added as an afterthought.

It was an indulgent-sounding afterthought, as if patient with age and with the sheriff's heavy anxiety and perplexity; the sheriff, however, said nothing; he nodded at Ruby. Ruby in the doorway, said to Sue, "I think you should have a lawyer. I'll speak to Wat and Jed. They'll do something."

She went away; the door closed. "What can they do?" Sue thought despairingly. Where was Aunt Caroline? What had it done to her?

Where was Fitz?

Henley returned and sat, bolt upright and erect, but looking tired nevertheless. His face was glistening and red. The glittering leather belt across his stomach was too tight; he eased it surreptitiously and said, "Now then, we'll have your whole story again, Miss Poore."

The sheriff made a kind of protesting motion. Henley snapped, "Again. Every word of it."

"She's told you everything she knows," the sheriff said. "There may be something, some detail . . ."

Some snare, thought Sue; some trap. "I've told everything," she said in an uneven voice which could not possibly carry conviction.

"Tell it again," Henley said inexorably and eased his belt another notch.

And surprisingly he was right; there did emerge a small fact, a tiny facet of the whole grim and tragic picture, which she had, up to then, forgotten. He interrupted her, to say: "And what did you do when, you say, you went into the room and found that he was shot? What was your first act?"

"I went to him."

"Did you know he was dead?"

"Yes—I—there was the wound."

"But the Baily woman had such a wound. She wasn't dead. She didn't die for nearly two hours."

"But he . . ." What had she done? She'd gone to him, she'd leaned over; she said, "He wasn't breathing. I held something to his lips; there wasn't any mist, any clouding —so I knew he was dead."

There was a silence except for that dull shuffle and murmur from the awakened street below. Both men were looking at her. Henley said then sharply, "You did not tell that before. What did you hold to his lips?"

"It was . . ." Exactly what was it? She thought back desperately; a small mirrored surface; hadn't it felt square in her hand like some sort of box? Certainly there was something thick and solid about it. She said faltering; "I don't know. It was sort of thick—as if it were framed or— it may have been a sort of box . . ."

"A box! What sort of box?"

"I don't know. A compact or a . . . a cigarette box or . . . I don't know . . ."

The sheriff looked at Henley; Henley said, "There was nothing of the sort on the desk."

"What did you do with—whatever it was that you picked up?" asked the sheriff.

What had she done with it? She could remember, although vaguely, the feel of it in her hand; she could remember the despair and terror with which she had looked at that small surface and found it bright and shining, reflecting only a part of her own white face. "I don't know. I must have put it down on the desk or somewhere. I can't remember anything about it. Not anything. All I could think of was Dr. Luddington and that—the place on his back and then I heard Jeremy galloping away. I don't know."

"It couldn't have been say, one of his instruments, some mirror—well, I don't know just what, but something that had a metal surface that shone like a mirror?"

She couldn't think any more; she couldn't remember

anything about it save that bright, unmarred surface. "I could hold it in my hand," she said. "It didn't have any sort of handle or anything like that. I—it was a sort of box. That's all I can remember."

"Is it in your pocket?" suggested the sheriff.

It was not. She searched. Obviously Henley did not believe that it was anywhere. It was in his eyes, in his red, impatient face. Yet how could it have been invented by Sue, or by anybody? How could it have served any conceivable purpose of deception, as Henley quite clearly believed that it did?

There was, then, a sort of commotion at the door of the outer office. Someone knocked; at the sheriff's word a trooper opened the door and thrust his head into the room. "Somebody's here to see Miss Poore. He's brought Judge Shepson. He says his name is Wilson."

Henley uttered an angry word and got to his feet. "They can both stay out."

"She's got a right to a lawyer. Judge Shepson's a lawyer," the sheriff said.

"Not yet," Henley said. "I'm not through questioning her. We haven't charged her. We haven't arrested her."

"We aren't going to yet, anyway," observed the sheriff. He rose and went to a desk in the corner: with deliberation, while Henley and the trooper and Sue watched, he took out an official-looking paper, lighted a match and held it to the paper. Henley started and jumped forward.

"That's the warrant! That's the warrant for her arrest. You can't do that."

"Oh, but I can," the sheriff said mildly. "Stay where you are, both of you."

The trooper didn't move. The sheriff held the flaming paper and as it quickly burned dropped the black flakes into an ash tray. Henley's face was bright red and furious. The sheriff said, "She just might have had some kind of row with Ernestine, but nobody can make me believe that this girl here shot old Dr. Luddington."

Henley started forward then, swearing; the sheriff stopped him, his faded eyes as cold as ice peaks. "I'm still sheriff of this county. If you want to do anything about it right now you'll have to go over my head. And I've still got friends in this county."

Henley caught an angry breath; he thought for an instant, "All right!" He whirled to the trooper. "Show in the boy."

Sue did not hear him. She was stunned and breathless. She was almost crying with gratitude and relief. So she had no warning—the trooper withdrew and closed the door, there was a sort of movement and the murmur of voices again in the outer room—but she was looking at Sheriff Benjamin and not really seeing him because everything in the room was blurred. She must telephone Caroline at once and tell her that she had, they had, at least a respite. Then Woody walked in at the door.

It closed behind him. He stood there in blues, very thin and young and tanned from sea duty. Captain Henley said, "All right. Here we are. Your brother, Miss Poore, was picked up in a garage in Dobberly, trying to hire a car. He was seen by a neighbor visiting Dr. Luddington's place surreptitiously only an hour or so before we got the alarm. Now then, we'll have your story, Mr.—Sergeant—Lieutenant Poore."

"Ensign," said Woody, looking very thin and young. "Hello, Sue."

12

He came across to her. Henley would have stopped him. The sheriff made a quick gesture. "Let them alone," he said.

Woody stooped and kissed her. "What have they been doing to you?"

"Oh, Woody, it's all right! Listen—they aren't going to arrest me . . ."

"*Arrest you!*"

". . . the sheriff says he does not believe that I could have shot Dr. Luddington and oh, Woody, I didn't, I didn't . . ."

Woody stood straight and slim in his blue uniform, his face hard, his eyes shooting sparks. "Sue—my sister— hauled up here and questioned and threatened, by God, sir, I'll . . ."

"Take it easy, Woody," said the sheriff and Sue cried, "But he's not going to! That's what he said."

"Now see here," began Henley angrily, "you signed that warrant for her arrest for the murder of Ernestine Baily, you can't tear it up now because of the Luddington . . ."

"I burned it," said the sheriff. "You said yourself the two murders were linked together, part of the same crime. That's what you said. Well, then, this girl just didn't murder Dr. Luddington; I don't believe it. So I'm not going to arrest her for Ernestine Baily's murder. Not now."

"The jury will believe it," snapped Captain Henley.

"And they're going to have a chance to listen. I tell you that woman is guilty. She killed Ernestine and she tried to influence the doctor to protect her and he wouldn't so she's shot him, too. She's a . . ."

"How would you like to have your head busted?" said Woody.

Captain Henley was scarlet with anger, his shrewd eyes furious. "Trooper!" he shouted, "Trooper . . ." and gave his belt a hitch. "I'll show you who'll get his head busted, you young . . ."

"Here now, here now," interposed the sheriff. "We'll not get anywhere this way." A trooper opened the door, put his head into the room and the sheriff said, "Get out."

He did so.

Woody, fists doubled, looked disappointed. They like to fight, Sue thought wearily, but with a glimmer of amusement: youth and the Navy, fast, quick scuffles in seaports, on shore leave and a quick getaway before the shore patrol comes running—and superior officers, later, who remember their own youth and fail to see black eyes and cut faces. "Woody," she said placatingly, "it's right. They were going to arrest me—I know how it sounds but they were—and now the sheriff burned up the warrant and they're not going to. At least not—not now and if you'll listen . . ."

"Then what's this guy talking about?" asked Woody, his eyes cold and again adult, fixed on Henley.

The sheriff said, "Sit down now, Woody, take it easy. This is Captain Henley of the State Homicide Department. He's doing his duty and you'll be doing yours if you answer what he wants to question you about. You'll also be helping out your sister. If she didn't shoot Ernestine—or Dr. Luddington—then the truth will prove it, and every detail, every scrap of information that leads to the truth is going to give your sister a boost. That clear?"

Anger and a desire to fight struggled with common sense and his ingrained respect for his elders; Woody looked at the sheriff and said soberly, "Yes, sir, but I think that my sister ought to have a lawyer. I don't know the law but I don't think it's right to haul her up here and question her and threaten her without giving her a chance for legal protection."

"All right. She can have a lawyer any time she wants one. But just now, Woody, we want to know something you can tell us, you see . . ."

Henley gave his belt another hitch and snapped, "What were you doing sneaking around the Luddington place just before he was shot?"

Woody whirled. "I wasn't sneaking."

"Go on. How'd you get there? Why?"

The sheriff made a kind of pacifying motion and then sat down to listen. Woody said, "I don't like the way you form your questions. But I'll answer . . ."

"You're damn right you'll answer, you . . ."

The sheriff got up. He wore old-fashioned congress shoes with elastic at the sides; they shuffled forward and backward and he sat down again. Woody said, however, more peaceably. "I've got nothing to hide. Yes, I was there. Who saw me?"

"Never mind that. Why did you go there?"

"Because I wanted to see Dr. Luddington."

"What about?"

Woody hesitated. The anger and look of defiance left his face. Sue, who knew him so well, saw that he was both troubled and perplexed; he waited a moment before replying and finally said: "Well—I wanted to see him. We— we've always gone to him for advice, Sue and I, and I—I didn't know just what . . ." he stopped there, stuck.

There was a little pause; a shrewd, exploring look had come into Henley's face. He said, "Had you talked to your sister before you went there?" The sheriff shot him a queer, surprised look.

And a new sort of alarm touched Sue. She said quickly, "You must have got into the Dobberly station from Richmond. We were expecting you. We had your wire from Memphis. Caroline would have come to get you. I suppose you wanted to ride up if Dr. Luddington happened to be going that way." She stopped abruptly; she had no idea why she had spoken so hurriedly until she heard her own words and they sounded like excuses, lifelines flung out quickly toward Woody.

It sounded like it to Henley, too, who said briskly: "No prompting, Miss Poore. . . . What did you want to ask his advice about? Come on, now—Ensign."

The sheriff shuffled his congress boots mildly. "Let's just have the whole story, Woody. You're on leave, I take it. Begin at the beginning."

Woody turned to the sheriff. "Yes, sir. From San Diego. I got a lift to Tuscon and another to Memphis and then the weather stopped me. I . . ." he swallowed; they could see his thin young neck move, "I wanted to get here before the trial was over. I thought they were making it pretty tough for Sue and I . . ." again he swallowed and said: "I thought it was going to be like this."

"Like this?" said the sheriff.

"I thought that—from the way it read. I got all the papers, I thought they were going to acquit Jed and I thought . . ." Again he stuck; the sheriff said quietly, his faded blue eyes steady, "What did you think?"

"I thought they were going to arrest Sue."

There was a short pause; someone down in the street shouted to somebody else. A car came racing along and stopped with a squeal of brakes just below the windows. Then Henley gave a kind of snort again. "Everybody knew that by the time the trial was over."

"I didn't," Sue thought queerly, "I didn't." Fitz expected it; perhaps everybody expected it. I didn't.

Woody refused to look at Henley; he moistened his lips and said, "So I wanted to be here. I finally got to Richmond and took the train here; it gets to Dobberly about five, it was a little late. Anyway, I wanted to see Dr. Luddington . . ."

"What about?" shouted Henley in exasperation.

Woody still wouldn't look at him. "I'm coming to that. First, though, Sue was right; I didn't want to phone for her or for Caroline to come to get me, and I thought Dr. Luddington would take me home after I'd talked to him . . ."

"*What* . . ." began Henley explosively and the sheriff said quickly. "Go on, son, tell it your own way."

"Yes, sir. Well, I left my duffel at the station—it's still there—and walked out to the doctor's place. It's quite a long walk from the station, I don't know how far . . ."

Henley got up angrily, his red face swollen with impatience, shot the sheriff a look and sat down again. Woody went on, ". . . I don't know what time it was when I got there; it's on the edge of town. It was raining. I didn't see a soul when I got to the street where he lives. The houses are sort of far apart there and with all the laurels and trees . . ."

Henley interrupted. "We know all that, but you were seen just the same!"

"Well. I wasn't trying not to be seen. But I didn't pass anybody that I remember, I'm sure. I got to the door and rang the bell and nobody came; I remembered it was Thursday, maid's day off." He stopped as if to collect his thoughts and again Sue knew his look. He was making up his mind not what to tell but what not to tell.

But Woody—*Woody* couldn't know anything of the murder! He'd been away, ever since the day after Ernestine had been killed, months and months ago. Woody couldn't know anything about whoever had come quietly out of the dusk, into Dr. Luddington's consulting room and shot him as he sat there unaware that murder stood behind him.

Woody said, "So I walked in. I didn't see anybody. The door was open into the waiting room. But the door into the consulting room was closed, and—and somebody was there with the doctor."

"*Unhh!*" said Captain Henley, startled.

"Somebody," said Woody, "in riding boots."

Captain Henley must have been tilting back in his chair;

it came down now with a crash. "You've been talking to your sister!"

"I have not!"

"Wait a minute, wait a minute," the sheriff's voice intervened again, "Now then, Woody, how did you know that?"

"Because he kept hitting his boot with a riding crop or something. I can't describe it but there's a sound, it was that sort of sound. I—well, I just knew it," Woody said rather miserably but with a stubborn sort of insistence that sounded true. "But I think whoever was there had just got there. I mean it sounded—well, short; I'm sure there were two voices but they didn't talk."

"What do you mean?" demanded Henley. "Either they were talking or they were not talking."

"No," Woody was stubborn. "You can say, hello, or wait a minute, I'm busy, or—or a lot of things. That's two voices but not conversation."

"I'm afraid," Henley said with heavy sarcasm, "that's rather a fine point."

"Well, it is true. And besides Dr. Luddington was typing."

"Now see here," began Henley, angrily, "you say the door was closed. You say . . ."

"I could hear it," said Woody. "So I thought that somebody had had a spill and maybe a sprain or something and Dr. Luddington was writing a prescription. I can't—well, that's what I thought." There was a longish pause; then Henley said weightily, "We've got a detective here. Through a closed door you decided somebody had got a spill and a sprain and Dr. Luddington was typing a prescription and—are we going to listen to this, Sheriff? I tell you the boy's been talking to his sister, he's heard about the fellow she says she saw . . ."

Woody picked it up quickly. "What fellow? Where? Who?"

The sheriff said, "He couldn't have talked to his sister.

She's been right here. What did you do then, Woody?"

"What fellow?" insisted Woody.

Henley got up and walked to the door with short, authoritative steps. Opening it he said, "Have you got that report on the Beaufort hunt yet?"

The sheriff said to Woody, "As she got into those woods back of the Luddington place she says she saw somebody from the Beaufort hunt, getting back on his horse. She says it looked as if he'd had a fall, there by the creek."

"*Who?*"

"She couldn't see his face. . . . What did you do then, Woody? Did you wait?"

"No, I didn't. I left. Right away."

"You . . ." The sheriff gave Woody a surprised look. "Now why did you do that?"

"Because I—I just did."

"But you'd walked all the way out there to see him. Couldn't you wait a few minutes?"

"I'd changed my mind," Woody said rather uncomfortably. "I—well, all the time I was going along through the village, I'd been thinking that really there wasn't anything he could do. I—I sort of began to see that I was the person to do anything for Sue, that . . ." he swallowed and said, "I'm the man of the family. I'm not a kid any more. The patient or whoever it was in his office decided me. I mean it was sort of the deciding last straw. If I could have walked right in to see the doctor I'd have done it; as it was I decided to go back to the garage and get a lift home and see Sue herself before I talked to the doctor or anybody. I was kind of nervous—I'd been cooped up in planes and trains and—well, anyway, that's what I did. I don't care whether it sounds like the truth or not, that's what I did.—And I don't know who was in there with Dr. Luddington and I don't know another thing about it."

Henley slammed the door and came back.

"Found anybody yet?" asked the sheriff.

Henley shook his head. "They've got the list all right,

but they can't locate everybody; they're either in bed and asleep, and refuse to be called, or rampaging around the country, eating and drinking. Oh, they've checked on most of them," he added grudgingly, "so far only three spills and none of them in the Luddington woods." He looked at Woody. "I heard what you said and it sounds fishy to me."

"It's what I did, just the same."

"Tell it again."

"All right, but it'll be the same story because that's the way it happened."

And it was the same story and this time Henley seemed not wholly to accept it, but at least to consider it. "Could it have been a woman in the doctor's office?" he asked at last.

Woody thought for a moment. "I thought it was a man. The voices were muffled; I couldn't hear any words. I never thought of it being a woman."

"Your sister," remarked Henley rather smugly, "was carrying a crop. She left it in the waiting room."

Woody paled a little, but his eyes did not flinch. "I'd have known my sister's voice anywhere."

"Even through a closed door?"

Sheriff Benjamin intervened, "I think he's right. I think he would have recognized his sister's voice. And if he had, he'd never have told this."

Henley seemed impressed by this reasoning but said nevertheless, obstinately, that it wasn't conclusive. "In fact, none of it's conclusive."

"It's what happened," Woody said, "and I'll swear to it."

"You'd swear to anything to help your sister. Well, don't count on being permitted to give evidence. Don't make up a story to get her out of it. Stick to the truth . . ."

"That *is* the truth!" Woody was white under his tan; his temper (like the frantic, stubborn baby temper he'd always had) was getting control of him. The sheriff said quickly, "You said you went away."

"I told you. I went to the garage. There's no taxi service in Dobberly but I thought I'd get one of the fellows to run me up home. They didn't have a car available just then; one of the fellows had gone home for supper. But they said he'd be back in a little while and then he'd take me. So I waited and I—there I was when a police car came along and stopped for gas and—one of them questioned me and as soon as he found out who I was he picked me up."

"Now look here," Henley said abruptly, "Come clean. You were in Dobberly the night the Baily woman was murdered! What do you know about her murder?"

And he did know something. Because Sue knew him so well, she knew that; she saw the flash of wariness in his face. But he said flatly, "I don't know a thing. If I knew anything I'd tell it."

The sheriff got up. "See here, Henley, if you want my opinion I'd say let the boy go, just now. We've got plenty to do; we can't do it all tonight—and as to that, it's getting on toward morning. Let the boy go." He paused and said, "Let them both go."

"I thought you were getting around to that! We've got nothing against the boy—nothing definite except he was there. He could have shot the old man. Or he could be covering for his sister and they could both be in it. However—I'll let him go. But not the girl."

After a long pause the sheriff said: "I think you're making a mistake."

"Let him go," repeated Henley. "We can get him if we want him. Let him go. But the girl stays. I want," said Henley, loosening his belt again as he settled back in his chair, "I want to hear the whole story again. This time I want a stenographer."

In the end the stenographer was brought in; the sheriff's disapproval was overridden; Woody was taken into the outer office and the door was closed and the questioning began again. It was by then very late; it was later and even Captain Henley's bouncing, red-faced energy and exuberance was a trifle dimmed, his spruceness definitely a thing of the past, by the time they finished. By that time, too, Sue felt like a sleepwalker going through motions that had no significance, saying words that had no meaning. When at last they released her, a trooper, at Sheriff Benjamin's quietly spoken word, brought her hot coffee. Her hands shook so that she could scarcely hold the thick white mug.

The sheriff went with her to the door of the outer office; the air was blue with cigarette smoke. Woody was there and Judge Shepson, looking sleepy and old, his fat jowls sagging, his curly, sparse hair rumpled; he got wearily to his feet.

"Go out the side door," said the sheriff. "I think the street is clear by now, but go out the side door."

Woody nodded. Their feet made dull and echoing sounds on the stairs; two troopers, looking sleepy too, let them past without a question.

The fresh air of coming dawn was cool upon her face. They went along the sidewalk, Judge Shepson puffing asthmatically. At the end of the sidewalk two cars loomed up, dark and ghostly. Jed and Fitz stood together, smoking, waiting; Camilla huddled in the second car, her face pale in the gloom as the long, light coat she had wrapped around her.

Sue's eyes ached from the dazzling light of the sheriff's office. Everything blurred; figures and sounds were confused. Judge Shepson was talking. She heard the words. "No arrest," and "nothing more tonight."

Jed was beside her, his arm around her; Camilla had got out of the car to listen. Sue was aware of Camilla's high voice, exclaiming in a hushed, yet shocked way. There was a low-voiced colloquy about cars, about going home; Fitz settled it by opening the door of his own car and putting Sue in the front seat. Woody got in beside her; she was between Fitz and Woody. She was dimly aware of Jed and Camilla and the bulky figure of the lawyer, fading off into the darkness.

Fitz started his car, backing around the graveled space. "How long have you been waiting?" Woody asked.

"Since I brought Shepson. Was he any help?"

"Didn't have a chance."

After a pause, Fitz said: "I was afraid he wouldn't have, but I didn't know what else to do."

"Who told you about it? The police?"

"I was at your aunt's when they told her. I'd been at Shepson's office; when I got home Jason said she'd phoned. Instead of phoning her I drove over and somebody, not the sheriff but a trooper, telephoned. He said the sheriff had told him to—I gathered at Sue's request. The whole county knows it by now."

"How'd Aunt Caroline take it?"

"As you'd expect her to. She's a sweetheart. . . . Then I went for Shepson."

They took the road out of town, toward the hill where she and Fitz had driven, toward the turn to Dobberly and home. Woody said clearly and suddenly in her ear, "The fact is Jed shot Ernestine."

The car gave a kind of jerk toward the side of the road and back again. Fitz said, "Do you know that or are you guessing?"

"I didn't see it, if that's what you mean. But just look at it! Sue swore to an alibi to get Jed off. She's in love with him! But she's got to be made to tell the truth now. No matter what it does to Jed. It's his life or hers now. I knew it was coming," said Woody, his voice rough and miserable. "I read the papers. Every word she said made it worse for her. Every word she said heaped up evidence against her. But she's got to tell the truth about Jed now."

Sue thought dimly, "I can't cope with this now. I'm so tired and Woody's so stubborn; I can't do it now."

Fitz said, "She did tell the truth, Woody. You'll have to believe it."

"I don't believe it! Jed did it. Sue made up an alibi for him and if she won't admit it we've got to make Jed confess."

13

Fitz said at last in an even, man-to-man way, "I'd better tell you everything that's happened, Woody. You haven't had a chance to hear."

He told it, from the day after Ernestine's murder, the day when Woody had gone back to his ship. The story of the evidence, the trial and in greater detail exactly what had happened since then. Woody listened until lights suddenly reflected themselves against the glossy surface of banked laurels. The car swerved, climbed to steps and white pillars. A light was burning in the hall. Chrisy was waiting for them.

She had put Caroline to bed hours ago. "I gave her some of those pills the doctor left last night," she said and took one look at Sue and led the way upstairs; Fitz almost carried Sue up the steps, with Woody coming along behind. "Hey, Chrisy, have I got any pajamas, or a razor? All my stuff is still at the station."

It was Chrisy who pulled off Sue's riding boots, untied her crumpled stock. How long ago—how quickly and anxiously she had put them on! "Don't you make any noise, Woody. You'll wake up Miss Caroline," Chrisy said sternly to Woody who had reached down and taken up a boot with apparently a desire to help and then stood there, holding the boot.

Fitz had disappeared; he came back as Chrisy spoke. "Here's some milk."

Chrisy turned her worried face toward them. "You and Woody go on downstairs, Mr. Fitz. You'll want to talk; but now don't sit up all night, either of you. Not that there's much left of it. Can you stand up now, Miss Sue, and I'll get these pants off?"

Woody and Fitz had gone; the milk was liberally laced with brandy. "How did Aunt Caroline take it?"

Chrisy's underlip thrust out. "We waited and waited; she was getting more and more nervous all the time, but you know Miss Caroline. She tried to hide it. And then Mr. Fitz came and then a policeman phoned and . . ." Chrisy shook her head with sullen and angry sorrow. "Mr. Fitz, he went for Lawyer Shepson. And then after a long time we heard old Jeremy and she went out with a flashlight and there he was, nobody riding him and a great slash along his leg. Miss Caroline, she liked to died. She was afraid you'd got hurt and they wouldn't tell her. So she phoned and phoned and finally got the sheriff and he said you were there in the courthouse. In the jailhouse!" Chrisy said in a kind of moan, holding up Sue's nightgown. "Now duck your head, that's right. And finally I remembered the pills. Now then, I'll turn out the light. I'll sleep right in the next room so if either you or Miss Caroline wants me, there I am."

Sue said from a vast distance, "Don't forget Woody . . ."

"My gracious, ain't I always seen to Woody?" said Chrisy and went out.

Sue did not know how long Fitz and Woody talked, downstairs in Caroline's study; she did not know until later that after Woody had gone to bed at last, Fitz was unable to leave; he stood on the steps in the gray dawn, looking down at his car and then went back, uneasy, afraid of something he could not define and spent what was left of the night on the shabby, leather-covered couch in the study, fighting old Reveller for possession of it. Chrisy found him there much later, gave him breakfast and watched him release the brake of his car and coast silently down the incline so as not to waken Sue or Caroline; he turned on the engine at the gate and drove home through a gray, clouded daylight.

It was a day that ushered in a series of days which again had for Sue and perhaps for others, a kind of sleepwalking haze; there were moments of sharp reality and moments of sheer, incredible unreality.

Much and little happened.

The machinery of police investigation, already unlimbered, rolled on slowly, thoroughly, and for the most part, invisibly—at least to Sue, to Caroline, to those most deeply concerned. Such machinery of defense as could be gathered together for Sue's protection was assembled; Judge Shepson came and went; she told her story, everything she knew of Dr. Luddington's murder over and over. Fitz and Woody and Jed, Caroline and Chrisy and—even—Ruby and Wat, sat in Caroline's study and debated and searched for ammunition for that defense, certain that the time would come when it was needed. Nothing new or revealing emerged from all that debate. The coroner's inquest was held on the first day.

It was brief, businesslike and merely a factual recital of the known facts of his death; very few people attended. Probably the sheriff had taken steps to prevent wide publicity and a jammed courtroom by holding the inquest so quickly and with little fanfare. It was like a cold, short repetition of Jed's trial; it was over so quickly that the announcement of the decision came as a surprise. But Sue was not named in the decision; he had come to his death at the hands of a person or persons unknown.

And then, there was nothing they could do but wait for the police to make a move.

The fact was, of course—Sue knew it because they told her, Fitz and Woody, Jed and Judge Shepson—the sheriff and Captain Henley were still in a kind of deadlock, the sheriff holding out against Sue's arrest, Captain Henley demanding it and both of them seeking for some clinching evidence that would resolve that deadlock one way or the other.

There were curious things, too, about those days; small yet sharply unreal things, such as the way newspapers disappeared; Chrisy spirited them away and as far as Sue or Caroline were concerned, newspapers, just then, did not exist. What were they saying, Sue wondered, in those columns of newsprint? She did not ask for them, however; probably Chrisy would have said there were none. Nobody telephoned; probably reporters were distracted, keeping close to Bedford and the sheriff's office, but the usual little thread of telephoning, the invitations, the chats, had cut itself off—not unkindly, perhaps only in mute or embarrassed sympathy—but it was cut off.

More significantly policemen, singly or in pairs, seemed to hover often at the gate or wander about the grounds; clearly they were keeping an eye on the house, which seemed to give Fitz and Chrisy some occult satisfaction although neither of them, then, could have said why.

On Sunday Dr. Luddington was buried; since it was Sunday everybody in the countryside could come and most of them did; the tiny church with its white steeple pointing up into the gray sky was packed; people stood along the sidewalk and in the vine and moss-grown cemetery outside, their heads bared. Caroline went, of course, and Sue and Woody and the usher, a boy from the filling station who knew them, seated them directly behind Wat and Ruby. It was a public declaration that as far as he was concerned Sue could not have shot Dr. Luddington and that all the talk was so much talk. Ruby, swathed in black, turned and spoke to them; she was composed but her usually white-and-pink complexion had a muddy look and there were dark pockets around her eyes. After the service Wat further marked their position in his eyes by giving Caroline his arm down the aisle, with everyone watching and out to the small, old cemetery, with its turf paths, it ivy and Virginia creeper, its moss and lichen-covered stones.

Fitz was there, too, standing near them and Jed and Camilla—also swathed in black. They drove back, all of them, to Fitz's place for supper—a quiet and also rather unreal hour or two, with Jason plying them with food like an anxious mothering old hen, with Jed in Fitz's red armchair, his legs stretched out, gradually acquiring an almost equally red flush in his cheeks from Fitz's bourbon, with the Kerry Blue remembering Sue and coming, after a serious moment of thought to put his black head on her knee. With Sue herself remembering too well the afternoon when she had fed cake to the Kerry Blue.

For a moment, there in the wood-paneled library, with the beat of the rain outside and the warmth and flicker of the fire inside, she had let herself look at that room and that house as it might have been for her, always. A gracious and dignified house, sheltering her and Fitz and a life together. She'd had a glimpse of what she'd known then was only a picture. The other woman in a murder trial had, even then, no place in it.

She had still less a claim to such a place now. She had not even the right to sit there, touching the Kerry Blue's black head, looking into the fire, letting herself dream.

She and Caroline and Woody left early; nobody said much of the murder; there was not a moment alone with Fitz but perhaps, Sue thought, doubting her own courage, it was just as well. As they drove away Camilla's blonde head showed in the lighted doorway beside Fitz.

The police, however, were busy.

There were at least two lines of inquiry that required much time and patience; one was the continued and rigorous check of the Beaufort hunt; the entire field of twenty-odd was interviewed, painstakingly and repeatedly. And Dr. Luddington's entire list of patients, his account books, finally the entire neighborhood, was canvassed for a person who had presumably been an emergency case, who had been in Dr. Luddington's office, who had been requested by Dr. Luddington to telephone to Caroline and ask for Sue to come; who had telephoned, too, to Jed and asked for him.

Jed hadn't known the voice; Caroline had not known it. Perhaps at that moment, even if there had been a tone of familiarity she would not have realized it, but certainly she had not recognized it. The telephone operators, two of them, interviewed at length, could tell them nothing; it was a fairly busy hour; the doctor's line was always in frequent use; there was nothing they remembered that was of any value.

There was a minute search of Dr. Luddington's office and cabinets of instruments. Jed and particularly Ruby, since Ruby had been alone in the consulting room for a moment or two, were questioned, without success, about the flat and shiny object, a mirror, a box, which had apparently disappeared. The only point of question was its disappearance; the police might have doubted its existence had its disappearance been of any possible aid to Sue. It remained a small unanswered question among many more important problems. Gradually, however, the motive the police had first ascribed to his murder began to gain in strength, as one after another possibility was ruled out. Certainly he had been alone with Ernestine for some time before her death; certainly she might have told him the true facts of what proved to be her murder. Certainly if that had happened, he had kept that terrible secret inviolate.

And certainly during that winter he had changed. They had attributed it to age, to the strain of the trial. Was it, instead, the sapping burden of that knowledge?

There was the detailed and deliberate laboratory procedure of cataloging the fingerprints on every available surface. The gun and the extracted bullet were taken to Captain Wilkins. All of this was a long and deadly patient process. There was, too, a long and tedious search through Dr. Luddington's account books; he had never kept a file. That was sometime Monday afternoon and Jed drove to Bedford and to the sheriff's office late in the afternoon. He came from there to Sue.

"The sheriff likes you. I thought he might be willing to tell us whether they'd found out who telephoned to us, or how things were going, or—or something!" Jed said. "He was friendly enough, but if there's any real dope he didn't tell me. All he said was they'd found enough unpaid bills to set anybody up for life if they were collected."

"Wat wouldn't want them collected."

"Not if he's going to run for Congress," Woody said crossly. He looked even younger in a white shirt with the collar open, faded blue jeans and moccasins than he had in his tailored, slim Navy blues; he'd been in the stables most of the day, puttering around with Caroline, criticizing the arrangement of the tack room, putting young Lij right (or wrong) about the proper way to give a rubdown, examining Jeremy's leg with an air of omniscience.

Woody now ruffled his streaked, fair hair and stared morosely at Jed and Jed said suddenly, "What's on your mind, youngster?"

"Unhh," said Woody startled.

"The way you keep looking at me. If you've got anything on your mind, spit it out."

But Woody balked. His face closed; he had nothing on his mind, nothing special, he said, and rose and sauntered away, softly as a red Indian in the leather moccasins, his hands in his pockets.

He had said no more of his feelings about Jed; if he had relinquished, or more probably merely shelved, his suspicions, he had not relinquished his dislike; it was in his silent and grudging withdrawal. Jed saw it, too, and guessed the reason.

"He doesn't like me," he said watching Woody go. "I can't blame him. I'm the one who's dragged you into this,

Sue. Because I let myself love you. I couldn't help it, I've dragged you into this."

He came to stand beside her near the railing of the wide porch, with the wistaria along it beginning to show purplish, fuzzy buds amid its bare brown branches.

The day was overcast again but warm. It was one of the Dobberly hunt days; a Dobberly pack was out twice a week up to the first week in April; it was, as a matter of fact, one of the last few hunts of the season; the Hunt Ball, by tradition, was to take place the last of the week. But that day again Caroline and Sue, Jed and the Luddingtons and some of the other regulars did not join the meet. There had been, Wat told Caroline, an offer to cancel the meet in deference to Dr. Luddington. He had refused to permit it; his father would not have wanted it; Caroline had agreed.

Hounds were somewhere now on the far side of Hollow Hill; they could hear the faint, distant music.

Jed stood for a moment, his hands on the railing. And then he said abruptly, "Let's get married now, Sue."

She turned quickly, surprised and troubled. His dark eyes sought eagerly into her own. "You're on the spot. I want you to marry me."

Fitz had offered that too; it was the fullest protection a man can give a woman. She was frightened and lonely; it moved her deeply. She couldn't speak for a moment; she put her hand out, on Jed's arm.

He took it for consent. He covered it with his other hand. "When, Sue? Right away?"

"No."

"What do you mean, no? We're engaged . . ."

"No, no. I've told you. Things are different. You must believe me."

"But you—but we . . ." Suddenly his face flushed; he caught both her hands, his eyes demanding yet still not believing. "You can't have changed. You stuck with me after Ernestine. All through the winter, all though the trial, you were loyal. You'd never have done that if you hadn't loved me. You still love me. You can't desert me now. Besides we're in it together. Whoever phoned to you and said he was a patient, and Dr. Luddington wanted you to come, phoned to me, too; he planned to have the police find us both. He—but we'll get out of it. What's past is past. We love each other and . . ."

She was shaking her head. "I don't love you."

For the first time he began to believe her; she could see belief—and incredulity and opposition—in his eyes. "Jed, I mean it. We're not going to marry."

"Do you mean—not ever, Sue?"

"Not ever. I'm sorry, Jed."

He did believe her then; she was sure of it, but he fought that belief too. "But Sue—you can't decide so—so quickly. You can't be sure, you . . ." He held her hands and cried, "Promise me to wait and think about it and . . ."

A car was coming up the driveway, between the laurel hedges. They both heard and saw it; Jed dropped her hands. "It's the police."

It was the police. But they had come this time to talk to Woody. It was Captain Henley and two troopers, one who drove the car and one who was a stenographer and made a record of every word Woody said. And they questioned him, this time, about the night when Ernestine had been murdered.

They let Jed remain. They let Sue listen. Henley was spruce and tightly belted but looked tired; there were deep hollows below his bright, shrewd eyes and his fat cheeks and chin seemed to have sagged; he walked as if his glistening black boots were too small for him. But his resolution was unwearied; he made it clear in every word that, if he had his way, he'd have been armed with a warrant for Sue's arrest.

He was, however, punctiliously, dreadfully, coldly polite.

Sue called Woody. He came instantly, as if he'd been watching from the tack room, with Reveller walking stiff-legged at his heels. They sat in the wicker chairs whose very creak was familiar. It was warm, yet Sue hugged her yellow sweater around her as she listened, for they began at once with Ernestine's murder. They had got out the files, the whole record, question-and-answer, of that investigation; they were trying to find some loophole, some flaw, some small up-to-then unperceived fact which might provide a clue to Dr. Luddington's murder, to Ernestine's. Sue had forgotten, if she had ever known, that they had questioned Woody the morning after Ernestine's death before he took the plane back to San Diego; merely, probably, because he and Caroline had come instantly when they heard of the murder to Duval Hall and Sue and were there shortly after the police arrived.

Captain Henley put on eyeglasses, pince-nez which looked odd and old-fashioned amid his general air of dandyism, leafed through a notebook and read Woody's testimony of that day.

It was brief and as far as Sue could see, valueless; yet she remembered her feeling in the sheriff's office the night she was questioned there that Woody was withholding something. Captain Henley had sensed that, too; again she was aware of his acumen and intelligence. Captain Henley was reading, ". . . and was at the hunt dinner. Sue had gone on ahead; she said she was stopping to see Ernestine. She had the car and when she didn't come back, I phoned the Bascoms and they stopped for Aunt Caroline and me. . . . No, we didn't think anything of it when she didn't come back for us. Why should we? . . . Yes, we expected she'd come with Ernestine, but I thought they'd turn up; maybe they'd stopped somewhere for cocktails. . . . I was dancing when somebody came in and said that Ernestine had been shot. I thought it was an accident. But I knew Sue was there. I borrowed a car and I drove with Aunt Caroline to the Baily place. The policemen were there and wouldn't let us in." Captain Henley's eyeglasses flashed as he went on down the page. "Oh, yes; and here's your dancing partners and the lady you sat by during the dinner. All that seems to be clear."

"All that is clear," Woody said.

"All very clear," Captain Henley said, handing the tablet back to the stenographer. "Except you didn't say that you and Mrs. Baily left the hunt that afternoon and met at the Hunting Horn Tavern. You left the hunt early and separately. But you met there by prearrangement, didn't you?"

The thin line of Woody's jaw looked like stone; his eyes were bright and fixed. Jed said something and got up. Captain Henley said, "A barmaid at the Hunting Horn left that evening to go to another job; apparently she didn't like it and returned to her old job last week. She saw the papers; she recognized Mrs. Baily's picture and your picture. The reporters knew, of course, that you had been picked up in Dobberly following your visit to Dr. Luddington's house and questioned. Now then, I'd like to hear all about this—this secret meeting with Ernestine Baily—only a couple of hours before her murder."

Captain Henley nodded at the stenographer who opened a tablet to a fresh page. Woody said, "Don't worry, Sue! We were at the Hunting Horn. But I didn't kill her."

14

Henley seemed rather taken aback; his bright, sharp eyes were fixed on Woody with a kind of surprise as if he had not expected Woody to capitulate so soon. If so, however, he recovered himself quickly; he said, "Do you know who did kill her?"

"Woody," whispered Sue and put out her hand toward him. "Don't . . ." She didn't know what she meant; don't say too much, perhaps. Henley's bright gaze observed it and her. Woody's face looked dirty but was really only very pale under his tan. He said, "I thought Jed did it. And I still think Jed did it."

"Woody!" Jed stared at Woody in angry bewilderment. "Woody, what do you mean? What . . ."

Captain Henley took control. "Wait a minute, Mr. Baily. Now then, youngster, that is, Ensign, just why did you think that? Did Mrs. Baily lead you to believe that she was—say, afraid of her husband? Had he threatened her?"

Woody blinked; the line of his thin jaw was bony and hard but he had lost some of his composure. "Well," he said finally, "no."

Jed started forward toward Woody, not angrily but in a helpless and bewildered way; Henley made an imperative motion that stopped him and said, "Exactly why, then, are you accusing Baily?"

Woody's throat moved as he swallowed. "Because I don't see what else could have happened. He—Jed—he and Er-

nestine didn't get along; she told me that. And Jed was
. . ." a little flush crept into his cheeks, ". . . Jed liked
my sister; he was always around, wherever she was; he—
everybody was talking about it. Sue was new here; she'd
just come home, she was away when Jed came here and
Ernestine and he were married and he bought the Duval
place and settled down, only he didn't settle down. Just the
minute he saw Sue, he was after her and . . ."

"Woody," cried Sue.

"I thought she'd see through it; I thought she'd see she
was getting into deep water and make an end to it. But
she—she's awfully young in a lot of ways," said Woody
looking very young himself, "and Jed's—well, I suppose
she got to liking him too. And then he—anyway when Ernestine was shot and I think Sue was afraid they'd turn in
a guilty verdict for Jed and I think she got to thinking that
if he did quarrel with Ernestine and lose his head and
shoot her, like that, I think that Sue got to thinking she
was responsible. So I think she made up that alibi to save
him and I don't think she'd care about herself, I mean I
don't think she thought about the kind of place it was putting her in, and even if she had she would have gone
straight ahead and alibied him, she's like that. You don't
know her," said Woody and stopped.

There was a silence except for the frenzied pencil of the
stenographer; he finished and sighed and gave Woody a
wary look as if the well of Woody's articulacy might burst
out again. Henley then said, "Well," and took a breath
himself. "Well. You did considerable thinking, didn't
you?"

Jed unexpectedly went to Woody. "Look here, Woody,
I had no idea you felt like that. I—the fact is, Woody, I
want you to know, I meant it; you are young; you don't
understand. It was the—the real thing with me and with
Sue. I wasn't just making a play for her. And I—everything, Woody, was honest and—it wasn't till that very
night, that evening when I met Sue, by accident there at

the gate, that I even so much as told her how I felt and then I said, everybody knows it, you know it, I told her I'd ask Ernestine for a divorce. Sue refused; she said she wouldn't let me. It all happened exactly the way . . ."

Woody said, a white rim around his mouth: "Ernestine was through with you, you know."

Henley made some kind of murmur which sounded startled. Jed, apparently holding hard to his patience, waited a moment before he said quietly, "No, I didn't know. What are you talking about, Woody?"

"You weren't kind to her," said Woody. "She told me. She was unhappy. She told me that; she didn't mean to, but I could see she was unhappy and it—it came out. Ernestine . . ." his voice suddenly was uneven; he tried to steady it; "Ernestine was wonderful. You didn't understand her, you didn't try to understand her. She said so."

Ernestine! Sue thought, Ernestine! Eight—no, nine years older than Woody, knowing him since he was a tousled, blond baby—then suddenly playing the enchantress, playing on the sympathy and the admiration of a grown-up Woody, who was attractive and more adult-appearing in his naval uniform, than in fact he was. She sought back desperately into her memory of Woody's last short leave, ending the day after Ernestine's murder. Why hadn't she watched him more closely? Well, there was a reason for that, she'd been absorbed with her own problem, with her own obsessing notion that she was falling in love with Jed and that she must stop it. (And she hadn't known what love was, she thought in a quick little stab of new knowledge. She had fled from a shadow.)

Where had Woody seen Ernestine? Everywhere, of course. He'd hunted; they had all hunted furiously and happily, almost every day; they had been in the same small group that gathered afterward for long post-mortems and dinner. If he had been often with Ernestine then she'd only have thought that Ernestine was being kind to a boy, Sue's brother, whom she had known since his romper days and for whom Sue would have expected Ernestine to have a grown-up, adult affection. Not—Henley suddenly stirred and supplied the word, "Quite a little flirtation," he said.

Jed whirled around. "Nonsense. My wife had known Woody always; naturally she was fond of him. So's Camilla. So's Ruby."

The adult look had gone from Woody's face leaving it rather lost and miserable. He said: "It wasn't a—a flirtation. Not the way you say it. She—I—meant it."

"Oh, now look here, sonny," began Henley and unexpectedly showed a grain of humanity at the dumb misery in Woody's eyes, for he amended his voice and his words. "Suppose you tell us just how it happened. I mean how you happened to meet her at the Hunting Horn and what she said and all that."

It was humanity; it was also intelligence.

Jed thrust his hands in his pockets and went to stand at the white railing and look down at the laurels and the green lawns. Woody cleared his throat, got out a cigarette and made rather an ado about lighting it. He said then, stiffly, "Well, that was all it was. I was going away the next day."

"I see," Henley said. "I see. Sort of a farewell."

"I suppose so. Yes."

"Well, go on. . . . You'd arranged to leave the hunt and meet at the tavern? Right?"

"Yes. About five. So we did. We had a drink or two. Then she—well, we knew we'd meet at the dinner that night but we might not be alone again. So she—we said good-bye and she said, she said we might never see each other again, or at least not for a long time and she said . . ." he swallowed. He lifted his cigarette with a hand that shook. "She said good-bye. She said I'd meet some girl but not to forget her. But she . . ." his voice became harder, "but that's how I knew she was leaving Jed. She'd

137

had enough; she couldn't take any more. I said I'd be home on other leaves; I asked her to write to me. And she said she wouldn't be here."

There was another instant of silence; then Jed swung around. "Wouldn't be here!"

Woody's chin was stubborn. "That's what she said."

"But she . . ." Jed stared at him incredulously. "Where on earth was she going?"

"Well." Some of Woody's certainty evaporated. "She didn't say. I asked her. I supposed, of course, she was leaving you. What else could I think? She'd told me she was unhappy, she . . ."

"But now see here, kid, I mean, Ensign . . ." Henley was taken aback too, but his eyes were sharp. "Didn't she say where she was going? Or why she wouldn't be here? Think now. Try to remember."

Woody took a long breath of smoke; Jed stared incredulously again at Woody. And out of the silence a memory of Caroline's voice floated to Sue's ears: "What do you suppose Ernestine was up to? What did she want?"

Jed said suddenly, "You must be wrong, Woody. Where could she have gone? She'd have told me; she'd have—well, she'd have asked me for money, you know. She . . ." A thought seemed to strike him; he said, "Camilla didn't say anything about any such plan of Ernestine's. She'd have told Camilla."

But Woody was still stubborn. "That's what she said."

"Is that—all?" Henley asked.

Woody nodded. "That's all. Except I think she had some —some plan."

"What plan?"

But Woody didn't know; he wouldn't say any more. Probably, thought Sue, there was no more to say.

"And you still think Baily shot her?" said Henley at last.

Again the little flush crept up into Woody's face. "Well," he said. "I think Sue lied to try to save him."

138

"That's perjury," interjected Henley, watching him.

"Yes, I—I mean she would lie if she thought it would save him. But . . ."

Sue said, "I was telling the truth, Woody. You'll have to believe me."

He wouldn't look at her. "Well, but if Jed didn't kill her, who did?"

It was an unanswerable question. It was the question they always came back to; Henley, however, was sure he had the answer. He heaved himself up, with a look at Sue. "That's what we're trying to find out," he said, and turned to Jed. "Can you remember anything—anything at all that your wife did or said that bears out what young Poore here has told us?"

Jed suddenly was flushed and angry; he looked almost as young as Woody with his dark hair ruffled and hands thrust in his pockets, facing Henley with a rather despairing defiance. "Don't you think I'd tell you if I knew? Don't you think I'd tell you anything that would help get Sue and me out of this?"

"Well, yes," Henley said. "I guess you would." He thought for a moment, hitched up his belt and started for the steps. The two troopers were instantly on their feet.

The car shot smartly down the drive. Jed, watching it, said, "I wonder where they're going." It disappeared along the road below and he turned to Sue. "Don't worry, Sue. Woody's in the clear about this. Ernestine—well, she didn't mean anything, you know. She liked admiration; who doesn't? Woody—every young fellow some time or other has had a sort of infatuation for an older woman. She was lovely and—he'll get over it."

"It wasn't that, I tell you!" Woody said. "I—I meant it."

Sue linked her arm through Woody's; he was trembling a little for all his stiff, white arrogance. Jed gave Woody a troubled look. "Woody, I didn't mean to—belittle or—I do see how it happened. That's all. See you later, Sue."

He, too, went away. Sue watched his car disappear along the road before she said at last, with difficulty, "Woody, I had no idea."

"It's all right." He stared out beyond the laurels and the sloping lawn toward the rim of blue hills. "But I don't think she was simply—having fun, you know; laughing at me. I think she meant it, too."

"Darling, darling," thought Sue, "you didn't know Ernestine; she never meant anything that wouldn't have been a gain for Ernestine. What could a boy with no position, no money, nothing—what could you have done for her except, in your admiration, feed her vanity?" She pressed his arm gently, "I'm sorry, Woody."

"It's all right now. I've got used to it. It was hell then—for a long time. But—Sue, she was going away somewhere."

"Where?"

"Well—I don't know."

"Do you know—why?"

"Only because of Jed. Because they were unhappy and . . ."

"Did she say they were unhappy, Woody?"

"Well. Not in so many words. I guessed. . . ."

"Did she say he didn't understand her?"

"Yes. And she—she needed me, Sue. She said so."

Often when they were children Sue had felt a gusty, quick anger with Ernestine, never since she became an adult. She had for awhile (frankly in her heart) envied Ernestine. Ernestine had everything—she had Jed, she had Duval Hall—but Sue had never until that moment felt the wave of fury that she felt then. Her own baby brother! How dared Ernestine! How dared she bring surreptitious meetings, false and cheap emotions into Woody's life? And how dared she let any move of the tawdry little game become a real and wounding thing for Woody?

She couldn't hate a dead woman, but she saw, for a moment, why someone might have hated Ernestine with a blind, destroying rage.

Woody said suddenly, "I—I guess I'll see how Jeremy's leg is making out. We're putting compresses on it. . . . Thanks, Sue."

He went away. She was still standing there at the railing looking out over the thick hedges when Fitz came.

This time no one was with him and this time he had news. Old Lissy Jenkins, who had cooked and cleaned and answered the telephone for Dr. Luddington for many years had, at last, told the police of a telephone call Dr. Luddington had made during that mysterious hour or so preceding his death.

"She wouldn't tell it before. She's got a dread of the police and everything about them. Say nothing and stay out of trouble. It's a sort of fixed policy of her age and color. You can't blame them really," he sighed and looked at her and said on a tangent, "I like that yellow sweater. You look more like yourself."

They hadn't been alone together since the day of Dr. Luddington's murder. Always someone had been with them. She found herself tingling under the look in the gray eyes of the man opposite her, feeling conscious of herself and of him. He said, "You've been going around as if you were in a dream."

"A terrible dream, Fitz."

"I know. Grief and shock—that's part of it. But the rest —it is terrible, yes; it's more than that. I think . . ." he lighted a cigarette and leaned back with a kind of sigh and said, "I'd better tell you, Sue, that I think somebody has stacked the cards against you."

"Stacked . . ."

"Whoever murdered Dr. Luddington deliberately tried to get you into it. Entangle you. Make it look as though you did it."

After a moment she whispered, "*Who* . . ."

"I don't know who; and I don't want to scare you. But I do want to—warn you. Only I don't know exactly why." He smoked for a moment thoughtfully, his eyes seeming far away. He looked tired and as if he hadn't been sleeping; there were sharp fine lines around his eyes and mouth and his gestures were quick and nervous. But then he glanced up and caught her eyes and smiled, "We'll get over the hill, somehow, Sue. We'll get through the woods. Now then, I want to tell you about old Lissy; this is her story—belated, but here it is. She took down the phone to telephone for a taxi. It was her day off and she went to the movie at Bedford. The telephone was in Dr. Luddington's consulting room but there's a kitchen extension; she answered his sick calls when he was out. When she took down the telephone he was talking. And he said, as nearly as she can remember—'I swore to false testimony; I perjured myself. I was never going to tell the truth but now I've got to.' She remembers those phrases fairly clearly—so she says—and I think she's telling the truth."

Sue was sitting upright, staring at Fitz. "But—who . . ."

"That's what Lissy doesn't know. She swears up and down that she doesn't know who was on the other end of the conversation. Then he said something about you; she's not so sure about that; she said—and I believe her there too—that she started to hang up; she thought she'd get on her hat and then make another call when Dr. Luddington had finished; she says it didn't strike her that it was important—that I doubt—but in any case her set policy of keeping her mouth shut would have operated. At any rate as she hung up she thinks the doctor said, 'Now that it's Sue I've got to tell the truth.' "

"But that—what . . ."

Fitz got up, walked restlessly to the railing, tossed his cigarette over into the laurels and turned around. "Obviously he meant that he perjured himself to get Jed free. It seems fairly clear too that he felt that, if you were to be arrested, he had to tell whatever it was that he knew. That it would free you. Therefore he may have been warning someone—someone who—well . . ." Fitz's brown face was hard, too, like Woody's. "It sounds as if he knew who murdered Ernestine and it was someone whom he wouldn't sacrifice for Jed and would sacrifice for you. That's what it looks like on the face of it. . . . Of course, it could mean other things too. And if it *was* that somebody that killed him, there's a queer sort of discrepancy about the way he died." He did not explain what; he stood still, his shoulders sagging wearily.

"Fitz, it was because of me. He was trying to help me out . . ."

"Nonsense," Fitz said roughly, "Don't get that into your head. There are several things he may have meant; we'll never know exactly perhaps. The police tried to check on the telephone calls he made. There was only one that they're sure of and that was to Ruby and the maid there talked to him and Dr. Luddington didn't say that to her. Then—listen, Sue, that shiny thing, the mirror, whatever it was that you picked up, can you remember what you did with it?"

"No, Fitz! It could have been anything! I—what about Jed and Ruby?"

"They still say they don't remember seeing it. Well, sometime you'll just think of it all at once. There's another thing I want to know. Are you sure you tied up Jeremy? I mean securely, so he couldn't possibly have got loose himself?"

She was sure of that and said so.

"Henley insists that you didn't. I think you did; I think it'd be second nature for you to tie him up so he couldn't work himself loose. No matter how worried you were. And if you did—well then who rode him away? Or did anybody ride him?"

He moved. "I'm going over to tell Shepson about this latest thing. The sheriff told me; he's been damned decent, Sue. But I don't know whether . . ." he stopped. She said, "Whether he can hold out against Henley much longer?"

He turned abruptly to look at her. He said, "We'll make him hold out," as if he were swearing a solemn oath. And all at once he took her in his arms.

He held her and kissed her. And then let her go and looked down at her with a kind of smile. "You look more like yourself. Why didn't I think of that sooner?" But then his face sobered again. "Listen, Sue—I'm not an old woman and I'm not fanciful or—but has Woody got a gun?"

"Why—why, yes, I suppose so."

"Not that that would help. The fact is, I'm not easy in my mind about—well, about this place."

The tight, stifled feeling came around her throat. "What do you mean?"

"Well, it's a nasty situation, Sue. Dangerous . . ." said Fitz. "Well—tell Woody what I said."

After he'd gone, she thought of what Woody had told of Ernestine. Probably there was nothing in it, yet if Ernestine had had some plan—if, as Caroline had said Ernestine had been up to something—then it could conceivably have had something to do with her murder. She would tell Fitz. She would not tell Caroline, unless Woody did so himself; it would only trouble and anger her unnecessarily. Yet it suggested again the question Caroline herself had asked. . . . "We'll get over the hill," Fitz had said. "We'll get through the woods."

The soft spring breeze was cool on her face. The shadows were lengthening around the house, under the tall thickets of evergreen, below the great hedges of laurel. The pine woods beyond, along the south side of the house, were darkening; blue shadows blended with green. Somewhere a honeysuckle was blooming early; a ghost of its fragrance drifted across the porch and touched Sue's face like a faint, small promise.

The tranquil evening light, the deep blue shadows under the pines, the distant rim of purple hills denied the thing that had walked through those very shadows.

She thought that; from the stables at the other side of the house, she heard Jeremy moving about in his loose box, his hooves like soft distant thunder. She turned to enter the house.

As she turned a shot came from one of the thickets of evergreens. The bullet missed her. Tiny splinters of wood flew from the pillar nearest her.

There was a second shot, rocking the evening air. Some birds flew, screeching, from the thick clump of pines at the edge of the woods.

Then there was complete silence until Woody came, running from the door behind her.

15

It was a bold attack, it was direct and easy and if its intent was murder, it was very nearly successful.

The clump of evergreens stood about fifty yards from the house at the very edge of the lawn; a wide strip of woodland, mainly pines, covering some thirty acres, lay on the Poore property, dividing it from the hilly Jameson farm beyond. The wood was irregular, with patches of thick undergrowth and thickets of laurel beyond whose broad and glossy leaves a man might easily conceal himself, with gullies and overhanging banks. It offered an easy refuge and an easy approach to the house. Sue, standing so still on the steps in her yellow sweater, had been a perfect target. They debated, later, the power of the gun which had been used; Woody believed it was a revolver, a forty-five. There was, however, no way of proving it. The first bullet had scraped the pillar beside her, knocking out splinters but had then dropped somewhere amid the shrubbery. They could not find any traces of the second.

And they could find no traces of whoever had stood there in the pines, stalking and waiting his chance. The troopers who had been ordered to keep an eye on the house had been withdrawn that day, not because Captain Henley's belief in Sue's guilt had weakened, but because he needed the men. Murder was murder, the county was aroused and complaining, his job depended on results—but at the same time there were all the usual chores of the daily routine.

It was also a quiet hour of the day, when there was little traffic anywhere. So whoever had come and gone had done so with ease and, as far as could be discovered, without observation.

Further, whoever was in the pines had time to escape, not much time but enough while Woody ran back into the house for his own gun. Woody searched the thicket—aided by Chrisy, willingly, black rage in her face and a fire shovel in her hand, and by Lij unwillingly, showing a disposition to hide behind his grandmother's ample skirts, and bellowing loudly when Woody fired once at what he took to be a man and was not. Caroline came hurrying from the stables; she went into the house and came back with an old, long-barreled army revolver, a Civil War revolver which had not seen service since. Sue took it from her.

"It's loaded," Caroline said. "It's loaded. I always keep it loaded."

Sue turned it prudently downward and started after Woody and was hauled back by Caroline. "If he fired at you," cried Caroline, "if he fired at *you*—Sue, stay here. Go in the house, Sue . . ."

By that time Woody was running back toward the house with Chrisy plowing angrily after him. "Phone for the police," he called out. "Hurry, Sue. They can block the roads."

Caroline, however, hurried after Sue into the house, along the hall with Sister Britches, caught by the excitement, shrieking and leaping and getting under their feet and when the operator did not answer at once, Caroline snatched the telephone from Sue and jiggled it up and down and cried, "Operator—police—operator . . ." until the girl answered.

It could have been only about ten minutes before the first police car arrived; they heard it screaming along the highway from the village. They went to the steps to meet it; they were like the inhabitants of a beleaguered fortress.

The trooper who got out first gave them a look of rather wild inquiry—Chrisy with her fire shovel, Sue with her Civil War revolver, Caroline armed with furious, terrified dignity. Only Woody's weapon drew a glance of respect.

Both of them looked also at the splintered nick on the pillar, listened briefly and searched the thickets of pines. Woody went with them. By that time another police car had arrived. The two troopers it brought had received the radio call; they joined the first contingent.

In the end they found no one and nothing to prove that anyone had been there; they searched with flashlights by that time, as it was rapidly growing dark, for rejected cartridges, searched all through the leaf mold and thick, slippery pine needles and found none.

They did find, however, a rather curious thing.

Sue did not know of it until later; neither, as a matter of fact, did Woody, for at the time when it was discovered he had come back to the house to telephone to Sheriff Benjamin. He told the sheriff eagerly, his sun-streaked hair tousled, a scratch from a low-hanging branch across his hot, flushed face, somebody had shot at Sue. It meant the murderer was at large and in the woods near their house and it proved therefore that Sue was not the murderer, it proved she was not and Henley must see it.

Sue had not thought of that. Chrisy, also listening, muttered approvingly. "Good out of evil. He don't touch Miss Sue and he get himself hung."

It was not, however, so simple; the sheriff was noncommittal, but said he would come and bring Henley. When Woody put down the telephone Sue took it and gave Fitz's number to an operator who by this time was excited and helpful. "He's not at home, Miss Poore," she told Sue agitatedly. "He's at the garage. He got a flat and phoned to his house for somebody to come after him in his other car, the station wagon, but Miss Duval was there, at his house, I mean, so she got on the phone and told him she'd pick him up in her car. Shall I try to reach him at the garage. Miss Poore, did somebody try to shoot you?"

"Yes, I—please try the garage. . . ."

"How awful! Oh, Miss Poore, we're all afraid to go home or anywhere at night—we—here's the garage. . . ."

But Miss Duval had already come for Mr. Wilson, a man's voice said. How long ago? Oh, fifteen minutes or so. . . . Miss Duval had Mr. Baily's car. He thought they were going to stop at Duval Hall. He'd heard Miss Duval say something about dinner there. The operator rang the Baily number and Camilla answered; yes, Fitz was there, they were having cocktails and about to have dinner. What did Sue want?

Her voice was not particularly pleasant. It was, indeed, so much like Ernestine's that again it evoked a shadowy presence of Ernestine—chill, defeated about something she had desired and determining to have it anyway. The image fled, however; Camilla gave a faint scream when Sue told her what had happened. Jed and Fitz must have been very near the telephone. Jed took it and Fitz was at his side; Sue could hear his voice. They would come at once. "Who was it, Sue? Didn't you see him? Don't you know who it was?" cried Jed. When she explained the little there was to explain he and Fitz both talked at once; Fitz took the telephone, though; he said, his voice shaken and rough in her ear, "Are you sure you're all right, Sue? Are you sure?"

"Oh, yes, yes . . . ."

"Did you call the police?"

"Yes, they're in the woods, searching."

There was a short silence; then Fitz said, "Have them search the house, too. And the stables. The car's at the door; we'll be there in five minutes."

It was, of course, more than five minutes; it was three miles by highway from Duval Hall; by the time they arrived Woody, with an odd, secretive look in his eyes had also telephoned Wat and Ruby Luddington.

"Why are you phoning them?" asked Caroline. "I think we ought to let Judge Shepson know, but Wat and Ruby . . ."

Woody, stubborn and secretive, did not reply. And someone answered at the stately, huge Wat Luddington house; it was an even statlier butler, imported by Ruby from New York; he would not be queried or hurried but he at last imparted the information that Mr. Luddington was out. Madam was out too and at Woody's insistence he said they were both expected home to dinner. Some quality of urgency in Woody's questioning did however penetrate his calm; he volunteered the information that he believed Mr. Luddington had gone to a political meeting in Bedford and that Madam was exercising one of the horses and ought to have returned by then.

Dinner at the Luddington establishment was at eight-thirty; it was a formal and worldly institution which had been looked upon with slight disfavor on the part of Ernestine and Camilla. Ernestine, however, had pushed the Baily dinner hour up to eight. It seemed very strange now to Sue to remember it and other trivial rivalries between the two women. Ernestine had been the undisputed leader, not only of that small quartet of friends—Ernestine herself and Camilla, Sue and Ruby, but of their little group in the county, the hunting and riding and gay little group—until Ruby with all the DeJong money had returned, married to Wat and setting up an establishment which far surpassed Ernestine's. The memory of those small battles was like the memory of a gay and sunny world which had never existed.

In that world there was no horror, no dark ways to murder; she thought of Ernestine in her yellow gown with her fingers pressed to her back and blood oozing from between them. She thought of Dr. Luddington. She thought of the shocking crash of sound from the shadowed pine thicket. Woody was telephoning now to Judge Shepson. Some of the police were returning from the pine woods. She could hear their heavy steps on the porch.

It had grown too dark in the woods to continue their search. In any case they were not likely to find anybody; there'd been time for whoever hid in the shadows to have escaped. They felt and said that further search was futile.

One of them, a sergeant, asked Sue if she had heard a car along the road.

"I don't remember it. But one might have come along. I might not have noticed it."

"You can't see much of the highway," Woody told him. "If you'll stand there on the steps you'll see. The laurels make too high a hedge."

"Mmm," said the sergeant and no more.

Woody got out bourbon for them which they refused rather wistfully. Chrisy bore in great platters of scrambled eggs and bacon from the kitchen and brimming cups of coffee which they did not refuse. The sergeant kept his own counsel, however, until the sheriff and Captain Henley arrived, when he drew them aside, out on the porch for a low-voiced conversation. They were still there when Fitz and Jed and Camilla came, the gravel flying under the wheels of the car as Jed braked to a quick stop; Judge Shepson, rather flushed and unnaturally vivacious from his before-dinner highball and his hastily eaten dinner, arrived a moment or two later. It began to seem like a kind of party, but a nightmarish party, with bright lights everywhere and revolvers strapped in leather holsters at the troopers' waists, adding a note of grim masquerade.

Except it was not a masquerade. The sheriff and Captain Henley, having finished with the sergeant took Sue into Caroline's study again, and with old Reveller eyeing them balefully from the couch, questioned her.

They let Judge Shepson listen; he puffed and crossed and uncrossed his fat old legs in their baggy trousers but did not have much to say. And certainly Sue did not have much to tell.

But she began to perceive, almost at once, that Woody's rosy and hopeful theory that the attack upon her would go to prove that she was not the murderer was, at least as far as Henley was concerned, merely a rosy and hopeful theory.

He was flatly, arrogantly frank about it. "Are you perfectly sure that this so-called attempt to murder you really occurred?"

The sheriff's faded blue eyes turned icily toward him; Judge Shepson stirred, opened his mouth, closed it again. Sue said: "Yes—yes—I told you . . ."

"Exactly," Captain Henley said. *"You* told us."

"But—but the pillar, the splinters . . ."

Henley got up. "That's not proof." He looked at the sheriff. "I frankly have had enough of this. There's no proof whatever that this attack occurred. It could have been designed with exactly this purpose in view, to make us believe that this girl herself is the object of a murderous attack and that therefore she herself is not guilty. In my opinion it's an outright attempt to deceive us."

"You can't deny the shot," said the sheriff. "Everybody heard it. Miss Caroline and Woody and the cook . . ."

"The boy did it himself. He'd do anything to help his sister."

"What about the horse?" asked the sheriff.

Judge Shepson leaned forward, his protuberant blue eyes blinking. "What horse?"

It came out then. The sheriff told them. The troopers in searching the woods had found no fugitive, they had found no cartridges, they had found no footprints, no cigarette ends, no matches in the pines—but they had found in the soft clay at the edge of a little gully the mixed, confused hoofprints of a horse.

"It was near a sapling; the sapling is barked a little about the height where the horse could have been tied.

The hoofprints are deep and, the sergeant thought, fresh; there's a little trickle of water through the gully. It looks as if a horse was tied there for maybe half an hour, maybe less, there's no telling about that, but there are hoofprints."

The lawyer's eyes were bulging.

"How far is that from the pines?"

"About a hundred yards; we'll look at it by daylight."

"What happened to the hoofprints? Which way did they go?"

"Apparently, as far as they can discover, the horse then jumped the gully; but the hoofprints vanish; of course it was dark by then; but there's another strip of pine. A carpet of pine needles doesn't show much."

Judge Shepson rubbed his hands together and looked at Henley. "You'll have a hard time disproving that in court!"

"You'll have a harder time proving that the hoofprints were made tonight," snapped Henley. He turned to the sheriff. "Look here, Sheriff—we're wasting time and energy and the taxpayers' money. Wilkins was right; that girl's guilty as hell. This is only a dodge . . ."

The sheriff got up too, unfolding his spare, old bones slowly. "You've got to have a case this time, Henley, that'll hold up in court. And I don't believe this girl killed Dr. Luddington and I don't think a jury'll believe it."

"You can't tell what a jury'll believe," Henley said angrily. He stood for a moment, his eyes sparkling, his red face shining almost as brightly and furiously as his boots; then without a word he jerked toward the door, in a kind of military motion as if snapping to attention at some drill command heard only by his alert ears, and went out. Sue looked at the sheriff.

But if she had hoped for a word of reassurance he did not give it; he looked tired and discouraged himself. He walked over to the couch and bent to scratch Reveller's ears; he said: "You didn't hear a horse, did you? Or anything like it?"

She shook her head. "There was only the sound of the

birds rising out of the thicket. I don't remember anything else."

"No—rustle in the pines. No breaking branches or anything like that?"

Sue thought back desperately; he saw failure in her eyes. "Well." He straightened. "Maybe we can find somebody who did see something. Maybe—you tell your aunt to try not to be too upset. And by the way . . ." he was at the door, his face very lined and white like a papier mâché mask, his faded blue eyes anxious. "By the way, that young brother of yours . . . tell him to keep a lookout but not to get too hasty with his trigger finger. I'm letting him keep his gun," he said as an afterthought and nodded and went away.

Judge Shepson gave a kind of sigh and grunt and got up too. "It's funny about that horse. And your aunt's old hunter too. You're sure you tied him up—Jeremy, I mean, there at Dr. Luddington's?"

Sue nodded. He sighed again, gave her a hazy smile and pat on the shoulder, said, "I don't see anything we can do tonight," and ambled away into the hall. He was, she knew, an able lawyer; he had successfully defended Jed. She wished, though, that he had been able to say something solid and heartening.

There were voices from the front of the house, the sound of departing automobiles. Woody came back to the study, followed by Fitz, and Woody was in a white rage; Captain Henley had asked for his revolver, had examined it, had smelled it and then asked Woody point blank if he had fired the shot.

"And the hell of it is, I had fired the gun! I fired it there in the woods. I thought I saw something move and thought I'd better fire first and inquire later. It wasn't anything, an old hump of dead grass Lij had left there after he mowed. But of course, my gun had been fired. He could smell the powder. One shot was gone out of the barrel." He appealed to Sue. "You heard me, Chrisy heard me. That damned fool, Henley . . ."

Fitz said, "Take it easy, Woody. We can't do everything all at once." He spoke to Woody quietly, but he looked at Sue and he was frightened. He tried not to show it. Somebody called to Woody from the hall and Woody, still in a rage, went out. Fitz crossed the room to where Sue sat huddled in the old armchair, one foot tucked under her. She looked like a schoolgirl with her brown tweed skirt, her white blouse and yellow sweater, her rumpled hair and he thought she looked not so much frightened as bewildered.

She said, "Why should anybody shoot at me? Why?"

He pulled up Caroline's footstool, moved to the floor three hunt magazines and a book about kennel feeding, and sat down beside Sue.

"We'll try to make them give you a police guard. If they won't Woody's got a gun and I'll stay here, too." He took her hand and turned it over and looked at it as intently as if he were memorizing every line of the pink palm and lifted it to his cheek. As he did so Camilla came flying into the room, her coat billowing around her, saw them and came to an abrupt stop. "Well, my gracious, Sue, do you have to have Fitz hold your hand?"

Jed followed her. Fitz said with a twinkle, "Well, it's a nice hand," and Jed, his eyes bright and anxious, cried, "Sue, what happened? Didn't you see anybody?" His anxiety was genuine; it occurred to Sue rather shame-facedly that as a rule, if Jed had deep feelings, it did not move her. "It's all right," she told him quickly. "I wasn't hurt. I have no idea who it was—or why," she added with a kind of chill in her heart. She turned to Fitz. "There must be a reason and there can't be! There's nobody who would—do—that . . ."

Wat and Ruby came in; Woody and Caroline came, too. Jed said, "It must have been an accident. Somebody shooting in the woods, afraid to come forward. Or some crackpot . . ."

Wat, pale and drawn, too, looking suddenly like his father, came to take her hand. "It's dreadful, Sue, dreadful." He stood looking down at her, swallowing and for once at a loss for words. But then he seemed to pull himself together, and resume his air of bright, nervous competence. And all at once everybody was questioning, exclaiming, offering opinions, and none of them had an answer.

Ruby's seemed the most logical and credible. "It's a tramp, it's somebody hanging around, hiding in the hills. It's somebody with a grudge and a twisted, horrible—oh, Wat," she turned to Wat with a white face, her hands catching each other, a throb in her voice which was unlike Ruby. "Wat, they've got to find him. They've got to . . . Can't you round up a posse and search the hills? That's what people used to do."

It was not, said Wat nervously but kindly, a bad idea; not a bad idea at all; except the police were perfectly adequate; they were on the job; they'd swear out deputies if they thought it necessary. He smiled a little, thinly, and patted Ruby's shoulder. "It's not like the old times, Ruby; you sound like your own grandfather. A posse," said Wat and gave the ghost of a chuckle.

"Something's got to be done," Ruby said.

"Something is being done," Wat assured her. "You'll see. It takes time."

Ruby, amazingly, began to cry; it was amazing because nobody, as far as Sue knew, had ever seen Ruby so conquered by emotion. Sue was touched and rather apologetic; she wouldn't have thought that a danger to herself would have so moved Ruby.

Caroline watched with the stricken expression that since Dr. Luddington's death, since the news of the warrant for Sue's arrest had fastened itself like a mask upon her face. Camilla touched her hair and slid out of her long coat; she had changed for dinner—for dinner with Fitz as a guest, thought Sue unexpectedly. The long pink-flowered dress looked out of place and ornate in the comfortable, shabby study. Jed, frowning, watched Ruby, Fitz leaned back on the footstool and linked his hands around his knees. "Look here," he said, "we've not talked like this before. Together I mean and—straight out. We were the people who were closest to Ernestine and to Dr. Luddington. Why don't we try to put things together? There are no policemen here; we can say what we please."

"What in the world . . . ?" began Wat, giving Fitz a startled look over Ruby's heaving shoulder.

"You begin it," said Fitz. "What were you doing tonight when somebody fired at Sue? Where were you?"

16

IF SUE had thought of it in advance she would have said that any implication such as that Fitz unexpectedly had introduced would have set off an explosion of major proportions; southern tempers ran high, with perhaps pride and a certain combative joy in the tide. Certainly, most of the people she knew had rather a flair for a fracas, particularly Woody, particularly Jed and certainly Camilla and Caroline in their different ways. Wat, of course, was always like a firecracker, waiting for a match. He flared up, but then, he fizzled out, too, as more prudent considerations overcame him. Woody thought as she did; he was standing in the doorway, his eyes lighted. "Whoops! By golly, Fitz. A free-for-all!"

Both of them were wrong. Nobody even glanced at Woody. Everybody in the room was looking at Fitz with startled, yet so far as Sue could see, perfectly genuine surprise. Everyone that is, except Ruby, whose face was still hidden on Wat's rather scrawny shoulder, but who had stopped crying to listen.

Then Camilla, who was nobody's fool, leaped several fences. "My gracious, Fitz, Wat wouldn't shoot his own father!"

Wat in his surprise hadn't gone that far; now the firecracker in him began to sizzle; his hatchet face turned bright scarlet, he disencumbered himself of Ruby by putting her down rather hard upon the end of the couch, which move Reveller protested with a low growl, and advanced toward Fitz, taking off his coat. "We'll settle this, Fitz Wilson! We'll settle this right now, man to man. You're insulting, sir, insulting. You've outraged my grief, my deepest feelings. You're not fit to call yourself a man, sir, you . . ."

"Calm down, Wat." Fitz did not move from the footstool. "Calm down. You're not making a political talk." There was a faint smile on his mouth but his eyes were extremely intent. He said quietly and sincerely: "I didn't mean to hurt your feelings, Wat. I don't think you killed your father; nobody does. Put your coat on."

Caroline said suddenly, "It's a very terrible thing to suggest that a man would kill his own father—or a woman her own sister or . . ."

Camilla gave a faint, shrill scream. Caroline went on with a grave solemnity that held them quiet ". . . or that a friend would lift his hand against a friend. But murder is a terrible thing, too." She looked at them with her blue, grief-stricken eyes for a long moment; no one spoke. Caroline said: "I don't think Fitz meant to suggest that you had fired that shot at Sue tonight, Wat. For one thing you wouldn't have any reason to. Nobody needs to be afraid of Sue; she wouldn't hurt anybody. Even," said Caroline looking down at her strong, small hands, "even if she knew something that could hurt anybody she wouldn't tell it, she's not that kind. But Fitz means that we—all of us here —knew Ernestine the longest and knew her better than anybody else. And we knew"—she bit her lip and said with a little quaver—"and we knew Tom Luddington, too. Of course, Ernestine knew other people, especially lately since the war and since it's got so fashionable around here, with all the rich New Yorkers and the people from Washington coming out here to buy places and hunt and all the—the politicians and the diplomats and the—everybody," finished Caroline with a sigh, "but I still think that if we tried we might—we just might get some idea, some fact

159

. . ." she floundered, seeking a word, pushing back her untidy wad of hair and Woody said with a gleam that was half amusement and half pride, "Clue . . ."

"Why, yes, that's what I mean. Clue. If we could just talk about it . . ."

"We have talked about it," Ruby said unexpectedly from the couch. "We've talked and talked about it. All winter."

"Yes, I know but . . ." Caroline's troubled gaze appealed to Fitz. "That is what you meant, isn't it?"

Fitz's brown face was closed and thoughtful. He said, after a second or two, "Yes. Yes, that's right."

Caroline said, "For instance, maybe Wat passed somebody on the highway, somebody that turned in at the woodland and . . ."

"I didn't," Wat said. "I went by the other road. Much earlier, too, unless the fellow was hidden out there all afternoon, or all day for that matter, waiting his chance."

Waiting his chance—creeping nearer and ever nearer the house, from one leafy covert to another. Something cold and inimical seemed to hover at the edges of the room, to walk on soundless feet along the hall, to peer secretively through the windows from the darkness outside. Sue rose, not knowing what she was going to do nor where she was going, and Fitz got up, too, and took her hand again. "It's all right, Sue. We're here with you."

She met his eyes which tried to reassure her; she sat down again, slowly, holding tightly to Fitz's hand. Caroline was making a valiant attempt to smile at her, giving her courage.

Ruby said from the couch, "I tell you it's a tramp." She was not in riding clothes. She had taken time to change to a red tweed suit; a diamond pin sparkled at the throat of her white blouse. She reached in one pocket and then another for a handkerchief; the shifting of her weight displeased Reveller who rose with an outraged look, got down from the couch and stalked out.

Jed saw Fitz's hand on Sue's; he also saw the look she and Fitz exchanged. He started forward and stopped, watching, his face tense. Camilla saw it, too, and sat up; her jaw seemed to widen and fix itself. It was again a look of Ernestine's. Sue was aware of that; she was aware of Jed, yet in a curious way she seemed to be aware of it without looking away from Fitz.

He said, "Remember, now you've been warned; now we've all been warned. So we can take steps, we can do something, we can . . ."

"Exactly what?" Jed demanded. He was angry. There was a deep flush in his handsome face, his shoulders squared aggressively and he flung back his black head and looked at Fitz with anger and defiance. "Exactly what? And exactly why and how have you constituted yourself an authority, Fitz? You act as if you own Sue. I'll take care of her. I don't need your help. And besides," added Jed suddenly, "you're not exactly in the clear about Ernestine. You were always hanging around after her; she told me so. Maybe you shot her yourself. Maybe she wouldn't have anything to do with you and you . . ."

Camilla stood up, her face white, her eyes far back in her head, "Jed Baily, that's not true! Ernestine always thought every man was after her. Ever since she was a little girl. She was just as vain as she could be. She always tried to take my beaux away from me. She just couldn't stand it if anybody liked me. You know that, Jed Baily. You know it was me you liked first, when you first came down here. You liked me but Ernestine thought you were a catch and a better catch than either of us was ever likely to get again and she just walked right in and took you away from me and you know it. You didn't have a chance."

Jed started to speak, stopped, thrust his hands into his pockets. Camilla swept on, "That's the way Ernestine was. She couldn't stand it if anybody got ahead of her. She was going to make the best match, and have the finest house and the finest position and when Ruby came back with all that money and Wat headed for a high position in Washington just as sure as anything, you know how mad Ernestine was. And then Fitz came, and he's famous with all that war-correspondent background; everybody knew who he was and what he'd done, and here he was, settling down to write his articles and all sorts of Washington people, statesmen and everybody—people Ernestine wanted to know—kept coming out to talk to him and she saw that he was important, and besides he'd inherited the Fitzjames place so he was Virginia, too—when she saw all that she just went after Fitz, too, and . . ."

"Camilla," said Fitz, but rather helplessly, too. "No. No, she didn't."

Camilla did not even take a breath. ". . . but I'll tell you this, Jed Baily. Ernestine was so vain she'd say anything but—Fitz didn't like her. He didn't like her one bit. She used to invite him and invite him but he wouldn't come and . . ."

Caroline said in an icy voice, "Camilla, it's not decent to talk like that. However . . ." she added, "now that you've said so much you may as well go on. You say Ernestine was interested in men; do you mean that she would have divorced Jed if another man had come along whom she liked better?"

But Camilla had thought twice. She stood there, her hands clenched at the sides of her flowing, flowered silk dress, her jaw firm. But her eyes, sunken so far back that there was only a dark glimmer had a rather frightened glimmer. She looked like Ernestine, her coronet of blonde braids was so like Ernestine's that from the back they would have been indistinguishable. But Ernestine was smarter than Camilla; Camilla only then saw that she had gone too far. She turned to Jed, her voice high and plaintive. "Jed, I didn't mean all that. I'm nervous and upset. But you—I never meant to hurt you, Jed, or to—you've always been so good to me. So was Ernestine, after she married you. Nobody could have been nicer to me than you. You gave me a home, and you gave me everything just as if I were really your sister. You—I didn't mean I thought you were in love with me; Ernestine was prettier and—Ernestine just naturally got whatever she wanted, she wouldn't give up. I . . ."

"Oh, that's all right, Camilla," Jed said. "I guess it's the truth, too. I did know you first, before I knew Ernestine. But then Ernestine—but I sort of disappointed her. I—I guess all I ever wanted was just to live in the country and ride and . . ."

Camilla flared again but this time in defense, "Why shouldn't you? What's the matter with that kind of life? Ernestine hadn't any right to nag you the way she did. Ernestine . . ."

"Ernestine had so much talent," Jed said, staring at the carpet. "She was made for a more—more glittering sort of life. Ernestine . . ."

"Ernestine," said Ruby, sitting bolt upright, "was a pig! There's no use in looking at me like that, Wat. She was. I know all about not speaking ill of the dead, but she was downright mean."

"*Ruby!*" cried Wat.

Camilla, thoroughly aroused and reckless turned on Ruby. "That's just because she wouldn't sell Duval Hall to you. You thought you'd come back home with all that money you got out of that old man you married and you'd just ride high, wide and handsome. You'd get Wat into politics and push him along with that money till he really got to be somebody important and you'd buy Duval Hall because it was the loveliest and oldest place anywhere around here and you'd set up the kind of establishment there that would make the rest of us feel like ten cents. You had a real quarrel with Ernestine about it, too. I knew it but didn't tell anybody because I knew you wouldn't really shoot her; it didn't mean anything that way. But you did quarrel with her. She knew she'd got the loveliest place in the county and it rightfully ought to have been hers, too; it was our grandfather's house. But you wanted it to get ahead of Ernestine. You've always been like that, you and Ernestine, ever since you were little girls, only Ernestine used to spit things out and you always just kept quiet and . . ."

Wat, spluttering again, went to Camilla. "You shut up, Camilla Duval! It's disgraceful for you to talk like that. Besides," he took a breath. "Besides, suppose Ruby did offer to buy Duval Hall and pay a handsome profit to Ernestine, too. What's wrong with that? You can make an offer for a house, can't you, without being accused of murder!"

"I didn't accuse Ruby of murder. I said she didn't. But they did quarrel and they kept right on quarrelling even after Ruby gave up and bought that huge place of the Chesters' with all that land and the stables and the greenhouses and swimming pool and," said Camilla running out of breath, "that English butler. English butler. None of us around here has an English butler!"

"Ruby!" Fitz said in a voice that sounded, by contrast to Camilla's, extremely quiet and friendly. "Did you really quarrel with Ernestine?"

Wat turned quickly to Ruby. "Tell Camilla she doesn't know what she's talking about! She can't go around making statements like that! It's—it's . . ." Wat hesitated and said rather flatly, "I don't know exactly what it is but we're not going to let her. Now you tell them the truth, Ruby."

But Ruby, after her burst of energy, had lapsed back into her usual rather cow-like stolidity. It was a troubled and anxious stolidity; she turned her great brown eyes to Wat and to Fitz appealingly, she knotted up the handkerchief she had finally found and diamonds winked on her fingers as she did so, but she wouldn't talk. Wat said, "You see? Ruby wouldn't quarrel with anybody."

"Woody," Caroline said clearly. "You put that gun right down."

Woody did have a gun, a heavy business-like revolver held in a very business-like way in his right hand. As if they were on a string which Caroline unexpectedly pulled, everyone jerked that way. Sister Britches behind Caroline got up and snapped.

She didn't snap at anyone, she snapped into the air, but she was suspicious and nervous; her amber eyes sparkled; Caroline's voice hadn't been right.

Woody said, "I'm not going to shoot anybody, for Heaven's sake, Aunt Caroline."

Fitz got up. "It's late. We'll see what the police dig up about the thing tomorrow. May I stay here, Miss Caroline, tonight? Woody and I can take turns watching."

Jed said, "You go on home, Fitz. This is none of your business. Sue and I . . . If anybody stays here I'm going to stay. You go on home."

Ruby got up and started in a stolid but determined way for the door. Camilla cried, in her thinnest, highest voice, "But Jed, if you stay here, I'll have to stay at home alone and I'm afraid, too. I'm afraid . . ."

"The servants will be there . . ."

Camilla went on plaintively and determined, gathering up her long coat, "It isn't that I mind your staying. I think it's right that you should. Sue is engaged to you; she's going to be married to you and it's your place to stay, but I'm afraid and I—Fitz, maybe I could stay at your place."

Fitz got out cigarettes and said nothing and Caroline pushed up her hair and said severely, "That's not a bit proper, Camilla. I'm surprised at you. Besides, there're all sorts of servants at Duval Hall and you can have Sam Bronson sleep in the house if you want to. He'd be protection—not that I think Jed needs to stay here or anybody —we can lock all the doors. I got new keys this winter and Woody—Woody," snapped Caroline, suddenly angry, "I told you to put down that gun."

Woody put the gun down on the table. Camilla, shrugging into her coat, said, "Sam Bronson, pooh! He's no account, half drunk most of the time. Besides he's not been near the place for days."

Wat, following Ruby, turned nervously to Camilla, "We'll take you home, if you want us to, Camilla. I suppose you could stay at our place, eh, Ruby?"

Ruby was already in the hall and out of sight; her voice came back like a disembodied sort of echo, but very calm and stolid, "No. I don't want her."

"But—but . . ." Wat's sharp face wrinkled up; he darted after Ruby. "But Ruby, that's not—it's Camilla —you can't . . ."

Ruby had progressed slowly but methodically down the hall; again her voice came back, although from further along. "I don't like what she said. I won't have her in my house. If you're coming home with me, Wat, you come on now."

"But you—you didn't say good night to Miss Caroline or . . ."

"Good night, Miss Caroline." Ruby's voice came back in an unmoved and unhurried way and the front door closed firmly.

Wat put his head in the door, blinked rapidly, adjusted his tie and said to Caroline: "I'm sorry, Miss Caroline, I— you know how women are. And Camilla wasn't nice. She wasn't one bit nice but still . . ."

Caroline, too, was aroused. "I don't think Ruby acted very nice either, Wat, and you can tell her so. Fitz, if you want to stay you're welcome to. Or . . ." she looked worried but turned to Sue questioningly. "Or Jed if—if, well . . ."

Wat disappeared into the hall; Jed put his arm around Sue and Fitz said coolly, "We're not going to quarrel about it as long as somebody stays and keeps an eye on the place. Not that I think whoever was in the woods is going to risk coming back tonight. . . . Do you want me to take you home, Camilla? I really think you'll be safe there. Sam Bronson probably has turned up by now."

"Well, he hasn't," Camilla said. "He's been gone for days now. Just disappeared without saying a word to anybody. Lazy, no account . . ." She took a breath and went to put her hand on Jed's arm. "Jed, you will forgive me if I said anything bad and cross, won't you? You've been wonderful to me, just like a brother. I didn't really mind about Ernestine and you, I mean I—I only meant . . ."

"It's all right, Camilla."

Fitz said to Woody, "You and Jed can fix things, of course—but it seems to me you might take turns . . ."

Jed's eyes had angry lights. "We don't need your advice, thank you."

"All right." Fitz turned in an unperturbed way to Sue. "Good night, Sue. I don't think anything's likely to happen tonight. Honestly I don't." He took her hand briefly. She couldn't read anything in his eyes or in his voice. It wasn't like Fitz to give up like that, resign her to Jed's fiery air of proprietorship. It wasn't like Fitz to walk calmly away and that was exactly what he did. He said good night to her; he said good night to Miss Caroline. Woody walked down the hall with him and Camilla hurriedly followed, the little ghost of Ernestine's perfume drifting after her.

Jed sighed. "Miss Caroline, could I have a nightcap?"

"Why I—why yes." Caroline gave Sue a troubled look, then rose and went out. Sister Britches, still worried, glaring at Sue and at Jed in a threatening manner, pattered after her. Jed said, "Sue, do you suppose—it just occurred to me—but suppose it was Sam Bronson. In the woods tonight?"

Of the bewildering factors that made up that bewildering night this suddenly seemed to Sue the most fantastic. She looked blankly at Jed. "But—but why? Why? Sam Bronson . . ."

Woody from the front door said loudly: "Okay, Fitz—we'll phone in the morning . . ." A car started down the driveway—Fitz's car with Camilla riding with him. Jed heard it, too. He said, "Sue, I wish you wouldn't—well, encourage Fitz, it looks . . ."

"Jed," she said desperately, "you must believe me. I've tried to tell you—everything's changed. You must believe . . ."

But he did believe her, she was sure of it; he had believed her, at last, that afternoon. His face, however, darkened; he stood for a moment regarding her with something of the sulky look of a boy in his dark eyes. He said finally, "So it's Fitz . . ." and Caroline came in with a tray in her hands and Woody followed and looked at the tray with raised eyebrows. There was a glass of milk for Sue, a dark-colored drink for Jed and another for Woody—a bow to his new maturity, but of a markedly lighter color. "And now," said Caroline firmly as they drank, "you are all going to bed."

Actually the two men arranged to take turns sitting up in the downstairs hall; Jed took the first watch, Woody the second. Caroline, Jed and Woody made a tour of the doors, locking them securely. Sue found cigarettes for Jed and Caroline gave him a light woolen rug and a pillow.

It seemed very late when Sue at last turned out the light in her own room. The room itself was reassuring. It was as it had always been; it denied such things as murder—as a shot from the pine woods. Certainly the house was safely locked and guarded; no one could possibly enter it and if anyone did Sister Britches would raise such a hullabaloo as to wake the dead.

It was an unfortunate phrase to use even in her thoughts.

But why should anyone attack her? It must be, it had to be, simply a stray shot, someone hunting in the woods, afraid to come forward in view of the state of something very like hysteria in the county, following Dr. Luddington's murder. The elaborate precautions they had taken began to seem rather silly and unnecessary.

The night deepened. It was a quiet night, dark with no moon and a curtain of clouds over the stars.

No one could possibly enter the house. Probably no one did. There was, however, someone about the place that night.

It happened in the quiet, dark hour just before dawn. Woody heard it and described it later; old Jeremy, he said, had what amounted to a fit. Woody went to investigate. He and Jed found nothing amiss until they returned to the house and a pantry window was open. The lock had been forced and Woody himself remembered having locked it the night before.

17

THEY DID not rouse Sue or Caroline.

"Why not?" demanded Caroline the next morning.

"Because there wasn't any point to it," Woody said rather sullenly as if he felt he had failed in his duty. "Whoever it was had got away. We looked all over the house, Jed and I, and all we found was the pantry window open."

"That was enough," said Caroline, who grew snappish when she was frightened. "What about Jeremy? Was he all right?"

"Oh, yes," said Woody. Jed said, "Honestly, Miss Caroline, there simply wasn't anything to do. We searched the whole place, except your room and Sue's and we knew you were both all right; Woody tiptoed in and listened. There wasn't a sound and Sister Britches barely opened an eye and looked at us so we knew nobody was around. We discussed it and the only thing that was really—well, evidence, was the pantry window. Whoever was here had got away. There was no use in frightening you and Sue at that hour of the night; there was nothing we could do and nothing the police could do just then. I think they ought to know about it."

"They'll not believe it," Woody said morosely.

Caroline got up. "I'm going out to take a look at Jeremy."

"Well, but Aunt Caroline, really he's all right. Something frightened him; that's all. And it really could have been a rat; you know how he is. He'd calmed down some by the time we got there, but he was still trembling and he looked scared."

Sue said, crumbling toast, "What exactly happened, Woody?"

He told it, still rather sullenly. "Well, it was—I don't know when, just before dawn. I hadn't gone to sleep; I'm sure of that, but maybe I sort of drowsed. I was sitting in the hall; the window beside me was open, the screen was fastened. All at once it sounded like thunder and I jumped up and Jeremy was kicking hell out of his loose box. I had my gun right there; I ran out along the hall and unlocked the side door and ran out; it was dark as pitch and all at once I thought how silly it was for me to start on a man-hunt, if that's what it was, alone. I wasn't afraid but it just wasn't smart. Jeremy was quieting down but still—I turned around and ran back and by that time Jed had heard it . . ."

"I'd been asleep on the couch in the library," Jed said.

". . . and he'd got to the side door, so we hurried then to the stables and turned on the lights and there wasn't anybody there. Jed started at the tack room and I went to Jeremy first; he was nervous and fussing around but there wasn't anything really the matter with him and just no-body around at all. We gave the whole place a quick look but then Jed said we'd better get back to the house; we'd left the side door open. A fool thing to do of course; nei-ther of us thought that maybe it was a diversion, I mean a trick to get us out of the house. So then when we did think of it we got back to the house in a hell of a hurry and searched there every place. We didn't miss anywhere. And there was only the pantry window open."

That was in the end all there was to it; if it was evidence it was a negative kind of evidence which led nowhere ex-cept to a question. Why should anyone make an attempt to enter the house? Was it an attempted repetition of the at-tack on Sue?

Caroline said thoughtfully, "I've always thought that Sam Bronson had a heavy hand with a horse. A poor stableman I'd have called him. And horses do remember things—it's astonishing—let a horse do a thing once and he'll always do it. And if he's once been really terrified . . ." she stopped and thought and pushed up her hair. "But I can't remember that Sam Bronson ever had anything to do with Jeremy."

Sam Bronson. Sam Bronson who had come, hurrying to the house that foggy dusky twilight when Ernestine had been murdered; Sam Bronson whom Sue had called, to whom she'd first told of the thing that had happened; Sam Bronson who had waited, his little dark eyes alert, his tight-lipped mouth silent, until Ernestine died. Sam Bronson who had, however, apparently given straightforward and honest testimony, who had had no quarrel—as far as anyone knew—with Ernestine; who had never said anything that indicated any special knowledge of Ernestine's murder. Who had disappeared, but whose disappearances were so customary that no one thought twice about it.

Jed had suggested that it might have been Sam Bronson hiding in the pine woods. She said to Jed, "Could it have been Sam Bronson?"

Jed, who had been pacing up and down, gave her a worried look. He was tired. So was Woody; neither of them had slept after their discovery. Jed said after a moment, "What would he want?"

Nobody could any more than guess. Woody said, "The only answer would be that he had something to do with Ernestine's murder and thinks that Sue knows it."

"If Sue knew it she'd tell," Caroline said. "She'd have told long ago."

"Maybe we can find him," Jed said. "Or maybe he's back by now. He does go off on these binges once in a while. Not often." He looked at Caroline. "He's not the best stableman in the world, but he's wonderful with a car; used to drive some for Ernestine."

Caroline's lips set themselves rather tightly together; it wasn't the way she'd have run her stables, if she'd had the means, that is, to employ a real stableman. Jed said defensively, "Besides I don't know that we could have done any better. Ernestine seemed satisfied."

"Where does he go when he—goes on binges?" Sue asked.

Jed shrugged. "I don't know. He lives alone over the stable. Nobody pays much attention to what he does. Although honestly he doesn't do this often; Camilla says he's been around all winter, every day. He's not such a bad guy, really. Yet . . ."

Yet it could have been Sam Bronson, waiting his chance in the pine woods, shooting to kill. Woody went to the telephone. "I'm going to tell the police."

Jed said, "Make them believe it, Woody. They as good as said it was a cooked up thing last night—that shot. Make them believe it."

"How?" said Woody morosely, giving the number.

"Well." Jed thought and said, "Fingerprints. There might be some on the pantry window."

Somebody answered the telephone. Woody asked for Captain Henley. Caroline said suddenly, "Jed—we have to say these things. How much truth was there in all that nonsense Camilla said last night? Such as that Ernestine"—she hesitated and said, "liked Fitz Wilson? Or that you might have married Camilla if it hadn't been for Ernestine?"

Jed stared at her for an instant. "I don't know about Fitz Wilson," he said then. "I have to apologize for what I said, Miss Caroline, about Ernestine and Fitz. I was . . ." he glanced at Sue and then finally at the carpet. "I didn't mean it . . . She invited him, yes. Often. But she liked parties. She invited other people too. And as for me and Camilla—Camilla's heart wasn't broken, I do assure you, Miss Caroline. Besides Camilla likes Fitz Wilson and he was . . ." he glanced at Sue again. "He has been very attentive to her. If Ernestine invited him it was for Camilla."

Caroline said rather tartly that Camilla seemed fully capable of getting her own beaux. Sue briefly debated her automatic decision not to tell Caroline of Woody's story of Ernestine and again decided it was the right one. And Woody ended that by-path by shouting furiously into the telephone, "But you've got to believe me! You've got to send somebody out here! What are the police for?"

He slammed down the receiver. "It was Henley and he doesn't believe a word of it. He thinks it's a trick to draw suspicion from Sue. He said he'd send somebody to investigate but that . . ." Navy oaths trembled on Woody's lips and Caroline knew it and dammed them up sharply, "Woody! You hush! . . . Why don't you go and tell Sheriff Benjamin?"

Woody's face cleared. "That's a good idea. I will. Want to go along, Jed?"

They went shortly after, in Caroline's puffing, laboring and valiant little car.

And after a while—after Chrisy had heard the whole story and commented on it with a sullen, black rage which thrust out her underlip dangerously and sent her, muttering, back to her work, after Caroline had gone anxiously to the stables and cossetted and consoled a now perfectly calm Jeremy, who thrust his long neck and neat, intelligent head out to accept apples with an air of taking only his due—after a while two state policemen came, not Captain Henley but a sergeant and another trooper. They listened to Sue's story and Caroline's; they looked over the house and stables in a rather desultory way, tested the pantry window for fingerprints and went away. It was done with an air of perfunctory routine.

They had barely gone when Fitz came. Chrisy, like an enormous dark angel with blue chambray wings, was on guard, saw his car coming up the driveway and contrived to meet him at the door and tell him the story of the night. She brought him then with an air of triumph to Sue and Caroline.

If the police had been coolly perfunctory and skeptical, Fitz was not. He concealed, however, the real depth of his alarm. "It may have been nothing at all. Jeremy may still be merely fussy from the cut in his leg."

"I think it was the same person," Caroline said blackly. "Fitz, that's what I think. That cut wasn't made by wire."

"Perhaps he fell—perhaps . . ."

Caroline was shaking her head. "It was made by something with a hard edge. It was a cruel and vicious blow and if the man that gave it to him ever approached him again— well, I know horses and I know Jeremy."

"Were there any new welts on him this morning?"

"Well, no. Not that I could find. But just the presence of whoever it was that untied him and gave him that blow would be enough to frighten him."

Fitz seemed to agree; he turned to Sue. "Let's take a look at the stables."

Anxiety leaped into Caroline's eyes. "Is it safe? That shot . . ."

"I think it's safe."

Her eyes plead with him for a moment; then she nodded. Sue took her blue suede jacket from the rack in the hall. She was wearing again a sweater and skirt; again she looked young and childish in spite of the pallor of her face and the small dark lines drawn under her eyes.

Actually, though, once in the bright sunshine with the blue sky and a few white fleecy clouds sailing briskly above them, with the red bud and dogwood very purple and very white amid the thin young greens of spring foliage, on the hills—with the distant sound of the Higginson hunt following the ridge behind the village—whatever had happened, or had not happened in the night took on a quality of unreality. She looked up at Fitz and his brown face, his crisp black hair with its thick white sprinkling. The way he strolled along quietly beside her, hands in the pockets of gray slacks, tweed jacket looking ordinary and comfortable, was, all of it, reassuring.

But there was no unreality about the splinters of wood

struck from a pillar, the crushing, rocking sound of a shot. She said suddenly, almost surprised: "Fitz, *why* would anybody try to—kill me?"

That, of course, was the main, the important question. He looked at her gravely, "Is there anything, Sue—anything at all that you can think of that could—well, could identify the murderer?"

She had asked herself that, too; she shook her head.

"I expected that, of course; that is, if you knew anything you'd have told it unless . . ." he stopped and she had an impression that he quickly rearranged what he had intended to say; yet he said at once, "Unless it is something that you know without knowing what it means. I mean—something that is dangerous to the murderer, but which you do not recognize as being dangerous. Think hard, Sue."

Sue had done nothing else; again she shook her head.

"Well . . ." he turned to resume their stroll toward the stables, so ordinary and accustomed, with their low white wings, the double doors for a row of loose boxes, the door to the tack room half open. The paddocks looked newly washed and clear in the bright sunlight. Jeremy put his head out and surveyed them reservedly; Geneva looked out too, inquisitively, her ears pricked forward. Fitz said, "I wish I could suggest something that would suggest something to you. But I don't know what exactly. Unless —well for instance, one thing that has struck me as rather odd is a kind of invisibility about whoever it was that killed Ernestine and killed Dr. Luddington. That sounds silly; a murderer always tries to make himself invisible, but as a rule he's not so successful. Then the question of accessibility. The driveway, the evening of Ernestine's murder—Duval Hall—Dr. Luddington's or your place— none of these houses is close enough to anything to make walking easy; I mean anybody going, say, to Duval Hall would be likely to use a car. Same to Dr. Luddington's, even for a villager, because his house is on the outskirts;

same here. Yet you didn't hear or see a car at Ernestine's that night; I mean another car besides yours and Jed's. You didn't hear or see a car while you were waiting at Dr. Luddington's. You didn't hear anything of the kind last night and apparently nobody else did. They'd have said so."

She remembered the silence in Dr. Luddington's waiting room, the quiet of the foggy twilight when she'd walked from the cabaña to the stately steps and door of Duval Hall. And if Woody the night before had heard anything but old Jeremy's hooves, he'd have said so. "No. That's right but I don't see . . ."

"Don't you, Sue?"

She looked at Fitz who was smiling rather wryly, and at Jeremy and said flatly, "Oh!"

Fitz said, "In a hunting, riding country there's an easy way of getting around—rather quietly, too, and with a chance of being unobserved because everybody is riding. You took a back way, across meadows and over fences to get to Dr. Luddington's. You or Caroline thought of it immediately and it worked; nobody noticed you, nobody stopped you or if they saw you thought twice about it. Maybe somebody else has had the same idea."

It seemed all at once glaringly obvious. Why had they not thought of it before? Then she saw a discrepancy. "But then, there were two riders. The man I saw, the one with the hunt and whoever it was who rode Jeremy. If, that is, someone rode Jeremy."

He did not answer for a moment; they reached the stables and he swung open the door of the tack room; sunlight glinted on satin-smooth saddles. He glanced vaguely around the room as if he were searching for something and yet did not know what he sought. "Do you remember what the rider you saw wore? I mean—coat and collar and—anything you can remember."

She remembered clearly; the flashing black and white staccato of collar and stock, his red coat, barely a glimpse of a hard hat. "Why, yes. He was wearing a red coat; black collar, white stock. He carried a crop; yes, I'm sure I saw that—"

"A cap?"

"No." That would mean, of course, a master or one of his family, a child or one of the hunt staff. Caroline would know the correct custom. "At least I don't think so. I think he wore a hat. There were willows; there happened to be a gap just at the level of his shoulders."

"But you couldn't recognize him?"

"No. Not possibly."

"Could it have been a woman?"

"Not in pink . . ."

"Dressed as a man," said Fitz.

A woman? But then, who? She said slowly, trying to read Fitz's eyes, "I never thought of a woman. I suppose it could have been," and waited for him to explain. He said, however, musingly, "Black collar. Funny. The livery of the Beaufort hunt is beige collar."

Something in his tone, absent and remote though it seemed, caught her; she said, "Beige—but this was black. I . . ."

He looked at her then. "The Dobberly hunt livery is black collar."

"But—but there are so many hunts—so many liveries— so many almost alike . . . The Leesburg livery is black collar, too. There must be many others . . ."

"I inquired. There were no visitors out for the Beaufort meet. Whoever you saw, Sue, didn't belong to the Beaufort and there wasn't another meet in this neighborhood that day."

"But then . . ."

"That's what occurred to me, too. A convenient sort of disguise. Which—if that's right—could mean that whoever shot Dr. Luddington had shot him some minutes before you reached the house and was in the very act of escaping when he took a spill, unfortunately, and you came along and saw him."

Hope shot up like a flame. "Then we can find him!"

He was shaking his head. "That's only my notion of it. It's what the police think that counts. And it may mean nothing. It might be sheer accident; somebody we don't know of but who doesn't want to come forward and tell that he was there; somebody riding—in pink which, of course, looks intentional but could have a simple and straightforward explanation—or somebody even trying out some new boots or a new horse. There are those fences, too. If anybody did ride to Ernestine's and come in across the fields, avoiding the driveway, he'd have to have a horse that was as good a jumper . . ."

Jeremy gave a snuffle and he said, ". . . as good a jumper as old Jeremy. Some of those fences at Duval Hall are high. Those, at least, that are close to the house; they're all post and rail, most of them low enough for an easy jump, but the paddock between the stables and the garden, near the house, over which any rider would have to take a jump to reach the garden and thus the room where Ernestine was killed—that fence is high. I looked."

Sue said slowly: "The fences across Wat and Ruby's place are low. So is the fence for the Luddington woods. . . . Oh, Fitz, there are the hoofprints in our pine woods!"

He nodded and said, still with a withdrawn, rather absent look, "Let's go in and visit Jeremy."

Jeremy, in the haughty manner of indulged old age, seemed, although austerely, to appreciate the visit. Fitz looked at the cut, which was healing, and poked around the loose box, rather curiously, looking into the feeding rack and the watering pail, examining the old small frame where once there had been a name plate. "Too bad he can't talk," he said finally. "Well, let's go back to the house."

They strolled back to the house along the sunny turf, between green hedges; they sat on the steps at the side entrance and talked of Sam Bronson, of the pantry window (Fitz rose and looked at it again, from the outside this time, pushing back the shrubbery and getting old lilac seed pods, unpruned from the previous summer, in his hair). Of, again, Dr. Luddington's murder, for Fitz questioned her, in as minute detail as if he had never heard any of it before then. She told him too of Woody's meeting with Ernestine.

"I wouldn't worry," he said. "I don't think Woody's feelings were very deep. He's a kid really in spite of all his airs of maturity. Certainly they can't suspect him of murder on so slim a basis and besides he had an alibi."

He said nothing, however, of Camilla, or of Jed's angry accusation that he and Ernestine had had more than a friendship. Probably he never would say anything of it.

When he left it was to drive out to the Hunting Horn.

"The Hunting Horn! *Woody!*"

"No, no. It's only a notion. May come to nothing. I'll talk to the sheriff. They are short of men but there ought to be one here."

"I'm not afraid," she said, and thought, "Why am I lying? I am afraid. I'm in terror—when I think of it, when it seems real."

"It's possible that somebody's only trying to frighten you. . . . When will Woody be home?"

"Soon."

He looked at her for a moment and then took her hand and pulled her to her feet. "I wish," he said suddenly and rather savagely, "that I'd made you marry me last week —last winter—before the trial, before . . . *Chrisy!*" He shouted toward the kitchen.

Chrisy came, prompt and vengeful. "Keep your eye on her," Fitz said. "And if anybody comes around the place . . ."

"Let him," Chrisy said dangerously. "Only let him!"

He smiled but his eyes were still cold with fear and with something of Chrisy's own rage when he went away.

It was by then noon. Woody returned in time for lunch, disgruntled and sleepy. The sheriff had listened but made no comment; Woody had left Jed at Duval Hall. Chrisy came in with dessert and the news that some troopers had been in the pine woods and had tried to take casts of the churned up clay bank which showed, they had thought, the marks of horses' hooves. She didn't know whether or not they had been successful. "I couldn't get that close," she said.

Caroline paled. "Chrisy, stay out of the pine woods!"

Woody gave her an admiring look. "Good for you, Chrisy. I didn't think of it myself."

It was in the late afternoon, with Woody asleep and tossing uneasily in his sleep, and Caroline sitting on an upturned feed box in the sun near the stables, her chin on her hands and Sister Britches drowsing at her feet, that Camilla came.

She came as she had come before, with a swift sweep up the drive and gravel shooting from under the tires of Jed's car as she came to a rapid stop.

She had come to see Sue. She had something to say; she went directly and with a certain obstinate strength to the point.

She did make sure that no one was within hearing distance before she spoke, but then she did not hesitate. "I just wanted to tell you, Sue, I've made up my mind you ought to know what I'm going to do." She had come in a car but she was wearing riding clothes. She pulled off her string gloves and looked at Sue with eyes that seemed to sink deeply into her head. "I know why Ernestine phoned for you that night. And if you don't stop leading Fitz Wilson on, and acting the way you act with Jed, I'm going to tell it. I'm going to marry Fitz Wilson."

18

SHE REPRESSED a childish, idiotic and obvious retort: "Does Fitz know it?" before the enormity that lay behind Camilla's words emerged. She had only a glimpse; it was a curious and rather terrible thing even half seen; it checked any words on her lips. She must be careful, go slowly, but find out what Camilla meant. "You'd better come in, Camilla."

They were at the steps; Camilla glanced toward the pine woods, gave a kind of shiver and said, "Well. Yes. If that wasn't Woody last night, just trying to help you out with the police . . ."

"It wasn't Woody," Sue said definitely and held the door wide.

Camilla took off the other glove and gave Sue an odd look; she would come no further than the hall. She settled herself in a stiff and uncomfortable chair; she had a riding crop tucked under her arm, absently, as she got out of the car. She was wearing jodhpurs and low boots; she crossed her knees and whacked one boot with her crop. Where had somebody done just that? Who had talked of it? Camilla said abruptly, "What are you staring like that for?"

"Am I? I didn't mean . . ." Woody, of course! When he'd entered Dr. Luddington's office, somebody in the consulting room had spoken, had whacked his boot with a crop. Camilla?

But that was not likely. Besides, anybody might do that,

absently, nervously as Camilla was doing it. Camilla's cold blue eyes seemed to have receded until they looked black. She was slim and elegant and erect, yet her features had thickness and obstinacy, her broad forehead with its projecting frontal bone, her blunt nose, her strong, thick jaw; in spite of her slimness and elegance there was an impression of heavy and insensitive force. She said, "You can say it wasn't Woody. But I'm not going to mince matters, Sue Poore. We've known each other a long time. I'm going to say exactly what I think and what I know and what I'm going to do if you . . ." She paused, whacked her boot and said, "If you don't show some sense. You see, *I* know that you killed Ernestine."

Sue stood up, half dazed, half incredulous. "What do you mean?"

"I wouldn't tell a soul. I didn't. Everybody has asked me if I know; even Jed and Fitz, and of course at first the police. But Ernestine was dead and it couldn't bring her back. Jed was on trial and I wanted him to be acquitted and I could see that if I told it would only make things worse for him, just then. Because—of course, I didn't actually see you shoot her."

"Camilla . . ." Sue sat down: she put her hands to her temples dizzily; she must find her way through a tangle she had not known existed and it was not going to be easy; it never was with Camilla. She wished for Fitz. She told herself again to go carefully. "Camilla—maybe you'd better start at the beginning. You said that you knew why Ernestine sent for me."

Camilla nodded and whacked the crop. "Of course I know. She and Jed had the most terrific row. I heard them. I was dressing to go to Fitz's house. Ernestine was furious; she was so mad she said she was going to leave him. She was tired of the kind of life he liked; she said he had no ambition and she was going to have what she wanted and she was going to leave him."

"But—but Jed didn't say that." And when Woody had

told his story of Ernestine's stated interview, Jed had seemed genuinely surprised.

Camilla said, "Oh, I don't suppose he believed it. Ernestine was always threatening him like that. Ernestine," said Camilla on a thoughtful note as if some time she had experienced it, "could be real mean. But then Jed said he was in love with you and wanted to marry you and Ernestine needn't think she was leaving him because the shoe was on the other foot. Or something like that . . ." Camilla paused and eyed Sue, as if trying to recall every detail of the scene she had overheard and said again, at last, thoughtfully, "It was a real fight. I kept thinking it was lucky the servants were out. And then Ernestine came into the hall and I heard her phone to you. And that's why."

"*Why* . . ." said Sue, feeling as if she were in deep waters indeed and Camilla replied succinctly, "To tell you to let Jed alone, of course. To tell you she'd put a stop to any divorce that Jed himself wanted. Why, my gracious, Sue, you knew Ernestine. She might not want Jed herself but she wouldn't have everybody saying that you took him away from her!"

Sue took a long breath. She forced herself to say evenly, "But Camilla, how do you know that that was what Ernestine wanted to say?"

Camilla shrugged. "What else could it be?" She eyed Sue again and said curiously, "Didn't Jed tell you a word of that?"

"I knew they'd quarrelled. I didn't know all this."

Camilla said, "Well, I suppose he wouldn't tell you. A man hates to admit that a woman has the upper hand. And then after she was shot—well, of course, he'd have sense enough not to tell it then. Judge Shepson wouldn't have let him. That's why I didn't. At the trial, I mean, or when they questioned me, all those police."

"Why . . ." Sue repeated still dazedly and Camilla flashed her an impatient look. "Well, for goodness' sake, Sue, Jed supports me," she said with fine simplicity.

If only Fitz were there to find a clear way through the rapid currents of Camilla's words; it struck Sue that there was something important, some inquiry that she ought to make and that something Camilla had said had given her an opening. Then she knew what it was, "I wonder what Ernestine was up to." She met Camilla's obstinate eyes and made herself arrange words carefully so as not to alarm her into silence.

"Do you think Ernestine was serious?"

"Oh, my goodness. Serious! She was furious. If you'd been there at that minute, Sue, I don't know what she'd have done. I've wondered," Camilla said, "exactly what did happen. But I think I know. I don't think you meant to do it."

Again Sue felt as if dark waters touched her. *"You don't think I meant . . ."*

"No, of course. Why, you wouldn't do anything like that in cold blood, Sue. My conscience hasn't hurt me one bit about not telling what I know. I think that when you came Ernestine was still just so mad she was beside herself; maybe she saw you and Jed meet and go to the cabaña, I don't know. But I think she just lashed out and she'd got out the gun to threaten, you know, put on an act, and I think you tried to take it away from her or something and it went off and—that's what I think. But why should I tell it?" Camilla got up and went to the door. "Even when they were going to arrest you and I was here when the sheriff phoned, even if they had arrested you, I'd never have told it. I decided right away: I went home and told Jed about the warrant, he was beside himself. I think he thinks you did it, too, Sue, only he'll never say so; and I poured myself a stiff drink and took it to my room and I'd finally decided I just never would tell, I could see it would mighty near convict you, and by that time"—her eyes changed, a queer, cold light came into them—"by that time I couldn't have stopped anything. You were so scared you didn't know what you were doing. But *I'll* never give you a chance."

"What . . ."

"I mean Dr. Luddington, of course! I was so upset. I hadn't even heard the car leave; and then to have Jed phone from Dr. Luddington's and tell me he was shot! It was dreadful—but it was the same as with Ernestine. How would it help for me to tell? But you—I'm not afraid of you because—well, I'm not."

"Camilla, I didn't. That's horrible . . ."

"You didn't mean to. I could see how it happened. Except I don't think you ought to have phoned for Jed and dragged him into it—except you were scared . . ."

"I tell you, I didn't. You've got to stop . . ."

"Oh, he'll never tell. He'll always say it was a patient."

"It was a patient. You've got to believe it. You can't think such a monstrous . . ."

"But I told you. I can see how it happened."

"Camilla, suppose I said that to you! Suppose I said I thought you did it! How would you feel?"

Camilla shrugged, and since she couldn't reach her boot gave the door sill a rap with her crop, for good measure. And Sue thought irresistibly, Camilla could have done it. She and Ernestine had quarrelled many times; suppose Ernestine had driven Camilla beyond endurance; she had no alibi for the time of Dr. Luddington's murder; she had said she was alone in her room. Had she a real alibi for the time of Ernestine's murder? Was there any way in which she could have shot Ernestine and then left the house, without being seen?

The unexpected hypothesis carried her that far, swiftly before she could stop. And Camilla said coolly, "Nobody thinks I did it. Everybody thinks maybe you did. Especially the police. But I won't tell anybody ever, if you'll leave Fitz alone. He—I'm going to marry him, Sue. You can't stop me. He's been around here all winter; he was sorry for you and he wanted to help. But I never dreamed of your liking him or—I thought you were in love with Jed. I thought you'd just have to have been in love with him to tell about the cabaña and everything, when all you had to

186

do was go home, as Dr. Luddington told you to do, and nobody would ever have known that you were there at all. Dr. Luddington and Jed wouldn't have told. But now you act as if you—well, if you ask me you're just throwing yourself at Fitz Wilson's head, and you say you won't marry Jed, and I'm not going to have it. Why, goodness . . ." a kind of plaintive frankness came into her face. "Why don't you marry Jed, everybody expects it, and I'll marry Fitz and we'll all be happy and just forget all this dreadful thing."

It was bewilderingly practical, Camilla-like; it was childish, shrewd, obstinate—and completely ruthless.

Sue helplessly groped back for the question, the important question. "But Camilla—do you suppose Ernestine really meant to leave Jed? I mean—well, where could she have gone?"

She said it as casually as she could; she watched Camilla. So she saw the birth of a new and rather startled speculation stir and move back in Camilla's eyes.

But she saw, too, when Camilla became aware of her own regard, a guarded look flashed down upon Camilla's face; she turned, as if absently, yet as if, too, she wished to conceal her own aroused surmise; she stared out of the door, down across the hedge and the lawn. She said, yet in a queerly tangential way, as if what she said only bore upon what she was thinking, "Ernestine was jealous about Fitz and me. That is—Fitz was a better match than Jed. She took Jed away from me and married him and then Fitz came along. And he could have given Ernestine what she really wanted. . . ."

"What," said Sue cautiously, "was that?"

"Why, you know! Washington, travel, important people. The kind of glitter that Ernestine always wanted. Jed's happy and content right here; he never wants to do anything else but ride and hunt as long as he has the money to do it. But Fitz . . ." she took a breath and said in a dreamy and speculative way, "Fitz upset Ernestine—I mean Fitz and me; she wouldn't have wanted me to make a better

match than she did and it made her jealous to think I'd be
getting, with Fitz, the kind of life she wanted. Not that
Fitz seems to want to live like that but he could if he
wanted to. Ruby upset her, too."

"Ruby . . ."

"With all that money, of course," said Camilla and
opened the door.

"Wait. . . ." There were paths of exploration which
Camilla had rushed past. "Camilla, what did you do then?
I mean after you heard her phone to me that night?"

Camilla looked surprised, and seemed to fish back. "Why
I—oh, I left my door open till she'd finished phoning to
you. Then she went back into the garden room but she
stopped—and I knew later, not then, she opened the gun
cabinet there in the hall. I heard the click when she closed
it but, then, I never dreamed she was getting out the gun;
I just thought the door of the cabinet had swung open, it
does sometimes, and she'd given it a bang to close it as she
passed. But then later I realized she'd got out the gun to
threaten you with it. She was really in a state. You know
her temper."

"And then . . ."

"Then I finished dressing."

"Yes, but . . ."

"Jed came upstairs before she phoned; he was changing
while she talked to you. I heard the shower. Wat and Ruby
were going to Fitz's too. . . ."

It was the first time in all the miles of typewritten testimony, typewritten and sworn to, and repeated verbally at
the trial, that Sue had heard that. She said: *"Were they at
Fitz's too?"*

"Oh, no. But they were going. They'd said they'd call
for me. So I waited. I heard Jed go downstairs. Ernestine
had dressed early. Very early," said Camilla, suddenly
rather thoughtful. "I don't know why—but I didn't hear
another sound out of her after she'd phoned to you and
gone back to the garden room. Jed slammed down the

driveway; my room faces that way, I saw him meet you at the gate and I saw you both go to the cabaña. You didn't know that, did you?"

Sue shook her head. Camilla said, "Well, I didn't tell it. There wasn't any need. I wasn't going to tell it, any of it. I was surprised when you did that, Sue—the cabaña! But then, anyway, Wat came for me and I left."

"*Wat* came for you! But I—we didn't hear his car."

Camilla laughed shortly and harshly: "You were in the cabaña with Jed."

Another memory of words floated to Sue: Chrisy's voice saying scornfully, them Duval girls never was no account. She said, "Wat came for you; then you both went to Fitz's house? Together?"

Camilla nodded. If there was concealment in her look Sue could not detect it. Then the scene struck her with a chill and dismaying incongruity: they were talking perfectly coolly and quite naturally and were accusing each other of murder—Camilla in so many words, Sue in her thoughts. She had to go on, though; she had to find a loophole, if there was one.

"Where was Ruby?"

"Oh, Wat said she was at home. Said she had a headache. He took me to Fitz's and let me out at the door but he didn't come in, I guess Fitz didn't even see him. Wat said he was going back to see how Ruby was and give her a headache tablet so she could go on to the dinner. Nobody asked me how I got to Fitz's house so I didn't say. I went in and Fitz and I . . ." She gave a queer frank sigh. "I thought maybe Fitz would say something that night; Wat and Ruby didn't come at all and we were alone and—but he didn't. And afterward, at the club they phoned and—since then—things have been different. I thought he was waiting till the trial and everything was over. I didn't dream . . ."

The look of anger and resolution returned to her face. "I didn't dream it was because of you! Not till last night the way he—the way you looked. I mean what I say, Sue. You tell Jed everything's all right and of course you love him and are going to marry him, and you tell Fitz that, too. If you don't—listen, Sue—we've known each other a long time. But I mean what I say. I've never told about you, and Ernestine; they've asked me, too, if you quarrelled with her. I never gave you away and I never will if you . . ." she stopped; she looked full at Sue and said, "I mean it. Fitz is mine."

She went down the steps and got into the car, sliding her riding crop beside her at the wheel; it was absurd and Camilla was perfectly unconscious of it. She started the car and without a word or a look drove rapidly away.

And the trouble was that, quite simply and ruthlessly, she did mean it.

Sue went back into the house; standing there in the doorway with the green mask of shrubbery, shining innocently in the sunlight, hiding the pine woods, she felt chilled and frightened. Camilla did mean it. And it would be exactly the convincing, the clinching, the new piece of evidence that the police were seeking in order to arrest her, Sue Poore.

The gun cabinet, and the click of its door. The quarrel with Jed over her, Sue. Jed had never told her of that specific quarrel; he wouldn't tell it now because it would give weight to the terrible arguments against her. And then she realized that Camilla's groping, speculative look when Sue had asked her what Ernestine had planned and where she had intended to go, was like Jed's look—the first morning after his acquittal, when they'd sat all four of them, Caroline and Fitz and Jed and herself, at Caroline's breakfast table and tried to map a course that would save Sue herself from arrest. Jed had looked like that, half startled, half speculative, when they asked him about Ernestine. And then Fitz had grown impatient and Jed had grown stubborn. Was it then, the memory of that quarrel with Ernestine, which he would not admit? He had not believed

Ernestine, Camilla had said; he had not believed Woody's later story of Ernestine's plan to leave, but had he begun to question his own disbelief?

She would ask him; she would tell him of Camilla's visit; she went back to the telephone. But Jed was not at home and neither was Miss Camilla, the maid who answered told her. Sue said on a queer and unexpected impulse, "By the way, has Sam Bronson come back?"

The maid's voice was unperturbed, uninterested, "Why, no, Miss Sue, I don't think so. Miss Camilla she took the car. I don't know when she'll be back. And Mr. Jed, he woke up just a few minutes ago, I guess he didn't sleep much last night and he wanted the car but Miss Camilla had it so he got on a horse and he went, I think, to the Luddington place. He didn't say when he'd be back. Shall I tell him you phoned?"

Sue said yes and thanked the maid; as she put down the telephone Caroline came in the side door and came to the study. "That looked like Camilla Duval driving away. What did she want?"

The telephone rang as Sue debated rapidly how much she should tell Caroline. The whole truth would terrify her. Sue answered the telephone and it was Wat. "Is your aunt there? Let me talk to her please, Sue."

She handed the telephone to Caroline and listened, but thinking of Camilla. Caroline, she realized vaguely, seemed to be expostulating but being talked over by Wat and it was something about the end of the season hunt. Caroline hung up suddenly and turned around. "Did you ever!"

"What did he want?"

"Well!" Caroline pushed up her hair angrily; her blue eyes were snapping. "But at that," she said, "I believe he's right. About the hunt—the hunt ball. And Wat wants to be M.F.H."

Sue considered it. "That sounds like Wat."

"Well, yes, of course. Partly politics, it won't hurt him, you know. Ours is an old and respected hunt. And it's partly because he and Ruby both seem to feel that it's—well, due them. Natives and—that great big place and—well, anyway, he wants us all to hunt tomorrow. It's the last hunt of the year of course . . ." Caroline paused rather wistfully. Sue said, "You never miss the last one, or the hunt ball . . ."

"No, well, I—I don't know what to do exactly. Maybe he's right. He says we all ought to go to show people that we—well, to show them. He said it was important psychologically—not that I think Wat Luddington knows a thing about it. But maybe we ought to show people that we're not afraid of anything that the police—of anything," finished Caroline, looking worriedly at Sue. "Maybe he's right. Of course, he said, he wants my influence." She gave the ghost of a chuckle, sighed and said: "And honestly—it doesn't seem just right, Sue, for us *not* to go—I mean, there's mourning and all that—Wat went into that—but he says it'll make a better impression if we go and if he—not that I care about impression," said Caroline suddenly snapping out the words. "But I'd rather fight than hide, any day. We haven't got any reason to hide."

Woody coming, yawning, in the door agreed with her. Sue listened to their talk, their arguments, their final conclusion to join the meet the next day; she listened to Caroline when she telephoned to Wat and told him—much apparently to his approval; she listened when Caroline put down the telephone and told Woody that Wat had said that Ruby had sold her famous hunter.

"Rocking Horse! What did she do that for?" asked Woody, amazed. "He was a terrific jumper; they could hardly build a paddock high enough to keep him in."

Caroline shrugged. "Ruby didn't like him. Said she couldn't trust him."

"I wonder what she got for him," said Woody, diverted, and Sue listened while they talked of that, too, both unconsciously but deeply grateful for the boon of a normal, usual topic of conversation. But she wished they would go to another room. She wanted to talk to Fitz and she wanted to talk to him alone.

They went from Ruby's hunter to Wat's wish to be M.F.H.—"her wish too," Woody said, "if I know Ruby. Wat and his oriental beauty! M.F.H. and his beautiful wife! I wonder how he intends to reconcile that with his political career. Either is a full time chore."

They were going thoroughly into the politics of the Dobberly hunt, when Chrisy advised them that dinner was ready and Sue still had not had a chance to telephone to Fitz, yet she began to be certain that before night he would come, if only to see that, somehow, they had taken precaution against any unwelcome night visitor.

It was full dark by the time they had coffee, lingeringly, in Caroline's study and again beside the telephone. Woody by then had got out Caroline's fixture card. Sue could ride Jeremy, he said; old Jeremy was safe and not nearly as lame as he pretended in order to get attention; Caroline, of course, would ride Geneva. He'd borrow a hunter from Wat; they would probably need no second horses. Unless, of course, they had a good run. The window beside him was open so all of them heard it when Jeremy began to kick.

Sister Britches, under the couch, shot out and skidded into the hall.

Woody gave a wild look at the windows. The screens were dark; they could see nothing. Sister Britches set up a clamor at the side door. Caroline started for the door; Woody cried, "Wait . . ." and ran upstairs. The thunder of Jeremy's wild kicks was like a drum; Woody ran down again with his gun in his hand. "Stay there, Sue," he shouted, "Don't come out of the house," and ran along the hall and out the side door. Caroline and apparently Sister Britches went after him, Sister Britches in a frenzy.

And then suddenly, the lashing of hooves against wood, the wild tattoo of that drum died away. Sister Britches stopped yelling. In the distance she could hear Woody's voice; saying something about lights. She went to the window and beyond the thick shrubbery lights were glimmering distantly in the stables. And all at once there was silence except for the faint, remote tinkle of Chrisy washing dishes in the pantry.

Things were, then, all right. The silence reassured her, but Caroline would stay there for some time, soothing Jeremy and trying to discover what had sent him into such a spasm of terror.

But it wasn't as it had been the previous night—or rather as they thought it might have been. Certainly if anyone had been in the stables or on the grounds, they would have found him; Sister Britches would not have quieted.

She did not, nevertheless, follow them; she went to the telephone and called Fitz's number.

Jason answered. His voice was trembling and high. She started to say, "Jason, it's Miss Sue. . . ." The trembling, shaken quality of the old man's voice checked her; she said, "Jason, what's wrong?"

He knew her voice. "Miss Sue—Miss Sue . . ."

"Yes, yes, Jason. What's the matter? What's happened?"

"Oh, Miss Sue—they've found him."

"*Found . . .*"

"The stableman."

"The . . ."

"Sam Bronson. The Duval stableman. He's shot, Miss Sue. Right through the head. In the Luddington woods. Two, three days ago. He's shot."

"Jason . . ." The room wavered around her; objects seemed to slide together; she cried, "Jason, is Mr. Fitz all right?"

"Oh, yes, Miss Sue. He's at Luddingtons'."

She said, "Tell him I phoned." She put down the telephone. She turned to the door.

As she did so, very quietly someone standing in the hall

moved aside, out of the doorway, quickly out of her range of vision.

Away off in the pantry Chrisy dropped a glass; there was the tinkling sound of the crash. There was not a sound from the direction of the stables, not another sound anywhere in the soft, deep night, in the pine woods, in the house.

19

She would scream. Caroline and Woody were in the stables; they could hear her in the deep quiet. Or would they? Were they actually in the stables at all? If so, they made no sound; would they hear?

The telephone! That would take too much time. . . . Walk out then, and confront whoever was in the hall. Whoever had waited and watched in the pine woods.

Why was he waiting in the hall?

But Chrisy was in the house; she'd scream. . . . Chrisy wouldn't hear.

There was a feeling rather than a sound, of motion, small movements, in the hall. What was he doing?

Then she heard a sound. It was a curious sound; it sounded as if something rather light had flipped tautly against the wall. It was like but it wasn't like the whack of Camilla's riding crop on her boot.

She wouldn't stay there like a hunted animal, frozen, hoping dumbly to be overlooked. He had seen her; he knew she was there. She thought of the windows; could she open a screen? Could she get herself—but quietly—oh, quietly—through the window and into the shrubbery below? There was cover there; and then her way was open to the stables—to Woody, to Caroline, anywhere.

Chrisy opened the pantry door with a wide sweep that sent it banging against the wall and came into the dining room with a tray of tinkling silver. Was there the click of the old-fashioned switch for the lights? She'd have to turn on lights in order to put away the silver.

But if she did—what about Chrisy? What would he do? Sue screamed.

She didn't know she was going to; the demand that she warn Chrisy dragged it from her throat. And Chrisy heard it and dropped the tray of flat silver.

It clattered and clashed down upon the hardwood floor; the tray went with it with a crash like doomsday and Chrisy came, charging heavily across the dining room so her footsteps shook the house, and amid the clatter and crash and bang there was another softer sound. Sue could barely hear it; yet she was sure that the side door had closed, stealthily and hurriedly.

"Chrisy—" she screamed, "look out. Don't come. Somebody's there. . . ."

Chrisy shouted, "Help—murder—help . . ."

Lights flared up in the hall. Somebody called from the stables; Chrisy charged through the doorway, searched for the telephone and shouted into it, "Police, help, murder—police . . ." She had snatched up, again, the fire shovel from the dining room fireplace.

Outside Sister Britches was in a frenzy which came, wildly nearer.

Woody, his gun in his hand, came running into the room; Caroline panting, followed him. Sister Britches thudded in beside her and dashed around the room, yelling frantically. Sue cried above the dog's clamor, "He was in the hall—he went out the side door—Woody, don't go. . . ." Woody had disappeared. Caroline tried to take the telephone away from Chrisy who wouldn't relinquish it and shouted, "Police—murder—police . . ."

The front door banged. If they heard the sound of his car none of them knew it; probably through the clamor and crash they had not heard it. Fitz, though, heard them; he came running along the hall.

It was Fitz who restored a sort of order, who took the

telephone from Chrisy, who gave Sister Britches a rather well deserved cuff which Caroline did not in the least resent and gave Sister Britches the shock of her life. She sat down and stared at Fitz and in her vast surprise stopped yelling.

Someone had answered the telephone; his voice crackled excitedly. Fitz cut into it. "I know all about that! But the murderer was here—five minutes ago. Send out a radio. Get hold of somebody. I'm telling you the truth, and they'll flay you alive if you make them miss this chance to get him. . . ." He put down the telephone. "The police are at Luddingtons'. I don't know whether he'll do anything or not. Where's Woody?"

Reveller, from away off near the stables, gave a deep bay. The side door banged and Woody came running again along the hall. "Fitz, I saw your car lights. Come on. He's outside somewhere. Have you got a gun?"

But Fitz did not answer; they were standing in the hall, he was staring at something on the floor. A leather strap, long and thin and tough lay there on the floor and it had been tied roughly into a sort of slip knot.

Caroline gave a kind of whistling sigh and reached out for the wall behind her; Chrisy got her onto the couch.

"Look out," cried Woody as Fitz picked up the strap. "Fingerprints . . ."

Fitz paid no attention; he rolled the strap together and put it in his pocket and from another pocket took out a gun which he gave to Chrisy. "It's loaded. Hold it like this." He put Chrisy's black, strong finger carefully around it. Then he and Woody were running along the hall again.

It was, of course, by then a futile search. Fitz knew it; Woody knew it, but they had to search just the same. Reveller joined them but was not in the faintest degree interested and returned presently to sit down at the side door, yawning and watching the flashlight. "What I need," said Caroline once, looking at Sister Britches, "is a watch dog." She said it with blue lips; but her eyes softened lovingly as Sister Britches came to her.

They found no one; whoever had been there had slid away into the heavy shrubbery, before Woody and Caroline had more than reached the stable path. There were a dozen, a hundred ways to escape the place unobserved, to reach thicket after thicket of shrubs; to take refuge in the pine woods or make a furtive way across the fields.

"Hundreds of ways," Woody said. "If the police'd get here . . ."

They hadn't come; they hadn't telephoned to inquire; it developed later that the man at the desk that night had decided, on his own, that it was simply another ruse, another trick to draw attention from Sue. Besides the sheriff and Captain Henley and all available troopers were in the Luddington woods.

"It wouldn't help if they did come," Fitz said.

Woody, angrily, agreed. "They wouldn't believe us anyway. Chrisy, did you see anybody at all?"

Chrisy shook her head. Except for the strap there was no visible proof of that presence. Woody held it to Sister Britches who sniffed it without interest, looked fondly at Fitz, the man who had cuffed her and gave an ingratiating wave of her stern. Reveller by then under the couch, sighed and stretched.

"What do you keep those dogs for, Aunt Caroline . . ." began Woody in exasperation and even Caroline gave a reproving look at Sister Britches. "If it had been a rabbit," she said weakly but stopped.

"How about phoning the police again?" said Woody and Fitz said, "They're at Luddingtons'. You didn't know . . ." and told them what he knew of Sam Bronson.

He had been found in the Luddington woods that afternoon late, by some troopers. He had been shot through the head. As far as Fitz knew they had not found the gun and had not extracted the bullet; perhaps it was not there to extract. He'd been dead, according to the coroner, for some days, it wasn't definite. Wat had telephoned Fitz; he had gone at once to the Luddingtons'. Jed was there, had been there with Wat most of the afternoon. The police questioned Wat and Ruby and they knew nothing; they were beginning on the servants and stablemen when Fitz had left. The body might have remained there for years; it was not far from the stream which Sue had crossed on her way to see Dr. Luddington and where she had seen a rider. The troopers had been requested by the sheriff to try to find hoofprints in the clay along the bank; if so, to make a moulage of them. They had found no hoofprints that were sufficiently well defined for a comparison with anything (and the sheriff had said that the hoofprints in the pine woods had proved to be too blurred and confused to show identifying marks, too, Fitz told them parenthetically) but they had found Sam Bronson—still in riding breeches and a turtle-neck sweater, but his eyes were no longer alert. It was then nearly dusk.

Chrisy was muttering, and rocking her vast blue chambray bulk to and fro.

Woody said suddenly out of a white, excited silence, "He shot himself! By golly, Fitz. He did it—he shot Ernestine, he shot Dr. Luddington—he—why, yes, he thought Sue saw him and recognized him there at the creek—he'd disguised himself in somebody's hunting coat, nothing easier —he thought Sue recognized him, he was afraid, he tried to kill her and then he gave up and lost his nerve and shot himself. . . ."

Fitz touched his pocket where a thin, tough strap lay coiled.

Woody lapsed into scowling, tight-lipped silence. Chrisy put her white apron over her head and began sobbing.

Again Fitz made a kind of order; he induced Chrisy to take Caroline upstairs and put her to bed. Sue and Woody and Fitz altogether searched the house, locked doors, bolted windows, picked up the wildly scattered knives and forks and spoons in the dining room. The police still had not come. They gave them up. Fitz went out and turned off the car lights and locked the car. He was going to stay.

Woody would have talked endlessly; Fitz sent him to bed. "I'll call you at three," he said. "Believe me, Woody, there's just nothing we can do now."

"Do you want my gun, too?"

"Keep it. I've got mine." Chrisy had put it down, gingerly yet rather reluctantly on a table.

Sue said, "I'm going to sit up with you."

She was prepared to battle if necessary to hold her ground; Fitz said, "Yes, I wish you would."

They talked, actually, far into the night—Sue on the hollowed, shabby couch in Caroline's study again, Fitz in the deep armchair with his feet stretched out on the footstool; it was a domestic scene—with a curious and unquiet note, Fitz's revolver, gleaming under the lamp on the table beside him. But they were taking unnecessary precautions, he said, to guard the house, he felt sure of it; whoever had been there would not try again that night. Sue took what comfort she could from that; there was more comfort in Fitz's presence, his brown face profiled against the lamp, his head leaning back against the cushions of the chair, the smoke drifting up from his cigarette.

He thought, he said, that the police might call Sam Bronson's death suicide and it might be; but the shot from the pine woods, the visitor that night, indicated that the murderer was not Sam Bronson—dead, at both times, in the Luddington woods. Reveller snored luxuriously under the couch. Fitz lighted another cigarette.

"If it wasn't Sam Bronson—and I don't think it was, the —the field, so to speak, is narrowed. We know that somebody—not Sam Bronson, made a murderous attempt last night from the pine woods and again tonight. So far the police don't believe it; the sheriff may insist on investigating. But if the field is narrowed—look here, Sue, I edged around to some questions last night with Camilla and Jed

201

and the Luddingtons, but I didn't get anywhere. That is —things came of it but nothing that seemed very important."

Sue sat up abruptly. "You can't mean one of them . . ." she began, and remembered her own question of Camilla and stopped.

"Well, that's what the police do. They get whole and complete stories from everybody concerned—alibis if they have them, what they were doing, where they were at the time of the murder. It'd be impossible for me to do that, of course—they wouldn't reply to inquiries from me if they didn't want to and besides the police have thoroughly covered the ground with everybody in the least connected with Ernestine's murder and they're getting it done about Dr. Luddington—at least they checked my alibi with Judge Shepson, simply because I was a friend and saw him the day before and Jed said they questioned him—he was at home—and I know they tried to check on Wat and Ruby; Wat was in Middleburg and they asked what men he'd seen and when and Ruby was riding again and said they'd asked her about time, and where she rode, and if she saw anybody. I can't do all that and anyway it's being done, thoroughly and well. But last night I suddenly thought that perhaps we could take that one hour or so, before and after the shot, and use it, say, for a test case. And got nowhere. At least . . ." he turned to reach for an ash tray and after a moment said, "Sam Bronson—exactly where was he, when you came out of the house after you'd found Ernestine was shot? Where was he, where was Jed, what did you say and what did they say? Who got to Ernestine first?"

She knew exactly. "Bronson was coming from the direction of the stables—across the lawn along the outside of the garden wall."

"And Jed?"

"He was coming along the driveway from the car. He

was fairly close to the door; Sam Bronson was closer. I told Bronson Ernestine was shot. He ran into the house; Jed saw me and ran to the door."

"Bronson was in the garden room ahead of you?"

"Yes." She thought she saw the trend of his questions. "But nothing was any different. He was bending over Ernestine. There wouldn't have been time for him to—to do anything. Change anything—conceal any sort of evidence, if that's what you mean."

"I don't know what I mean. Sue, I know he didn't but—just to make absolutely sure—Bronson didn't approach you at any time did he? I mean later. I mean—well, in any way that could be construed as a hint at a payoff?"

"No! No, Fitz, never."

He thought for a moment and said, "The stables are on the side of the garden room. If anybody did get to the house by riding across the fields and jumping that paddock fence on the other side of the garden, Sam just might have seen it."

"Camilla," she said suddenly, "saw Jed and me; and she heard Ernestine phone me and she came to tell me . . ."

She told him the story, omitting only, with instinctive, feminine loyalty, Camilla's offered bargain. He guessed that, however; there was a kind of twinkle in his eyes.

"There wasn't any sort of price put on her silence?" he said, eyeing her and suddenly, as she felt a flush creep up into her face, put back his black head with its crisp white threads and laughed.

"Fitz, stop, you'll wake Caroline!"

"Oh, I know—I won't . . ." He tried rather unsuccessfully to stop. "But it's so damned funny. Listen, baby—Camilla may be rather practical about economics and an unattached male, but I've trifled with nobody's affections, except I sincerely hope, with yours and that's no trifle. Camilla is not serious—but," he sobered, "I rather think she's got the kind of temper Ernestine had; if she should go to the police with this . . . Henley's looking for something exactly like that to bolster up his case. And there are some queer bits in her little piece. She's spoken it rather late but still—you see, it's always seemed to me perfectly possible that Ernestine did get that gun out herself. But I don't think she meant it for you and—what did Camilla say about her dressing early?"

"Only that. She didn't know why . . ."

"Maybe Ernestine expected another caller. Somebody she was afraid of. Somebody she was prepared to deal with —with a gun if she had to . . ." he stopped and thought. "And somebody she fully intended to get out of the way before you could possibly arrive. Therefore somebody she could have seen in the garden room while you and Jed were in the cabaña."

Sue whispered, "Somebody who killed her?"

"How are we to know?" he said rather hopelessly. "But that gun—it's always seemed to me that the murder must have been unpremeditated, because Ernestine wasn't dead. If it had been planned it seems to me whoever shot her would have seen to it she was dead. So it looks like, not an accident exactly but a struggle. . . ."

"But she was shot in the back."

"She could have been shot anywhere if there was a struggle over the gun."

Camilla and her temper like Ernestine's. Irresistibly, ashamed, Sue said, "Fitz, when Wat brought Camilla to your house, did you see them arrive?"

"No." He gave her a long look. "Oh, you mean, was there a time gap between Wat's bringing Camilla to my house and Jason's letting her in? Long enough for her to get back to Duval Hall? She'd have had to ride—saddle a horse . . ."

"She was in evening dress," Sue objected.

"But she's a brilliant horsewoman." He paused, thinking. Sue, irresistibly again, thought of Camilla and her mysterious flowering beauty and vitality since Ernestine's death. Ernestine who had always outshone Camilla!

But then sincerely ashamed again, she rejected it. "She didn't do it! She'd never do that. It's not fair to talk of it, even."

"Somebody did it." Fitz got up, went to the window, listened and the night was quiet. He came back. "And somebody—but this time intentionally, this time with pre-meditation, shot Dr. Luddington. And that somebody tried to drag you into it. If only we knew more of what the doctor did during that hour or so. He telephoned Ruby and told her to come. Presumably he told some patient to call you and Jed and have you come. I'd believe that—and so would the police—if they could unearth the patient. Dr. Luddington's old cook heard him say something which indicated that he knew who murdered Ernestine, that he had shielded somebody, at the gamble of Jed's life, and that he was now going to give up whoever it was he shielded, in order to save you from arrest. He'd held out—if all that's true, until he had the news of a warrant actually sworn out against you. That broke him down; if it was a terrible struggle with him between love and duty it accounts in a way for the telephone call Lissy Jenkins overheard; he was either warning somebody or taking somebody into his confidence. If he'd named names—but of course he wouldn't over the phone in so serious a thing. But the very fact that she heard no names, that it was so guarded, could have deceived whoever was at the other end of the wire. So he— well, I cannot believe that Dr. Luddington was afraid of whoever shot him. And . . ." he finished suddenly, "I had no idea that Wat was floating around; he's never said a word."

"He wouldn't. He'd not want to get into it."

"He will soon," Fitz said rather grimly and went into the hall; she could hear his footsteps the length of it and back again. He brought a light woolen scarf from the hall and put it over her. "Now then, go to sleep. I'll feel better if you're right there so I can see you. . . . Are Caroline and Woody hunting tomorrow?"

"Yes. All of us. At least we were planning to when this . . ."

He tucked the cover around her feet. "I'm going. So are you."

Something in his voice puzzled her; he glanced at her and caught the sharp question in her eyes and shook his head. "I don't know what I'm doing and I only hope it's right. . . . Go to sleep, Sue."

"I can't—I won't—what do you mean?"

"I wish I knew," he said in a suddenly rather harsh voice. He went back to the armchair and stretched out his feet, put back his head and firmly, convincingly closed his eyes. And inconceivably, against her will, she did go to sleep and awakened in the morning with Fitz gone from the armchair, the table light turned out, the woolen cover on the floor and somebody whistling shrilly in the direction of the stables.

Woody came bouncing in from the hall; he had breeches over his arm, a newspaper in his hand and a completely different, a carefree and natural expression on his face. He brandished the paper, "Look, Sue. Look. They say it's suicide; the police say it's suicide. You ought to wake up. Fitz has gone home ages ago. Breakfast's over." He eyed her in candid brotherly fashion. "You look awful. You ought to see your hair."

"Give me the papers."

"Okay." He scowled at his breeches. "Hunting's an expensive pleasure. Do you suppose Chrisy can get that spot out?"

He didn't wait for an answer. Chrisy was, in any case, an expert at brushing and cleaning. He went away, whistling, toward the kitchen, and Sue snatched the papers. The headlines were clamorous and said, mainly, suicide. Suicide of murderer in Baily case. Mysterious murderer who

206

has terrorized the county found shot in Luddington woods. Suicide. Suicide. Suicide.

There were columns and columns of fine print. It was a sensation.

The murderer of Ernestine Baily—and of Dr. Luddington, was the stableman, Sam Bronson; he had worked for the Bailys; he had had some grudge against Ernestine Baily; he had shot Dr. Luddington who must have guessed his identity; he had then shot himself. Remorse or fear—it didn't matter what was his motive, for the Baily case and the Luddington case were over and, the columns of print almost said in so many words, satisfactorily over. Everybody, including the police apparently, believed it.

Sue did not.

20

Woody came back in, this time with brightly polished boots; his spirits were high. "How do you like it, Sue?"

"But Woody—who shot from the pine woods . . ."

He turned to the window and examined his boots. "Somebody shooting squirrels. Accident. Scared and got away."

"How about Jeremy?"

"Sam Bronson slashed him. Scared him."

"I mean—last night. The night before."

"He's still nervous, scary. Aunt Caroline indulges her dogs and horses till they've got the temperament of a prima donna."

Did he really believe, in the light of morning, that the case was over and closed? She could not see his face. "Dr. Luddington wouldn't have protected Sam Bronson at the risk of the trial going against Jed."

"Now Sue, listen, you can't tell what he might have done or mightn't have done. Stick to the facts and the fact is they say that Sam Bronson shot himself . . ."

"What about last night? What about the—the strap?"

Woody's face darkened. "Sue, for God's sake, don't you want to believe it? Don't you see what it does for you? The police say so, don't they? Or at least they don't deny it. Would Henley ever admit it if he didn't believe it? Or the sheriff? You ought to be thankful and . . ."

"What does Fitz think?"

"I don't give a hoot in hell what Fitz thinks! You'll be late if you don't go and get yourself together. I'll bring up your breakfast tray. Wat has sent over a hunter for me. A honey, too, by the looks of her; little chestnut mare. I wonder how Chrisy's making out with my pants." He went off to the kitchen.

She had, however, dimmed his exuberance; there was a sort of pleading note in his voice when he brought her tray up to her room as she got out of the bathtub. He pounded on the door. "Here's your breakfast. And listen, Sue, everybody's telephoning. You ought to hear them. Everybody's read the papers and telephoned; it's gone like wildfire and they're really so thankful, Sue, about you and Jed, especially about you. Caroline's friends and yours and mine and even Judge Shepson phoned. He said it was all over and congratulations and—now do be reasonable, Sue, and don't keep thinking about—things. Leave that to the police."

There was a clatter as he put down the tray. Things, thought Sue. Such as a patient who could not be identified, who phoned to tell her to come, who phoned to tell Jed to come. Well, that could have been Bronson, his motive to drag her and Jed into it as suspects. But there was Dr. Luddington's conversation over the telephone with somebody —who? She shouted through the door and the splash of the emptying tub. "Why would the doctor telephone like that? The way Lissy Jenkins said . . ."

Woody's voice was still rather pleading. "Old Lissy Jenkins! She thought that story up days after Dr. Luddington was shot! Now, Sue, *don't* talk like that to anybody else. Let them believe it. Don't raise any doubts."

But how could Woody believe it? Or did he only want to believe it? Yet his advice was sensible; it was more than sensible, it was urgent. His voice wailed pleadingly through the door again. "Besides that's what Fitz said."

"You said you didn't give a hoot . . ."

"I didn't mean it, like that. You kept arguing and—Sue, he said for us to act as if we believed it. And it could be true, you know. Perhaps, those other things are—are accident, somebody, some crackpot . . ." His voice dwindled rather dubiously, then he said, "But *please* don't say things like to anybody."

"Of course I won't. I've got sense enough to see that! Thanks for the tray."

He clattered out. And as she was finishing breakfast Caroline came in. A different, normal and a very dignified Caroline, in a shining, newly ironed silk hat, her hair netted with inordinate neatness, her stock tied expertly. She always rode side saddle. Her heavy skirt was brushed and neatly draped, her blue eyes were shining. "Sue . . ." she said and came to her and kissed her.

Caresses were rare with Caroline. This one said all the things that Caroline herself was too moved to say. Sue looked at her and could not have uttered one word of what she had said to Woody.

"It was a hard ride, Sue. Some tough fences. But it's over. Everybody's been telephoning. It seemed queer to me that nobody did before but now I see why; it was their way of showing sympathy, of not intruding. It . . ." she couldn't say any more. She went to Sue's dressing table. "I had Chrisy put out your things. I'll tie your stock for you. Have you got your mother's safety pin?"

The plain gold safety pin her mother had used to pin her stock. Caroline had kept it; had, when Sue was sixteen, gravely presented it to her. "Of course."

Caroline, with a rather amusing reversal of roles, eyed Sue's hair. "Be sure to make your hair neat, dear. A neat head and a well-tied stock . . ."

"Yes, darling."

"I think Jeremy will be all right. Favor him at the fences; if he seems to want to refuse them then he's going lame again. In that case, I've already arranged with Wat, you're to shift to one of Wat's hunters."

"I'll be careful."

"And remember now, Sue, all the things . . ."

Suddenly the infectious, happy state of belief swept Sue. She chanted, "Fast at water. Slow at woodland. Show him the fence and let him take it. Choose your line and stick to it. And always, always, stay away from the hounds."

But this was serious business with Caroline; she did not smile. "And if you're going to buy a piece of land, remember to put your chin down on your chest."

She meant, of course, if she took a fall. Sue concealed an inward shudder; she would never be the expert and fearless horsewoman that under Caroline's teaching she ought to be. She'd fallen many times, too many, and always it happened so swiftly that she never had time to remember anything except an instinctive scramble to avoid horses' heels. She knew, however, what Caroline meant. A stiff straight neck meant sometimes a broken neck; she said with false lightness, "Of course I'll remember," and wished she need not hunt.

But Caroline at the door dispelled that wish; she gave her a happy glance in which there was a suspicion of tears. "I'm so glad, Sue—I'm so thankful, and somehow it makes the hunt and—and the hunt ball so soon after Dr. Luddington . . ." she stopped and took a breath and said, "all right. Doesn't it?"

Sue understood; she said firmly. "He'd have wanted it this way." Caroline, satisfied, nodded and wiped her eyes with the back of her hand and went away.

And suppose she was right; the police had apparently accepted it and in the end the police were always right. Sometimes one didn't know their reasons but there were always reasons—solid and valid. Suppose there did exist some explanation, odd and illogical as Woody had suggested, but still an answer to her own questions!

She dressed on a wave of that infectious, happy theory and under its spell tied her stock so neatly that it met with even Caroline's approval.

They were waiting when she came downstairs, already in the saddle. Woody was not a club member because he was away from home so much and a subscription was expensive, but he was always a welcome visitor; he wasn't in scarlet but he looked very slim and attractive in his dark riding coat. Chrisy had succeeded and his breeches were spotless. Caroline, mounted on Geneva, was a part of her, flexible and balanced, her hands, Sue knew, light and sure. She had taught Sue to ride astride; Sue looked with hopeless admiration at Caroline's beautiful seat on a side saddle which to Sue would have been perilously insecure. She liked to be able to grip hard with her knees—and that was not very secure either, for old Jeremy took that grip (and quite properly) to be a command to jump and often did. She must remember that. Jeremy rolled a pleased eye at her, Geneva gave a cavorting little step out of sheer glee, Lij stood by to give her a boot up and Chrisy stood at the side door, waving, her dark face alight with joy.

Caroline, all of them, waved back as they set out.

It was, Caroline said, a perfect morning for hunting, cold for the time of year and rather still. The laws governing scent, Caroline had told them many times, are mysterious; there are theories and theories none of which quite suffice to explain it and all of which were, at least to Sue, rather abstruse, but Caroline looked happy and satisfied. The fixture was the parkland in front of Wat and Ruby's magnificent house. They hacked over, Sue's spirits rising at every step. She was no expert horsewoman; she never would be. But she liked to ride and the creak of the saddle leather, the feeling of smooth and controlled power beneath her, the air in her face, the sense of well being, of a pulse of excitement was all of it exhilarating and deeply, gratefully, joyous. A softness and pleasure wiped out the lines of strain on Caroline's face; she leaned over and gave Geneva a lingering, gentle pat. Woody felt it and with difficulty kept himself from giving the borrowed mare a short test of her speed and spirit and told Sue happily that she was a love and there was something about a horse that was like a ship.

Sue thought, I suppose there is; and perhaps it's something deeper than sheer physical well being and the delight of balance and motion; perhaps it's a feeling of being close to the earth and the creatures thereof. She did not say so to Woody who would have been embarrassed for her and probably given his lovely borrowed mare a short fling merely to cover his shame that she could think or speak such nonsense. They arrived by dirt road at the Luddington place.

Sue thought again, "How I've missed it; all of it. It's my country. They are my people." The riders in scarlet and black, the horses, excited, pleased, knowing as well as their riders what it was all about, hounds—gathered so closely together that while the traditional blanket might not actually have covered them, still several blankets of a rather large size might have been stretched to do so. It was the dog pack, a beautiful one; Caroline looked them over with proud scrutiny for she had had much to do with the selection, breeding and management of the kennels. The Dobberly packs were now mainly bred from good English foxhounds; deep-chested, their sterns rather bushy, with springy well cushioned feet, muscles like whipcords. They were now, twenty and a half couple, eager and alert, waiting the huntsman's signal.

It was a comparatively large field; the Dobberly hunt was small and that day, except for Woody, there were no visitors, but all the regulars were out and, all of them, they made it clear, felt as Caroline did. They crowded around Wat; they crowded around Caroline and herself. Bob Hallock again, huge and kindly, pressed Sue's hand without a word. They didn't say much, any of them; their feeling was like a banner over the whole hunt. Jed was talking to the present M.F.H. (retiring by his own request that season); he waved and started toward them and was stopped by somebody who obviously was congratulating

213

him. Camilla was there looking, as usual now, like Ernestine, slim and elegant in her saddle, controlling her hunter with ease. She was gay and vivacious; she waved at Sue. Before Jed could reach them the hunt moved off. Sue fell in beside Caroline and Woody. Jed, ahead of them in the narrow lane, turned to find Sue and to wave; Fitz was nowhere among the riders.

She looked for him and looked for him among the scarlet-coated men and controlled Jeremy who was beginning to wish they'd get on with this tiresome preliminary business. They avoided the Luddington woods—probably it had been agreed—unless, of course, hounds found near them and the fox led them into the woodland. They turned off across Luddington meadows and finally drew up as the huntsman cast hounds into the covert below a ridge of low-lying hills. Ruby came up to them so suddenly that it startled Jeremy who gave an uneasy prance. Sue kept her balance and Ruby said, "You ought to tie a red ribbon on his tail, Sue. I didn't know Jeremy was a kicker."

"He's not, really," Sue said jerkily, trying to quiet Jeremy who was executing a neat waltz turn.

Ruby looked beautiful and stately with her severe, dark hair in a bun, her silk hat, her beautifully tailored, dark riding coat and beige breeches. She said, "I wanted to tell you, Sue—it seems heartless but I'm so thankful about Sam Bronson—although to tell you the truth I never liked him anyway."

"Listen . . ." said Caroline sharply, watching the distant covert.

Ruby would not; Jeremy, crossly, backed.

Ruby said across Caroline, "But it clears everything up. I wasn't sure that Wat was right about insisting that we join the hunt today but now I see that he was. Do you know," said Ruby suddenly dreamy, "this reminds me of the day Ernestine was killed."

"It's Rambler—he's speaking," cried Caroline sharply. "Do hush, Ruby. Listen—he's never wrong."

A clear bell-like note came from the covert; both Caroline and Rambler were right. His voice was honored by another and another; there was a sort of excitement, among the riders, a gathering up of reins, a tense listening. Sue's heart beat rapidly; she was half excited, half afraid. And then all at once the gone away sounded clear and strong.

Always to Sue it was a moment when she passed from the state of being herself, Sue Poore, to another being who didn't have time to do, or be, or think anything aside from sticking on her horse and trying to remember Caroline's teachings. Choose your line; don't thrust. She was thudding across meadow land, conscious of other riders as the hunt spread out. Someone viewed the fox; she caught a flashing glimpse of a rider, standing up in his stirrups, his hat lifted on high for the huntsmen to see. It was a wily fox, this one, leading them swiftly across meadow and then stubble; he slid under a fence, hounds after him in a tumult of flashing white and brown and eager waving sterns. Show your horse the fence.

She felt, as always, a kind of catch at her throat in the split second before Jeremy, his stride perfectly timed, lifted with fine power and landed easily and neatly. He was all right then; no lameness yet. They headed for Bob Hallock's place and plowed ground; choose the furrow where water stands; it's hardest. There weren't any furrows with water standing and anyway the fox was swerving again, Jeremy was pounding along. Sue felt as if she had no breath left in her body. They swerved again, backwards along a rather marshy strip of hay lands. The going was slower; she couldn't see Caroline or Woody: indeed the whole panorama of the field flashed confusingly outward, fanlike, in a chaos of scarlet and black, of thudding, galloping horses, of sound and life and color.

The fox led them into the Luddington woodlands.

They were there before Sue realized it and then she was so occupied with Jeremy——ride slow at woodland, ride slow at woodland——that they were in the woods before she knew it, in the woods with the hunt and all its color and motion disappearing, vanishing, disseminating into leafy, thin young greens.

She slowed Jeremy who didn't like it and fretted, tossing his head. They reached a bend of the same little stream that Sue had crossed on her way to Dr. Luddington's and before she could think of any of Caroline's admonitions, Jeremy had jumped it with such zeal that he nearly unseated her; the willows whipped her cheek and knocked her hat awry. She checked Jeremy, to his fury; her arms ached by the time she brought him to a standstill. She caught her breath and straightened her hat and listened; from the sound the hunt was veering to the right, away from the village and toward the ridge of hills again. She glanced around and realized with disgust that, again, she was tagging the field. Woody, an apter pupil, and Caroline would be away ahead; they'd be in at the kill if there was one. She repressed a secret, heretical hope that there would not be.

Then she realized that she was not, as she had thought, alone in the rear of the hunt. There was another rider, out of sight in the brush, keeping pace with her.

She was not at first uneasy. He was a straggler from the hunt as she was. She spoke to Jeremy and he moved on rather slowly through the uneven, slippery territory.

The other rider did likewise.

Jeremy put up his head sharply; his ears flicked back. Without any warning he began to run.

21

SOMEHOW SUE clung to his back.

They were over the stream, Jeremy taking it like a bird, they were out of the woodland, plunging across meadow land again. He wasn't running away. Let him run—let him run then—he'd steady down. She realized dimly that another rider was galloping towards her, not from the woods, though, from some other direction. Another rider, in a scarlet coat came up with her and Jeremy began to steady, into a gallop, into a canter, stopped and stood there panting and trembling. She was trembling, too, patting Jeremy with a hand that shook, speaking to him in a breathless, uneven voice. Fitz rode up. "Okay, Sue?"

She nodded.

"What scared him?"

She nodded back toward the woodland. "Somebody was there—quite near—somebody . . ."

"Wait for me here."

She got her breath and slid out of the saddle; it seemed as always a long way to the ground; she held Jeremy's reins and was walking him slowly along, talking to him, when Fitz emerged from the woods again and came at a gallop back to her. "Who was it?"

"I don't know. He'd got away. I ought not to have taken any chances. I was following you; I thought if it *was* somebody hunting today—but then you had such a sudden burst of speed that I lost you." He swung down from his saddle and came to her and put his hand on Jeremy's sweating neck. "He's all right now. Sue, do you care about the hunt? Will you come to Dr. Luddington's house with me? It's not far and the hunt's gone off toward Piney Ridge. I'll give you a lift. . . ."

Jeremy was now as steady as an old carthorse; Sue kept a weather eye on him, however, as, with a boost from Fitz, she got back into the saddle. He got into his own saddle. They rode together back toward the woods but further down, nearer the village, nearer Dr. Luddington's house. She said, "Fitz, everybody thinks it was Sam Bronson. The papers, the police . . ."

"I know. At least—they're letting everybody think that's what they think. And there's one thing certain; act as if you believe it, Sue. If anybody is scared, thinks you know too much, is threatening you—if you could convince such a person that you believe it was Bronson, that there's no question in your mind—if, in short, you convince whoever was in the pine woods that you believe it was Bronson and nobody else, then that person would have no reason to— well, you'd be safer. I hope," he added.

"Fitz, you look as if—what do you think? Could it have been Bronson?"

"If I told you what I think just now, you'd . . . Look out. Here's where we cross. Show me where you saw the rider that day."

She did, identifying it as nearly as she could. They rode toward Dr. Luddington's but now Fitz was ahead. She couldn't talk to him; they reached the stables and Dr. Luddington's house. They came to the gate where she had dismounted and Jeremy pricked his ears forward, snorted and waltzed. Fitz came back; he held Jeremy, he told Sue to get down. She opened the gate and Fitz led Jeremy through it and there Jeremy would go no further; he put back his ears and pranced and Fitz at last led him around, back of the stables, out of sight of the house and the place where

Sue had tied him. He tied him there and tied his own horse beside him. "Isaac Bell will stand. Come on, Sue."

"Isaac Bell?" Sue said, looking at the beautiful dark chestnut hunter he rode.

He glanced at her, amused. "Named for a famous sportsman. Don't let your aunt hear you ask that."

She said suddenly, as they walked toward the house: "Fitz, do you really like hunting?"

"I like the riding. I like the breeding of fine horses and hounds. I'm not sure about the fox."

"But the fox . . ."

"Enjoys it? I'm not sure about that. Yet actually no wild animal has a safe life. This way the end is merciful. And of course they really are a pest to the farmers. Here we are; let's go in the back door." He knocked but Lissy Jenkins had gone home; she wouldn't stay in the house. No one answered; he tried the door and in true Dobberly fashion it was not locked. They went in. The kitchen was neat and orderly, which was obscurely comforting to Sue. Fitz said, "I hate to ask you to go in there but . . ."

"What do you want me to do?"

"I don't know exactly. But—show me where you stood, what you did, everything."

It was not easy, but neither was it as hard as she'd have thought. The place was dusted and neat; the curtains were open and daylight flooded the consulting room and the waiting room. She stood beside the desk, with light flickering upon the glass-enclosed cabinets and told everything she could remember and then Fitz questioned her.

About Jed and what he had said, minutely. What she had said? Exactly what had she said? " 'Why did you come back like that?' " What had Jed said then: why had he urged her to leave?

"For the same reason I tried to make him leave."

"It would have been the worst thing either of you could have done."

"He wanted to get me out of it. That telephone call—he said I didn't understand how necessary—and then Ruby came."

"Did she seem suspicious?"

"Oh, no! I think she'd have agreed not to tell the police that I'd been there. While we were talking the police came and . . ."

"Wait a minute. How did Ruby take it? Was she excited?"

"Oh, yes; she doesn't show things as most people do; but she—I remember she stood there in the waiting room and said something about the fern needing watering, so I knew that she didn't know what she was saying . . ."

"Fern," said Fitz. *"Fern!"*

But she didn't believe it, not even when he examined the great spreading fern, when he plunged his hand into it, when he gave a kind of cry and pulled out a mirrored, flat little box that winked and shone. He cleaned off soil and peat moss. "It's Ruby's."

And it was; her name was engraved on the other side of it, the metal side, with below it "Happy Birthday from the Doctor." It was a trinket, a very flat, small cigarette case; one side had actually a mirror set in it. The other, except for the engraving, was plain. Fitz opened it and there were three cigarettes and a few flakes of tobacco.

"So she'd used it. When's her birthday, Sue?"

It took her back to the days when birthdays were of primary importance, of secrets, anticipation and birthday cakes. "October. October second."

Ernestine had been murdered on the ninth.

Fitz put the trinket in his pocket. "All right, I'm going to the Hunting Horn. Want to come along?"

"What for? I mean—yes, I want to go with you. But why . . ."

"I'll show you when we get there. I want you—if I'm right—to hear it with your own ears."

They went back out of the neat, quiet house, across the

graveled drive to where the horses waited, calmly and contentedly together. Fitz again gave her boot a lift. The hunt had gone far to the left along the ridge; time had passed. Fitz swung himself on his own horse, "We'll lunch there." He thought for a moment and added, "I'll take you along the byways; no use inviting the attention of any troopers." But he wouldn't talk and his face was so queer and grave that Sue did not question him. Ruby's cigarette case—why had she hidden it? There had to be a reason.

They turned onto a dirt road, they wound amid low hills, they passed a remote farmhouse or two and followed a dirt lane and came out onto another road which wound along a quiet valley. The Hunting Horn was in a remote and secluded spot yet actually not far away. Sue had been there at some time in the past; she remembered it dimly when they rode up at last into the courtyard. It was small and old with gabled windows and early, red geraniums flowering in window boxes.

"It's a fine place," Fitz said rather grimly, "for a rendezvous." And helped her from the saddle.

"A rendezvous," she thought. Ernestine had met Woody here. Fitz saw the look in her face; he said gently, "It wasn't Woody Ernestine came here to meet. At least—not more than once. Come on, Sue."

A boy ran out to take their horses; clearly the Hunting Horn catered to just such chance visitors. They went through a low door into a taproom, mellow, low-ceilinged, paneled in wood, with hunting prints on the walls, low tables and chairs and a well polished bar behind which a barmaid stood and smiled. "Why, good morning, Mr. Wilson. I didn't expect you so soon." She smiled at Sue. "What will you have?"

"We'll have lunch in a minute, but just now . . ." Fitz pulled a newspaper—a Bedford newspaper, Sue saw the familiar masthead—from a pocket. He unfolded it; he handed it to the barmaid and the barmaid stopped smiling.

"Is that the man?" Fitz asked.

She said slowly, all the beaming smile gone from her round face. "That's the man—I suppose I'll have to swear to it. It does seem terrible. But that's the man."

Sue craned her neck; there was a photograph, upside down. Fitz said, "It's Wat. He and Ernestine used to meet here."

"*I—can't* . . ." Sue took a breath. "*I can't believe it.*"

"You will, when you hear what she's got to tell."

Two hours later when they rode slowly away she did believe it. No one else had drifted in to lunch; they had the small room entirely to themselves. The barmaid's story was lengthy, prolonged by exclamations, regrets and inquiries of Fitz as to whether or not the police were going to be unpleasant because she hadn't told it sooner. "Why didn't you tell them, when you told about Woody—that is, the young man she met here the afternoon before she was killed?" Sue asked curiously.

The girl flushed and her eyes sparkled defiantly. "Because I didn't like that man."

"What man . . ."

"Henley," supplied Fitz with a twinkle.

"He wasn't nice to me," the girl said indignantly. "He acted as if I wasn't telling the truth. I'd read about the murder but I was in California; I was working in a store in a little town there and the papers I saw didn't have any photograph and I didn't know her name, that is, Mrs. Baily's. I was interested but that's all. But then I got homesick and came back here and the very day I got here Mr. Baily was acquitted and then right away the newspapers had all those stories and pictures and I saw that it was Mrs. Baily, I mean she'd come here often. And then I recognized the young man—Woody?—his picture was there, too, and I knew that I ought to tell the police that they were here that very afternoon. But that was the only time I remember that she'd met *him* here. All the other times it was"—she motioned to the newspaper Fitz had brought and said—"him. I was going to tell the police about him, but I started with the afternoon before she was murdered, because I thought that was most important and then . . ." her eyes snapped angrily, "he made me so mad, that police captain, that I wouldn't say another word. But it was sort of on my conscience, too. I was glad when Mr. Wilson came yesterday and asked me if Mrs. Baily had been here other times and with anybody else besides the young man. And . . ." she finished with an air of triumph, "I just hope it shows that Henley."

Without its voluble trimmings the story was short and simple. Ernestine and Wat Luddington had been meeting at the Hunting Horn for some time—not often but often enough; they had come sometimes together, as a rule separately. "And," said the girl, "she was after him. I could tell; it's the way they looked and sometimes I'd hear something."

The only thing, however, that she'd heard that was of real significance had been said by Ernestine, two or three days before her murder. The barmaid, bringing them a second drink, had heard it clearly and remembered it so perfectly that there was not much doubt as to its accuracy. Ernestine had said '. . . and when we get to Washington, the world will be ours. Nothing can stop you. With me to help you.'

"She was leaning over the table; she didn't see me coming. She was sort of—I don't know—anyway I knew that she was the one that wanted whatever it was she was talking about. Except I think she was beginning to make him think he wanted it too."

What a chance listener thinks of what he hears is, of course, not evidence. To Sue and Fitz it was utterly convincing.

"Wat!" cried Sue.

Fitz nodded. "And a glittering career."

The girl looked at them inquiringly. Sue said, "But money . . ."

"Ruby had money. Tons of it."

"She wouldn't give it to Wat so he could divorce her and marry Ernestine and get into politics and go from triumph to triumph as Ernestine probably was determined he should—her will power and Ruby's money . . ."

"I don't know," Fitz said. "I don't know . . ."

It was past the middle of the afternoon when they went away, Fitz promising to do what he could to intercede with Henley. "Not that I really care," the girl said. "It serves him right!"

Again though, as they hacked homeward, Fitz said very little and when Sue asked him what he was going to do he said that he didn't know.

"But if Ruby was at home with a headache . . ." began Sue, after a long silence broken only by the jogging of the horses and the creak of the saddles, "even if she'd found out about Ernestine somehow and . . ."

"Ernestine was expecting somebody and somebody she expected a bitter quarrel with. Although honestly I think she meant the gun for some kind of bluff."

He took her home across the Luddington pastures and then by way of the dirt lane. Woody and Caroline had not come home yet. Chrisy welcomed them with sputtering anger. "Them policemen have been here again! All afternoon they've been here. All over the place, house, barn, tack room, everywhere. And I couldn't do a thing about it. It was that Captain Henley and the other one. With the mean face—the one that was here before and went away."

Sue's heart sank. Fitz gave her a quick look and said to Chrisy, "Captain Wilkins?"

It was Captain Wilkins; Chrisy nodded angrily.

22

THERE WAS nothing they could do. As far as Chrisy knew the police had found nothing; she did not even know why they had been searching.

Fitz at last went away. "Go to the hunt ball as if nothing had happened. If you have a chance, you might try to muzzle Camilla. I don't want her coming out with all that just now." He turned to Chrisy, "I don't think Miss Caroline needs to know that the police have been here."

Chrisy, relieved, agreed. "No sense in worrying her. . . . Now, Miss Sue, what dress you want to wear tonight?"

Fitz rode away. Sue got out a dress for Chrisy to press. Fitz would either question Wat himself or tell the police. Somehow she didn't think that he would approach the police first. But the presence of Captain Wilkins, the evidence of renewed investigation, was ominous.

Caroline and Woody returned late; they were tired, happy and full of talk. They remained in the stables, seeing to every detail of the scraping of feet, the cooling, the rubdowns, even the feed of their horses before they came happily into the house where, by then, there was barely time for them to change. The house was full of commotion with Woody shouting the story of the hunt from his bathroom, Chrisy forgetting Wilkins for the moment and thundering happily up and downstairs, hurrying Woody, helping Caroline—and at last seeing them all into Caroline's car. She was beaming by that time and proud. Woody was resplendent in uniform and black tie; Caroline looked like a duchess in black lace and her only jewels, pearls and a brooch set with diamonds, rose cut and small but brilliant, that had belonged to her mother, Sue wore white, a dress she had bought—and saved for—in New York, a soft white with a tight bodice and full billowing skirt; a long red cape that swirled to the floor went with it. Woody whistled when she came down the stairs and gave her and then Caroline his arm with exaggerated courtesy but pride in his eyes just the same; his womenfolk were doing him credit. All the way to the club he and Caroline talked only of that day's run, endlessly and happily. They had missed Sue but thought nothing of it; Sue was never an enthusiastic hunter. They had lost the original fox after a stiff run; found again and after various checks and numerous stirrup cups, had at last had a really fine run.

Sue was listening and not hearing much of it; they reached the club, brilliantly lighted and festive; already an orchestra was playing inside. Dance music floated out to them; as gay as if so dark a thing as murder—and fear of murder—could not exist.

And, again, inside, it was at once evident that a special kind of gaiety, something warm and friendly, surrounded the hunt ball as it had hovered over the hunt. The pall of the winter was vanquished; friends greeted friends with an extra cordiality and all of them greeted Caroline and Sue and Woody as if they'd been away on a long and dangerous journey. And indeed, in a queer way they had been.

Usually the Dobberly hunt ball was preceded by a dinner or dinners; this time an elaborate buffet was in the long, low-ceilinged dining room and an elaborate bar was set up at one end. It was not an imposing clubhouse. It was supported mainly by a handful of residents, but its very unpretentiousness was both dignified and endearing. Caroline was whisked away on the arm of the present M.F.H.; Woody, however, remained rather closely at Sue's side—closely, she suspected, until he made sure that in this, her first party appearance since Ernestine's murder (since the trial, since she had become in a horrible sense, notorious, the other woman), she would meet with kindliness and a welcome. She was sure of it when Jed came, his head high, handsome and arrogant in his scarlet coat, smiling and triumphant, for Woody would not let her dance with him. "No use reminding everybody."

Jed's eyes flashed. "They'll think it's queer if we don't!"

"They'll think it queerer if you do!"

Jed unexpectedly gave in. "Maybe you're right. But I've not had a chance to talk to you alone, Sue, since they found Bronson. Can't we get out of this mob?"

Woody was shaking his head. "Everybody in the place will see."

"Just out on the porch."

Woody was firm. "Not a step. Besides, I think Camilla wants you." Jed turned and Sue followed his look. Camilla was crossing the floor toward them, in yellow which had been Ernestine's favorite color, which she'd worn the night she died; the deep red gleam of the old-fashioned Duval garnets encircled her throat and her wrists.

'Muzzle her,' Fitz had said. But how?

Yet hadn't the announced fact that Sam Bronson was the murderer, that he was consequently a suicide, muzzled Camilla by removing the threat she had been able to wield like a weapon over Sue's head? In fact it was still valid, but Camilla did not know that.

There was, however, a deep, cold sparkle in Camilla's eyes; she said directly to Sue, "Have you seen Fitz?"

Woody replied, "Yes, he's come. He came into the hall a minute ago but then somebody called him."

"Oh," said Camilla. "Oh." And swiftly attacked. "You'll want to dance with Jed, Sue. I'll wait for Fitz."

Jed said sulkily, "Woody doesn't want her to dance with me."

Someone touched Woody's shoulder; it was a waiter. "Please, Mr. Woody—Mr. Wilson asked you to bring your sister—I'll show you. There's some—some gentlemen with him."

There was a short queer stillness in the little group; the orchestra swung softly and gayly into a rumba. Then Jed said, "Gentlemen . . ." and the waiter, looking troubled, said, "Police . . ."

Camilla was marble white; Jed took the waiter roughly by the arm, "What do you mean?"

"Wait, Jed—if Fitz wants me . . ." Woody was white, too; he looked at Sue and Sue said—yet somehow could not hear her own voice; she was vaguely surprised when the others apparently did hear it—"We'll come. Thank you," and moved to follow the waiter. Camilla said, "I'm coming too," and Woody said in a savage whisper, "Stay where you are, both of you. Come along later if you want to. People are already looking."

Camilla hesitated, bit her lip and turned to Jed; they moved off in a dance step. Woody said in Sue's ear, "Smile —talk to me . . ."

She must have obeyed; someone in the hall stopped her and spoke to her and she replied and did not know how she extricated herself. The waiter led them back along the wide central hall to the steward's office.

Fitz was there and was at the door to meet her. He looked very gay and festive in his scarlet coat and white tie; there was strength in his figure and his arm around her, but what could he do? For Captain Henley was there, standing beside Fitz, and Captain Wilkins, lean and saturnine and suspicious, arose reluctantly from a chair. The sheriff was not there. As Fitz said something to her, Woody moved aside and Wat and Ruby came into the room.

The sound of the rumba was everywhere. Ruby in pale blue and diamonds stood like a beautiful statue done in stone. Fitz reached behind her and closed the door.

It shut out the sound of the dancers. The music continued to drift in from the long windows across the room that gave upon the encircling veranda. Fitz said, "Sue, these gentlemen came to your place shortly after you'd left; they came on here. Meantime Chrisy telephoned to me here and I met them as they arrived; they do not wish to do whatever they are going to do in a public way. They seem to feel that they have some—new evidence."

Henley seemed about to speak; Fitz went on quickly, "I've told them, just now, one or two facts that I happened upon and they were kind enough to listen. Now then . . ."

Captain Wilkins said: "In my opinion that strap you showed us was like the famous shot. You'd better tell the girl, Henley."

Captain Henley cleared his throat and would not look at Sue; he stared at the window, he stared in an embarrassed way at his boots and said, "I have a warrant for your arrest, Miss Poore. I really am sorry that it happened just like this but . . ."

"Sorry!" snorted Wilkins. "The girl's guilty . . ."

Fitz said: "That isn't quite all, Wilkins. I—Ruby . . ." He took the mirrored little box from a pocket and put it on the table so the light winked upon it. The distant music changed to a faster rhythm. Ruby sat down and began to cry and said, sobbing, vehement, "I told you we ought to tell the truth, Wat! I told you—I told you—and I'm going to tell it now."

Wat's hatchet face was white, too, and shrunken; he went to her after a moment. He put his hand kindly on her lovely bare shoulder. Then he lifted his head. "I'll tell them Ruby. The fact is . . ." he cleared his throat huskily. "The fact is, gentlemen, I was a fool. I—let myself—I was a fool. And Ruby discovered it and . . ."

Ruby cried, wiping her eyes, "No, no, I'll tell it. It was all Ernestine's fault. She wanted him—Wat. She wouldn't let him alone; she roped him in. She—wanted him; she got him to talk of divorce—a divorce from *me!*" cried Ruby suddenly wailing again. "And he's my husband and I love him."

Wilkins, looking startled, got up. Henley and Woody and

Wat were talking all at once. Fitz said imperatively, "Wait, please—Ruby," his tone was gentle. "Ruby, you told Ernestine you'd had enough of it, didn't you? You told her you were coming to see her? You were upset—you said things . . ."

"I was wild," cried Ruby, her great eyes flashing. "I don't know what I said. I telephoned, I said I was coming straight to Duval Hall. I threatened her, I told her I'd kill her . . ." she caught her breath and shot a terrified look at the policemen and cried, "But I didn't mean it. I didn't kill her. She had the gun."

Wat moaned: "Ruby—Ruby . . ."

Fitz said, "Of course you didn't mean it. But you were furious; you were going to stop any plan Ernestine had . . ."

"That was another thing." Ruby was vehement and outraged. "She was going to do everything—go to Washington to live, or all over the world if she wanted to, push Wat along in his career—and she had him half believing she could, too—and she was going to do it with my money. *My money!*" cried Ruby clutching the table with angry, jeweled hands.

"How?" asked Fitz softly.

And when it came it was utterly simple, utterly ruthless and profoundly in character with Ernestine and with Ruby and all that had gone before in their long rivalry. It was also, thought Sue, utterly fiendish. For Ruby looked up, her face streaming with tears, like a child; she cried, "By letting *me* divorce *Wat*."

Fitz did not understand. Perhaps none of the men understood. Ruby wailed, "Letting *me* divorce him! And making me pay for it. She knew I'd just die if he divorced me and everybody said she'd taken him away from me."

It was the truth. It might not have succeeded; it had not; but it was what Ernestine had offered. Probably no one in the room except Sue quite believed it. Wat came the nearest to comprehension; he said to Ruby, "I wasn't going to

—I wouldn't have—I never loved her, Ruby, the way I love you. I was a fool but I wouldn't have divorced you— Besides," he added, suddenly practical, "I couldn't have. You never gave me any grounds . . ."

Ruby's eyes flashed. "If you'd ever asked me it would have broken my heart. You know that, Wat. And so did Ernestine. And she didn't care; that's what she wanted. I'd have been so heartbroken—and so humiliated—yes, I'd have given her anything—if you'd done that to me—just anything she wanted so people wouldn't know that she'd taken you away from me. And Ernestine knew it."

Wilkins, off guard, gave his head a bewildered shake as if he was coming out of water. Henley's mouth was open. Woody felt sorry for Ruby and said, "Now, Ruby, Wat wouldn't have left you, he loves you . . ."

Ruby flashed around. "Don't you dare to talk, Woody Poore. She had you in her clutches, too. Ernestine . . ."

Fitz said, "You rode over to see Ernestine. You told her you were coming. You told her you'd kill her if she . . ."

"I didn't mean it," said Ruby and took a breath and added, "except maybe I did, when I said it."

"Ruby!" Wat tried to intervene.

Fitz said, "You rode your jumper; you took him back ways, while Wat came to Duval Hall and got Camilla and took her to my place. So as to avoid the gate near the stables you took your horse over the paddock fence and left him there; then you reached the house by way of the garden and Ernestine was there . . ."

"And she had a *gun,*" Ruby said as if conventions, but merely conventions, had been outraged. "Think of that!"

Again confused voices began and stopped. Fitz said, "What did she do with it?"

"She said I needn't threaten her; she said she wasn't afraid of me. She said if I was hysterical and tried to hurt her she'd really shoot. She said she'd never give him up and that I'd be lucky if she didn't marry him right away, but she said if I was sensible—*sensible,*" cried Ruby in a snort as cynical as Wilkins' best, "if I was sensible I'd make a division of property with Wat. Then she'd go away; she'd divorce Jed some time, not soon, and after some time had passed, long enough for people to think I was the one who'd left Wat, not that he'd left me on account of Ernestine, then—maybe—she and Wat would marry. It was that really that I just couldn't stand," added Ruby simply, "Ernestine acting as if she'd marry Wat when she got good and ready, just as if she could have Wat any minute . . ." She looked at Wat, said, "It would have broken my heart," and began to cry again.

Wat patted her shoulder and murmured. Woody paced the floor; Sue started toward Ruby whose distress was overwhelming, like a mountain flood, and painfully genuine and tragic and Wilkins finally rubbed his forehead in a rather frenzied way and said, "This doesn't change things, Henley. My advice is to execute your warrant, get our business over with."

"You can't arrest Sue," cried Woody, wheeling around. "Fitz—stop them . . ."

Jed said from the porch, "Unlatch the window, Woody."

He'd heard, of course; Henley whirled around, swearing. Woody unlatched the window and Jed stepped over the low sill.

Wilkins stared at Jed, turned to Henley and snapped, "Arrest that girl and get it over with before the whole damned hunt is in here making a fuss."

"I shot Ernestine. Sue didn't. If you so much as put your finger on her—I shot Ernestine," Jed said, his head high and arrogant.

Henley shouted, "You can't do that. You've been acquitted."

"Chivalry," snorted Wilkins. "Let's get the girl out of here."

And Ruby wailed, "I didn't do it. I had my cigarette case, the doctor gave it to me for my birthday so he knew it was mine. And I tried to be cool and calm, I did, Wat.

I took out a cigarette and—but then I put the case down there on the table in the garden room and forgot it and he saw it and of course he knew it was mine. And then I never knew what happened to it. I kept waiting for somebody to find it and the police to question me. All winter—but he'd found it himself and taken it to protect me and Wat. And then I think Ernestine, before she died, told him that I'd been there. And told him why and what I'd said so he thought I'd shot her but I didn't. I didn't—I didn't . . . And then he was shot—Dr. Luddington—and there was that awful cigarette case right on his desk. I lost my head. I didn't know what had happened, or who knew about it, and the police were at the door and I didn't know what to do so I hid it and then I was afraid to go back for it, but I didn't kill him—I didn't . . ."

Fitz said in an aside to Woody, "Bolt the door."

Woody moved to bolt the door and then, with a glance at Fitz, swiftly to the window but he was too late; Camilla in a flutter of yellow was already stepping hurriedly into the room. She looked at Sue and Fitz who stood together, turned to Captain Henley and said, her eyes cold but her voice shaken with anger, "There is something it is my duty to tell you."

23

THE ORCHESTRA changed to the light gay rhythm of a waltz; it brought with it a flashing picture of the dancers, the mingled colors of swinging skirts and scarlet and black jackets. Someone passed along the corridor outside, a girl and a man; they could hear his murmured voice and her high, light laughter. Then everybody spoke at once.

Jed said, "If you mean that quarrel with Ernestine, I'll tell it myself. It can't damage Sue or me now."

Wat said, "Ruby, darling, of course you didn't kill him."

Henley shouted something angrily at Jed. Wilkins got up and said, "Serve your warrant, Henley."

Fitz said to Ruby, "Is that why you sold your hunter?" And Woody had a gun in his hand. Sue thought fantastically, "Fitz passed it to him. When he went to bolt the door. I knew when his arm moved, when Woody paused just for a second behind me."

Ruby answered Fitz, sobbing, "Of course, that's why. There wasn't another horse in the county, at least not many, that could take that fence near the house. I was terrified for fear somebody would think of it—but I didn't do it . . ."

Wat said, "Nobody says you did, Ruby." His hatchet face glistening with sweat.

Jed strode up to Henley, "You've got to listen to me . . ."

"Chivalry," snorted Wilkins again. Henley, whose red

face was glistening too, turned to Sue, "Now then, Miss Poore . . ."

Jed's voice rose above the others. ". . . I tell you I shot her. I'll tell you exactly how. I—didn't mean to. It was the gun. I—I left Sue in the cabaña; I didn't go down the driveway at all. I went into the house and I was going to have it out with Ernestine then and there. We'd had a row just before Sue came. I imagine Camilla heard it but she never told anybody if she did. It . . ."

Camilla had had time already to regret. She cried, "Oh, no, Jed, I didn't mean—I went too far—I take it back . . ."

"No, that's the truth; Ernestine said she was going to leave me and I told her I was in love with Sue and to go ahead and leave me. She said she'd have nothing like that; *she'd* leave *me*." Jed glanced at Wat and interrupted himself in a way that sounded truthful—and reminded Sue of the sudden speculation in his face the morning Fitz had questioned him about Ernestine—"I'd guessed there was some man; I didn't really believe her, yet—but then later I knew that if I suggested another man it would add to the case against me. But I never dreamed it was Wat."

Camilla said with a gasp, "She never said a word! But there was something about her—only I didn't think of Wat until—*but Jed, you can't—you mustn't* . . ."

Jed went on, "I changed and left to go to the club. Then I met Sue, and then after we talked, as I say, I went from the cabaña back to the house. And Ernestine had the gun."

Ruby gave a loud gulp. Jed said, "And that really is about all. I mean it was an accident. She waved the gun at me. She was furious. Ruby wasn't there. She must have gone by then. I didn't even know she'd been there. But Ernestine was in a rage and when I saw the gun I tried to take it away from her and in the struggle—it went off."

There was a heavy silence; nobody moved. It sounded so true; it was what Ernestine had said, yet there were gaps. Jed said, "You don't believe it."

Fitz said, "What did you do then?"

"What—well, I didn't think I'd hurt her much, but I—got into a panic; I left. I went out the door to the garden and ran through the garden and got over the fence and around the house. I was heading for the car—oh, I know how it sounds, running away, but that's what I was doing when—when I heard the door bang and turned and there were Sam Bronson and Sue. So I came back." He took a breath and said, "It was an accident."

Again it sounded true. It was exactly the way it might have happened. It was a vivid and completely whole picture, without any missing segments. Sue cried: "Oh, Jed, how can you—you were in the car—I saw you . . ."

Jed gave her a long deep look. Then he came to her and caught her hand. "Sue, you haven't changed. You loved me; you still love me—you had me believing it was Fitz—I was wrong . . ."

Camilla sized up the situation, swiftly, and as swiftly made amends, "There you see! Captain Henley, surely you're not going to believe him! Why, he's doing it for her. Like a true southern gentleman . . ."

"Like a true southern—or northern—or any kind of idiotic fool," snapped Wilkins. "Cut this short, Henley."

Jed said, "But it *is* Ernestine's murder that you're arresting Sue for—isn't it? And I tell you she didn't . . ."

Henley gave his chest a puff; it was an authoritative gesture which was belied by the worried look in his face. "There's new and direct evidence against the girl for your wife's murder."

Fitz said, "What do you think about it, Wat?"

Wat's white, glistening face looked anguished. "I don't —I didn't . . ."

Ruby flashed, "He doesn't know anything about it. Except that I told him about going to see Ernestine. He knew that and of course he couldn't tell it."

Wilkins got up. "Why don't you show them the letter?" he said to Henley.

That was news to Fitz. It was news to every one, apparently; Fitz said, "Letter!" and Henley unfastened one of his neat buttons and dove into his well-padded chest and pulled out a folded paper. "Don't give it to any of them," said Wilkins shortly.

Henley shot Wilkins a bright and rather impatient glance. "Do you think I would? I'll read it. Listen. It begins"—and read " 'My dear child'—that's the way it begins."

"Well—well, read the rest of it," said Wilkins.

"I was about to. 'My dear child. But then you are all like children to me. Except surely no father has ever had such a terrible choice to make. I made it once. I gambled with an innocent man's life; I perjured myself by refusing to tell the truth. I thought there'd be an acquittal; I prayed for it and there was. But now they are going to arrest Sue; this time I can't gamble for an acquittal and win. Before she died Ernestine told me you'd been there and why; if anyone is to blame it's my son. I found the box when I went downstairs after she died and took it. It's unfair, it's wrong; it must have been an accident. But I can't sacrifice Sue, even for my son, even for his wife . . .' " Ruby was standing, her jeweled hands outflung, her face blazing white. Henley said, "That's all."

Woody cried, "That's what he was writing! That's what I heard—then he was shot and didn't finish . . ."

"He wrote that, Dr. Luddington wrote that . . ." began Fitz. "It proves . . ."

Henley stopped them both. "That letter was written on his typewriter; but Miss Poore wrote it . . ."

"I didn't—I couldn't have . . ."

"Nobody else talked of any sort of box; nobody else saw such a box; it was an obvious attempt to divert suspicion . . ."

"But I found it," Fitz cried. "You've heard the truth!"

Henley's impetus carried him on. ". . . we'd heard all these stories of somebody in the stables. Somebody mysteriously frightening the horses, somebody who wanted to attract our attention so we'd search and *find* this letter . . ."

Wilkins cut it short. "It was found in the tack room, hidden but not very well hidden, in a drawer full of tins of soap and leather polish."

His eyes peered out from under their black ambush at Fitz. "What Mrs. Luddington has said does change the interpretation of the letter. It does not clear the girl."

Fitz said, "Dr. Luddington was not afraid of whoever it was who murdered him."

Woody cried in a high, excited voice: "He wasn't afraid of whoever it was there with him, hitting his boot . . ."

Fitz left Sue; he went in a quick stride to Wat and took him hard by the shoulder. "Tell them the truth, Wat. It'll be on your conscience all your life . . ."

Wat looked at them; he moistened his thin lips. He seemed about to speak and everyone waited and then he shook his head.

Captain Henley moved impatiently. "You're not getting anywhere, Wilson. You've had all the time you asked for. The story Mrs. Luddington tells does change it but"—he glanced at Wilkins and said, "the intent was the same. The girl could have guessed, she could have written it herself . . ."

"I didn't . . ." Sue whispered and no one heard her.

Wilkins said, "Maybe though—it wouldn't be a bad idea to question this"—he eyed Ruby and said in a grudging way—"this lady."

Ruby gave a short scream; Wat's face was livid. Fitz said, in a queer strained voice, "It *is* new evidence, Henley. Listen—suppose Lissy Jenkins' story was true . . ."

"The Luddington cook?" asked Wilkins, his eyes gleaming from behind the masses of black eyebrows.

"Yes. Suppose she told the truth and suppose Dr. Luddington did write this letter and he was writing it to Ruby —because he'd tried to phone to her and couldn't reach her. Suppose the phone call Lissy Jenkins heard was to somebody else . . ."

"Obviously it was," Wilkins said shortly, "if the cook's telling the truth." But he eyed Fitz closely nevertheless.

Fitz went on, "Suppose the doctor wanted to take somebody into his confidence, somebody he trusted. Suppose whoever it was the doctor talked to was actually the murderer. But the doctor was talking over the phone. He couldn't name names, be specific; consequently the general sort of terms Lissy Jenkins heard could be misunderstood. Could sound like a warning. So the murderer construed it —and came to the doctor's house."

"But . . ." began Henley.

"Look at the picture like that," Fitz said. "If you look at it like that the figures in the picture shift around. First Dr. Luddington was mistaken."

"Of course he was mistaken!" cried Wat in a strained, gasping voice. "He thought Ruby did it and she didn't."

"If whoever came to see him was the person Dr. Luddington believed shot Ernestine, would the doctor have turned his back like that and let himself be shot?"

Jed turned stubbornly to Wilkins. "I tell you I shot Ernestine. You can't arrest Sue for it. Why won't you listen to me . . ."

"Did you shoot Dr. Luddington, too?" asked Fitz, "and Bronson? Are you going to go that far?"

Jed looked angry and baffled. "Certainly not," he cried.

Wilkins made an impatient gesture. Henley said, "Keep out of this, Baily. No jury in the world would believe you. Your motive's too clear."

"Well, but it's Ernestine's murder that you're arresting Sue for. It's not Dr. Luddington's or . . ." Jed turned toward Fitz, his scarlet shoulders outlined against the dark window behind him. The distant waltz tune floated over them and Jed cried angrily, "Why don't you help me, Fitz? You said this'd help . . ."

"Oh, so you planned this together," snapped Henley, his eyeglasses glittering. He pulled them off with a jerk and folded up the letter. Fitz said, "Please look at it that way, Henley—Wilkins. Dr. Luddington believed that Ruby shot Ernestine. He protected Ruby at the trial because she was his son's wife. In effect he perjured himself and that was no light and easy thing for him to do. But then, with Sue's arrest he sees that he's got to make—as he said there —a terrible choice. He does what he thinks is right. First he takes somebody into his confidence, he phones somebody but, in fact, actually warns that person. Then he phones Ruby to prepare her. She's out; he starts to write a letter to give her. And in the meantime the person he phoned is scared and comes—and then only afterward reads what the doctor was writing and sees what the doctor really meant. But sees too—how valuable it could be later and—don't you see it . . ."

Henley said flatly, "I see we've got to do our duty and arrest this girl."

Wilkins, however, didn't move; Fitz turned to Wat, "Tell us this, Wat—did Sam Bronson ever come to you or to Ruby and tell you he'd seen Ruby? Or you . . ."

Wat moistened his lips, "I parked out in the road to wait. I was going to stop Ruby. He couldn't have seen me and if he saw Ruby he never hinted it—he never approached either of us. I'm telling you the truth, Fitz. I didn't shoot him."

Subtly and suddenly Fitz's manner altered. Sue didn't see why, but she knew when he spoke that the strain in him was a different one. He said, "Suppose, Henley—if you look at the picture this way—suppose Dr. Luddington took the wrong person into his confidence. Suppose that person came—in secret, in hunting clothes, riding because anyone would think only of a straggler from the Beaufort hunt; suppose the murderer knew that Sue was involved and believed that safety lay in involving her still further;

thus the telephone call purporting to be from a patient . . ."

"But that," Jed interrupted, "involved me too." He whirled around to Wilkins. "Maybe Fitz is right. Maybe that was the intention. Sue and I were already involved—this would look as if we were both in it again."

Fitz said, "I'm not presuming to tell you what you ought to do . . ."

"Oh, by no means," observed Henley with heavy sarcasm, but he rubbed his nose worriedly all the same. Fitz went on, "But I think the sheriff would like to know about the new evidence . . ."

Henley looked at Wilkins who said unexpectedly, "There must be a telephone around here."

"I'll show you," Fitz offered quickly. Wilkins got up and stopped beside Henley who looked red and worried. "If I were you I'd get the Luddingtons and the Duval woman, too, into the police car. The troopers can keep an eye on them . . ."

"Me!" screamed Camilla, her yellow skirt swishing. "Me!"

"As a witness," added Wilkins and went to the door. Henley hesitated then he agreed. "Right. Come on this way, please . . ."

All of them objected and suddenly all three, with Ruby struck dumb and no longer sobbing, Camilla expostulating frantically and Wat gray and drawn as a deathshead, were out of the room. A burst of louder music came in as the door was opened. Fitz's eyes caught Woody's. "The telephone's out in the kitchen hall, isn't it?"

"Why, it's . . ."

"Show us, will you?"

Woody gave a kind of jerk and followed Fitz; someone closed the door. There was a murmur of voices from behind it. Jed said, "I promised you that I wouldn't let them arrest you, Sue, and I won't."

"It doesn't help, Jed. They didn't believe you." The room seemed very quiet after Camilla's exit. The dance was still going on; music drifted lightly through the windows. "Wat?" Sue thought. Would any man sacrifice his father for his wife? A terrible choice, Dr. Luddington had said. Had Wat had an even more terrible choice? Jed was staring at the floor, his head bent, but his scarlet-clad shoulders square. Sue sat down, slowly, leaning her head on her hand.

The door opened and Wat came in. His hatchet face was a grim and dreadful mask. "They said to tell you I'd parked outside on the road, at Duval Hall, to wait for Ruby. I was going to try to stop her. She'd said she was going to see Ernestine but I never thought she'd ride. I started to walk to the house finally and then I saw Jed's car and got in it to wait. I saw you at the door and I left. I didn't hear the shot; I left because you were there. If Ruby was already in the house, you'd stop anything. And then later I didn't tell it—I didn't want to get Ruby mixed up in it or myself— and hell, I didn't really know who did it. But then after my father—I've been in hell—if I told the truth they'd say Ruby did it. And now I . . ." Wat seemed to hear something in the hall. He cast a nervous glance over his shoulder and backed toward the door and said, "I was the man in the car."

She didn't understand him, yet she did, for she got up, stumbling in her long skirt. *"Wat . . ."*

Wat was in the hall. He closed the door. Jed's eyes were blazing. "Stick to it, Sue. You've done it so far. You've been a wonder. Stick to it . . ."

She was standing, leaning over the table. *"Jed—you* were in the car."

Jed smiled. His face lighted, yet there was something watchful in it, too. She saw that and cried wildly, "But it's the truth—I saw you . . ."

Jed said, smiling, "That's my girl. I knew you'd never give me away. You had me scared there for a while—when

242

you acted as if you'd got over liking me. When you said you wouldn't marry me you had me scared. I thought you were going to admit that you made up that alibi. That was so smart of you and so quick—and damned loyal, my dear. I knew I could count on you . . ."

"You—you . . ."

"You had me scared, but I needn't have been; I ought to have known I could count on you. I was sorry about Dr. Luddington but as I told you then, you must see how necessary it was. Why, Sue . . ." Triumph was agleam in his face; he laughed softly, "Why, Sue, do you know when I began to make love to you I didn't mean it for a minute —oh, it wasn't hard, you're cute and attractive—but I really only wanted to get even with Ernestine. I knew she was seeing somebody and—but I'll be damned, Sue, you've been so sweet and loyal and lying like that for me and so quick about it, too—why, you'd lie for me till hell freezes over. What more could I want of a woman?" He moved toward her. Sue cried, "I wasn't lying! I believed it! If it was Wat in the car—*where were you?*"

Jed stopped. A look of deep wonder came into his face. He made a sudden motion with his hand and knocked against the steward's desk; he gave it an impatient glance and saw the telephone. It stood, black and efficient, on the steward's desk.

His lips drew back. Fury surged into his face like a blast. (Had he looked at Ernestine like that?)

"Why, you lying, little . . . This is a trap! . . . But they won't get away with it. I ought to have got you before; I tried to. You can't get away this time—you . . ."

He lunged toward her, his hands reaching for her throat.

Wilkins was quicker than anybody and got through the window first. He had planned it all swiftly, the instant he had caught a glimpse of the possible identity of the central figure in the picture Fitz had drawn. Outside he had questioned Wat and then sent him back to tell Sue the truth— that the man dressed as Jed was dressed, in Jed's car, was not Jed. Then Wilkins stationed himself and Fitz so they could hear what was said between Jed and Sue, knowing that Sue would realize her mistake, would question Jed and that Jed's reply would either convict or clear him.

There was, for Sue, a chaotic moment of sound and motion and then suddenly of quiet. She was in the corridor; Woody was with her. The hot, steamy air of the clattering kitchen struck her face. A frenzied chef did not look up, a hurrying waiter brushed her elbow; they were out another door and on the veranda. Woody was talking: ". . . downstairs bar—nobody's there . . ."

They went down stone steps, into a tiny bar. A white-jacketed waiter leaned, lonely, against it whistling. Woody said, "Give us two brandies. And they want you upstairs."

"Yes, suh!" The waiter's face lighted. Glasses clicked as they were put on the table. The waiter whisked away. Woody said, "It's all right, Sue. He'd have . . ."

"Don't . . ."

"Well, but—do you understand?"

"Oh, yes. Oh, yes." She was beginning to understand many things but chiefly how fear may be a terrible black horse taking his rider into a dark abyss from which there is no retreat.

"Jed thought you made up his alibi. He thought you lied because you were in love with him. Then when you said you didn't love him and you wouldn't promise to marry him, he was afraid he couldn't trust you—he was afraid you'd tell the truth and from that minute on he was determined to eliminate you."

From the moment Jed began to believe her—scarcely two hours later a shot had come from the pine woods.

Woody said, "Maybe you don't want to talk."

They sat in silence for a long time while the waltz overhead stopped. There was the pattering of applause and then the music began again, with somebody singing. But the song had ended and another and another when Fitz finally came.

"Have this," Woody said, offering his untouched brandy. Fitz sat down. He looked at Sue and put his hand hard over her own.

Woody burst out, "Oh, for gosh sake, Sue, you weren't in love with him. You never were! He's a heel and a . . ."

"She's sorry for him," Fitz said.

"Sorry for him!" Woody's cry was like a howl of anguish. Fitz gave him a warning look. Woody subsided but said still wrathfully: "By golly, when I think he nearly killed her . . ."

Fitz said, "Ruby and Wat took Camilla home."

"Poor old Wat; he must have gone through hell thinking if he'd told the truth in the first place his father . . ."

"Well," Fitz said, "it might not have helped. And he wasn't sure it was Jed. He was only sure that the alibi Sue gave Jed was mistaken."

"Fitz." Woody leaned over the table, his face eager and very young. "The rider that afternoon . . ."

"Jed."

"Wait a minute. The doctor phoned to him. He believed Jed was innocent and Ruby did it . . ."

"And he believed Jed was sincerely in love with Sue and that he ought to know."

"But Jed took it as a threat—got into riding clothes, took back roads, yes, he would have to! Phoned for Sue, disguising his voice and pretending to be a patient, waited to be sure she came—damned near waited too long . . ."

"I expect he thought she'd drive."

". . . and went hell for leather home, changed—there was time for all that, and came back . . ." Woody stopped. *Why?*—Oh, I see. He was scared Sue wouldn't hold out for him when it was the doctor. He wanted to involve her, fix it so she'd feel she had to stick with him."

"Jed was in a dangerous spot; he needed wily tactics. He had to bind her to him, by marriage or heroics or in any way he could. Failing that . . . And after the unsuccessful shot he was terrified for fear she saw him, or guessed. But

245

then she didn't. She was just the same. He suggested Sam Bronson, he tried to avert any possible suspicion—

"The pantry window! Jeremy! The letter! Gosh, he must have thought Sue was really so much in love that she'd never dream . . ."

"I told him I wasn't. I . . . ." Sue stopped.

"But still you tried to make him leave the Luddington house. It was to him a continued resolve to shield him."

"Dr. Luddington!" Woody said. "Well, then he drove back, quietly by the lane behind the house to find out what had happened. He saw Jeremy and untied him, hit him a lick with—oh, anything. Something out of his car—so as to make it look as if somebody had ridden him. Then he drove the car right up to the door and came in. . . . Fitz, did you suspect Jed?"

"No, I didn't at first, at least not until the shot. And then I only began to question."

"Question?"

"To whom would it make the most difference if Sue's testimony changed in any way. To whom would it make the most difference if Sue herself had changed. So I saw how important it would be to Jed—if he were the murderer—to get Sue to marry him. But from there . . ."

"From there, there were some high fences. Bronson threatened him."

"Probably."

Sue said all at once, "Was that Jed in the woods this afternoon?"

"I think so, yes. I couldn't see enough of him to identify him."

"What . . ." began Woody and Fitz said, "Listen, Woody, there are many things we may never know. I think Wilkins and Henley will clear up the main points; they've got enough now. Better not talk about it now—Sue . . ."

Sue lifted her eyes. Fitz said, "We're over the hill, Sue—and through the woods . . ."

Woody wriggled. "Oh, look here. If you'd rather be alone . . ."

"We'll be alone as much as we want to be for the rest of our lives," Fitz said.

Woody became instantly and sincerely formal—and very young. "You have my consent, Sue. We'll get out Uncle Willie's port as soon as we get home."

"Caroline . . ." Sue cried and got up.

"I'll see to her." Woody jumped up, too.

But Fitz said quietly, looking at Sue, "We'll all go," and Sue led the way, her white skirt flowing around her, her red slippers tapping softly up the steps, with Woody and Fitz coming behind.

They reached the floor above; the scene struck them all perhaps with bewilderment because it had not changed. Dancers whirled past, scarlet and black coats and women's white shoulders and gay dresses. Caroline danced past— Caroline, who danced as well as she rode, and whose partner was a boy of twenty who looked as if he liked his partner and the dance. Caroline saw them and gave them a happy little wave and went on. "Let's not tell her now. Let's . . ." Fitz looked at Sue. "Can you do it, Sue—for her?"

She lifted her arms and Fitz took her lightly in his own. They moved out onto the dance floor.

704